MW00488539

DEATHFORM

BENJAMIN ALLOCCO

SEVERED PRESS
HOBART

DEATHFORM

Copyright © 2016 by Benjamin Allocco
Copyright © 2016 by Severed Press

WWW.SEVEREDPRESS.COM

All rights reserved. No part of this book may be
reproduced or transmitted in any form or by any
electronic or mechanical means, including
photocopying, recording or by any information and
retrieval system, without the written permission of
the publisher and author, except where permitted by law.
This novel is a work of fiction. Names,
characters, places and incidents are the product of
the author's imagination, or are used fictitiously.
Any resemblance to actual events, locales or persons,
living or dead, is purely coincidental.

ISBN: 978-1-925493-86-3

CHAPTER 1

Standing at the airlock door waiting for his ship to be boarded, Jack Kind fights the disorienting pull of memory. Twenty years old again, sheened in sweat, he wears nothing but a pair of piss-speckled tighty-whities. The barracks has already emptied. Stomping boots echo through the bulkhead. Screams rebound. When FROST soldiers burst into the room, he drops his weapon and dives to the floor with his hands on the back of his head.

"You alright?" Dino says.

Back to the present. This is his freighter. The war long over.

"Fine," Jack says.

The airlock prep chamber is filled with equipment. Reinforced lockers house helmets and hardware. There's a bench bolted to the center of the floor, a reminder that this is little more than a high-tech dressing room. Not the most glamorous place to die.

The proximity alert went off during dinner. A ship beelined toward them, small and armed with an illegal plasma cannon. Jack hailed but there was no response. He ordered the rest of the crew to the panic pod, but Dino stayed with him, so now they wait, while on the other side of this door unwelcome guests scrambling along their hull like insects seeking blood.

The way Dino's standing, Jack can tell he's ready for a brawl. Because at 6'6" with long tangled hair and the facial features of a caveman, Dino Vitale has never lost a fight.

Jack has. Plenty.

A mechanical whirring draws their attention behind them, to the far corner of the prep chamber where a defense turret takes aim. Jack frowns into the lens. He clicks the portable communicator dangling around his neck, a black cube about the size of his palm.

"Hunter," he says. "I told you to stand down."

Her voice buzzes through the speaker: "Just trying to cover our bases."

"Don't. We're complying."

"Well, shit."

He can't blame the crew for being upset. They've held to their delusions of dignity. The notion that there are lines which cannot be crossed. It's a feeling he has come to resent.

Hunter says, "They're opening the outer airlock."

Jack wipes his hands on his jeans. "How many?"

"Five."

"Armed?"

"Yes."

He says to Dino, "Do not fucking move unless I say."

"Okay."

"I'm serious."

"I realize that."

They have faced their share of touchy situations. Close calls with law enforcement. The kind of people you throw money at until they let you on your way. Plus the occasional raiders with their clunky ships that can barely escape Earth's gravity, but they always quit once they scan Bel and find the turrets.

This is different.

Hunter: "They're pressurizing. Fifteen seconds."

For a moment, he wonders if he will throw his body to the floor in surrender.

The door zips open. Frigid air rushes in with that faint electric burning smell that lingers after a spacewalk. Bodies and movement. Men with rifles pointed. They wear blue formfitting suits, like soldiers wear, though these lack insignia. A leader breaks from the pack, comes forward shouting.

On reflex, Jack hikes his collar to hide the tattoo.

The leader jams his rifle into Jack's gut and shouts, but the words are muffled inside his helmet. His face is small and red. He forces Jack into the corner next to a fire extinguisher, and for a moment, Jack is back at Camp Gertrude, awaiting a beating from the guards who would only leave once he was face down on the white concrete, frozen blood sealing him in place. Then the man in the spacesuit grabs his hair and yanks him upright, and Jack sees that he is not one of the guards he used to fear so badly. He is a goddamn pirate.

The man lets him go and steps back and opens his hands. An impatient gesture.

"I can't hear you," Jack says.

The man's face screws up.

Jack screams, "I cannot hear you!" He taps his ear.

The guy lowers his rifle uncertainly, slaps at the clasps around his neck. Another pirate helps him. When the helmet comes off it reveals a head of sweaty black hair and Asiatic features. The guy is young. Mid 20s at the most. A pink scar runs from the left corner of his mouth to his ear where a patch of hair is missing, folds of thicker scar tissue there instead. When he speaks again, his broken English places him somewhere in Venus's system. "Where is a cargos?"

Jack hitches his thumb toward the inner hallway.

*

As freighters go, Belinda is on the smaller side, but the cargo hold is still stadium-sized. Rows of grav suspension containers— 26 of them, though she can hold up to 100 of the 40-footers—rest under a high ceiling of white strip lighting. Jack takes the pirates inside, wondering how they intend to load these massive crates aboard their vessel.

They ignore the cargo, fan out and walk the rows. Jack and Dino look on, helpless.

The leader circles back. He holds his helmet under his left arm, rests the rifle in the other, hip-level. "Where is a cargos?" he says.

"Not sure I follow," Jack says. He gestures at the containers, but he's got a terrible sinking feeling.

"Other cargos, Mr. Kind. Do not play game."

Jack winces. There's no sense in pretending.

He leads them to a blue crate with a black circle on its side, walks the perimeter and stoops to release the straps. "Stand back," he says.

Hesitantly, the pirates obey.

3

He clicks his portable. "Belinda, target container 1187 for selective Zero-G."

Nothing happens.

"Belinda, you there?"

Belinda has been glitchy for years, ever since he switched off her AI. According to Stetson, it's something to do with encrypted files and fragmentation. You're not supposed to tool around with such complex software, but Jack prefers things old-fashioned, with a human at the helm.

He tries again. "Belinda. This is Jack Kind. Target container 1187 for Zero-G." Under his breath, he adds, "Please."

"Yes, Jack." Her voice comes monotone through his portable.

The air shudders.

Dino helps him heave the container from the floor. Even in microgravity, the thing is hard to lift. Something twinges in his back as he strains. The container rises, rotates slightly. It floats, suspended, about chest height in mid-air. They hold to the bottom handles and guide it a few feet down the aisle. Jack has to hang off the side to pull it back down. He asks Bel three times to reengage the gravity before she does.

There is a silver door in the floor where the container had been. At gunpoint, Jack lifts it open. It's heavy and drops with a bang, revealing a darkened compartment with a ladder built into the side. The pirates hop down one at a time. Jack shoves his hands in his pockets, an attempt to stop their shaking. Hunter and the others will be watching from the turret above. The pirates already noted and dismissed it. They know he's too smart—or maybe too stupid—to give the order. Make a run for it and hope Hunter has been practicing her aim. Hope there's nobody watching from the attack ship.

No. He has caused enough death in his lifetime.

He hears the hiss of pressure releasing from the suspension crate down there. The pirates hoist up their take. Five rectangles, the largest ten-feet tall by seven-feet wide, each wrapped in white foam and delicate brown paper. Paintings. Art. Cultural artifacts. Stolen from the catacombs of cultures shattered by the war and reduced to contraband to be sold on the black market. He doesn't know what the paintings are of or who they're by or what they mean and he doesn't give a shit. They equate to a great fuckload of money. That's what matters. Because even if the pirates don't execute Jack, there will now be a buyer on Earth who has paid for something that will not be delivered. And the seller—one of the most dangerous men in the solar system—will hold Jack responsible.

The pirates tear through the paper and padding and gape. *Ooh. Ahh.*

Satisfied, the leader says, "I think we will be go now." He smiles. Big white teeth.

CHAPTER 2

The freezers, dining room, and kitchen are nestled on the top level at the rear of the ship. He surveys slabs of frozen meat shrink-wrapped in their cases, selects tenderloins and mixed veggies. Bel carries about five short tons of food for any given run, enough for the six crew members to eat comfortably for a year, much longer if rationed. He'd been a cook in the military, and one of the first lessons he learned was how important food is for morale. As for hoarding so much of it, that's just one more compulsion he developed in the prison camp. Like keeping a full canteen on his belt at all times. The cooking takes his mind off things, anyway. He prefers a simple meal. Home kitchen quality with a slight kick. A red wine mushroom sauce to swirl across the steaks, a pile of veggies with a dash of garlic and parmesan. Rolls don't survive the suspension tanks, so it's flatbread for grain.

They've been in near-Earth orbit for three days now, awaiting clearance to dock and unload their shipment. The legal one. It's large enough not to raise eyebrows, but not exactly profitable for a trip across the solar system. He's been avoiding the crew since the pirates. A decision has to be made, but it's much easier to hide in his quarters with a bottle of bourbon. He's been doing this for ten years. Smuggling contraband for criminals. This should have been no different from the rest. Hard to believe this might be his final meal with his own crew.

Footsteps behind him.

"Don't go thinking too hard," Hunter calls.

Watery blood runs along the grill. He swipes it with the spatula. Few more minutes.

"We're worried about you, Jack."

He grunts without looking back at her, in no mood for this conversation.

"I'm serious, buddy. You alright?"

"Fine."

"You don't look fine. You look a little drunk."

"I'm fine. And a little drunk."

She comes around the grill, slides next to him and looks into his face. If he pulls away, she'll just harp on him worse. Nothing escapes those blue eyes. They torment young boys.

"Talk to me, Cap."

He sighs. "Later."

"We're not idiots. We know what you're gonna say."

"And?"

"And it's stupid. We're sticking together."

"You don't speak for everyone."

"No. But I know them. Whatever comes next, we face it together."

"We're not talking about an obstacle course here. We're talking about Jim Dandy. Plus the buyer. We'll have a bounty on our heads in a matter of days."

"So we're just supposed to call it quits?" Her mouth hangs open, jaw offset. He knows better than to argue with her. She's been with him from the start, longer than any others. Before he took her as his pilot, she moved from system to system hotwiring ships at port, bringing them to dealers still packed with cargo. She was a pro, but it was messy and dangerous. Black market transport is a cakewalk by comparison. At least with her onboard.

"This might be our last trip to Earth," he says. "You know what that means for me?"

She thinks a moment. Her features soften. "Aw, shit."

"It's my own fault."

"You don't know what's gonna happen. The buyer might go after Dandy."

He cocks an eyebrow.

"Okay. Maybe not," she says.

"Like I said, my own fault."

"Well, I don't know. But we're here. You'll have time to see him."

He says nothing, playing the scenarios out in his mind. *Hey there, son. Haven't seen you in more than a year. If you thought that was a long time, just you wait! And wait, and wait, and wait...*

"We're not dead yet, buddy boy."

He just shakes his head.

"Hey Jack."

"Yeah."

"The steaks are burning."

*

Sitting around the table, nobody says a word or touches the food. They look into their laps, except for Hunter. She glares at him. She never was one for the subtle approach. He wanted to wait until after the meal. Oh well.

"Fine," he says. "I'll make it quick. We were planning a two-week stay on Earth, but things have changed. The buyer expects us to bring his shipment 24 hours after touchdown at the latest. I'll be taking Belinda back out by hour 23. I won't ask anyone here to come along. I'll pay what was agreed upon when I hired you. As of now, all contracts are dissolved."

There's a palpable sense of discomfort around the table.

Dino speaks first. "I'm not leaving 'cause of some shithead pirates."

His response is no surprise. He's been Jack's personal security guard for a little over eight years. They met at a dive bar on Earth after Jack had gotten maybe just a little too drunk, and maybe had fallen toward some guy and accidentally spilled his beer, or maybe was looking for a fight and intentionally smacked it out of the guy's hand. Either way, as the guy reared back to swing at Jack, his elbow connected with the back of Dino's head where he was in the middle of sipping a rather expensive glass of amber fluid, and when the fluid splashed down the front of his shirt and the crotch of his pants, Dino turned around and laid the guy out with one punch. And when the guy's two big friends stood up and charged him, he laid them out too. Jack had been looking for some muscle and offered him a job on the spot, but he was out of prison on parole and couldn't leave Earth for another six months. Jack told him to get in touch the day his parole ended, and that's what he did. Since then, he's been nothing but loyal.

Hunter leans back, crosses her arms. "You already know where I stand."

Stetson just shrugs. "Won't be the first time I've had a bounty on my head."

Hunter slaps him hard on the back of the head. "Atta boy."

He rubs the spot. "Quit it!"

Hunter grins.

That's three out of five so far. Maybe Hunter was right, Jack thinks.

Darius, the ship's medic and newest member, places his hands on the table. He takes a breath. "I know I'm odd man out, and I've enjoyed working with you all. But I've got a family. I want to see them again." His gaze falls on Jack.

It might be a sidelong insult, but it's understandable. Darius never meshed right. This was his first time on a freighter. Months or longer from the ones you love. It changes things.

Jack says, "Okay."

This is more what he expected from the others. It's the smart choice. Self-preservation.

Last of all is Justin, Jack's nephew. At 21 years old, he's been with them a year and a half as an extra hand. Mostly he just follows Dino around. Something about their similar backgrounds. Living with his parents—Jack's brother and sister-in-law—on Atwood Station over Neptune, he was on course to become a delinquent. Theft, dealing HOP, some other minor run-ins with the law. He contacted Jack about two years ago wondering if there was a space on his crew. Jack said no. A year after that, the kid showed up at a nearby delivery point alone, saying he was wanted by a local gang and if Jack didn't hire him he would sneak aboard the next cargo ship to Earth. One of two things would happen in that case. He'd either fail to find an available grav tank and be crushed to death when the ship jumped, or he'd be found out and arrested. Jack contacted his brother, Justin's father, whose response was, "I couldn't give two tons of shit what happens that boy." It was all the same to Jack. The kid promised to work cheap and stay out of the way, and he has followed up on that for the most part. They don't have much of a relationship otherwise, a common theme in the Kind family.

When Justin realizes everyone is waiting for his decision, he shrugs and says, "I'm up for whatever, man."

So that's it. They won't disband, but they'll need a new medical technician. That shouldn't be too difficult on Earth, and Jack already has someone in mind.

An automated voice drones over the loudspeakers: "Attention crew of B-class freighter Belinda. You are confirmed for docking at 1600 hours SST. Please confirm your reception of this message."

"That was quick," Stetson says.

"Eat up," Jack says. "And if you've got shit to do planetside, make arrangements fast."

He's talking more to himself than anyone.

*

Belinda has two airlocks. The first is in her bow. The second below the cargo bay. An enclosed loading tunnel connected to this airlock peels away from her belly and attaches to another ship's dock, a bit like a giant straw. To move cargo, Jack's crew operates bulky machines called shovers, which do exactly what the name implies. About the size of a compact car, they work just like any extravehicular maneuvering pack (EM-pack), spurting compressed air to move them through Zero-G. The four front forks clamp the end of a shipping container and away it goes. They're slow moving and difficult to steer, and Jack only has two of them for the time being, but it's better than cracking the ship open and using a crane. Dino has been training Justin how to operate them, so it takes a bit longer than usual. Nearly three hours after they began to unload, they strap the shovers back into the rear airlock chamber and prep for reentrance to Earth's atmosphere.

Their regular landing zone is an Upstate New York nowhere town nobody's ever heard of. It's winter in the Northern Hemisphere. They come down in a field where the snow is three feet deep, exit through the loading tunnel with their hands held against the wind. The air shocks them, cold and refreshing and somehow *full*. To Jack, arriving on Earth always feels a bit like coming home, and that makes him edgy.

There's a hypertram stop two hundred yards to the west, a tram already idling.

They clamor inside and take their seats, leaving gaps between themselves. Strangers on a bus. The world zips by at 600 miles an hour, a white blur. The car rattles and groans.

In 20 minutes they reach the Rockwall tramport. It's crammed full of pedestrians with suitcases. Parents dragging children along the moving sidewalks. Color and noise and blaring advertisements. Holograms calling you by name. One image repeats on all the screens—a generic video feed of deep space. Field of steady pinpricks.

They agree to meet back in exactly 22 hours. That will give them a window of two hours before the buyer knows for certain that something is wrong, and will come looking.

Darius and Jack split off from the main group. The others are, according to Dino, "Going to find some fit young men to fuck."

"You can have all the men you want," Stetson says. "It's holo ladies for me. STD free electricit-*y*."

Darius does not say goodbye. Just disappears into the crowd.

Jack doesn't linger, either. He leaves the others to their vices, finds a rental place and reserves an autocar, the domed kind usually reserved for couples. Best not to search between the seats. It waits in the pickup area of the parking garage. It pops the door for him and he slides inside, crinkles his nose at the chemical stink of new-car spray over the tang of cigarettes and alcohol. He lowers the window half an inch.

"Hello and thank you for choosing Autocar Supertime Transport!" a voice from the speakers says. "Where are we—"

He states his destination.

"Great," the car says, then repeats it back and tells him to buckle up so they can get moving. "If you'd like to purchase refreshments for an additional—"

"No."

"Great."

They pull out of their spot.

"Are you interested in watching a film for an additional—"

"No."

"Great. How about the news? You'll get all the breaking stories. Did you hear the latest out of the Kuiper Belt? Some are saying—"

"No."

"Very good. For an additional fee, you can use the touchscreen to select—"

"Will you please let me sleep."

"Great. I'll let you sleep. Let me know if you need anything."

Families stand at crosswalks. Holding hands. They watch Jack and Jack watches back. Strangers going about their lives. Here and there a face he recognizes. His heart swells and then he shudders. Dead men, ghosts. He blinks them away, rubs his eyes. Just strangers.

He rolls the window fully down, inhales deep. He's been feeling a bit spookier than usual. That run-in with the pirates may have jarred something loose. It's been a long time since he's felt so trapped.

Anijira lives with her new husband in Nulleport, a city too small for hypertrams to pass through. He sets his arm on the window frame and lays his head.

He jolts awake a moment later as the seatback screen trumpets out an ad. "Jack Kind, isn't it time to smell like a *real* man?"

He can't find the volume.

"Jack," the car says, "you seem to be searching for something. How can I help?"

"The fucking volume. Turn the screen off."

"I'm sorry. Video advertisements are just one way Autocar Supertime Transport earns important revenue that helps keep your transportation experience super. Would you like to pay an additional fee for an ad-free experience?"

"For shit's sake. Yes."

"Great. I'll fix that for you."

The screen goes blank.

This is what so many men and women fought and died to preserve. An ad-free experience. For a fee.

CHAPTER 3

The portable buzzes against his chest and when he hits the holodisplay Jim Dandy's face appears in the middle of the car, a still image. Orange-blonde hair, rosy high cheekbones. Lips puckered slightly and accented pink. All for effect. The first time Jack met the Dandy was on Juno Station over Jupiter. The man had been wearing a blue dress with a fan of peacock feathers stuck in the top of his head like an insane Geisha. Jack was unloading munitions with his crew, eyeing this odd figure vaping and muttering to a lackey. He knew who he was based on his fashion. Yet there are plenty of other reasons to know the Dandy. Turns out there was some kind of religious uprising in Jupiter's system. Dandy was buying the munitions from a third party and selling them to both sides, making a fortune. That was his idea of a good time. He's the kind of guy who'd have no problem cutting the throat of a thief. Say, a smuggler arriving on Earth and failing to meet the buyer.

The call goes to voicemail.

Dandy leaves no message.

Jack looks out the window. He's nearing Nulleport. Defunct roadside diners and charging stations, dilapidated houses with chicken coops frozen in the snow. The Space Boom was especially rough on small towns. He has a theory why Ani's new husband built his mansion out here. He's a world-renowned lawyer. Travels the country defending famous athletes and politicians and actors. Ani stays here, watches the kid and drinks her wine while he slips between hotel sheets with "enhanced" blondes. Jack knows this because it is what he used to do.

He considers again what he might say to his son. Nothing feels right. Last time he saw him, his cheekbones seemed more defined than ever, the baby fat melting away. Somewhere in there was a budding young man, just a few years away. The thought stings now. He feels ill.

The house could be a restaurant. Jack's been inside once or twice, but stayed by the front door for fear of getting lost. It's set back from the road at the end of a winding driveway, blocked off from the street by a security gate. The car lets him out there. He keeps the meter running.

He stares into the green eye of the security camera until something goes *click* and the gate squeaks open.

He heads up the drive toward dimly lit windows, careful not to slip on black ice.

She leans in the doorway wearing a pink bathrobe cut high above the knee. It's been years since he's seen those brown legs. She holds a wine glass in one hand. The other is cocked on her hip. She sneers. "He's not here."

"Nice seeing you too."

"I'll say it again. Kip is not here." She shifts her shoulder and slips off the doorframe and stumbles onto the porch, righting herself and spilling wine on her toes and the snow. "Fuck." She backs inside and wipes her feet on the hallway carpet.

"Where is he?"

"Where everybody else is, Jack Kind." His name sounds like a curse when she says it. "Up their own asses. Taking your lead."

She's not usually this bad. Most visits, she shows only her best self. A trophy wife at the company mixer, all quips and materialism, trying to impress him. *Look at all you lost.*

This is sad drunken Anijira, depressed millionaire. She's no better off than before she left him. It shouldn't bother him, but it does.

"Ani, are you alright?"

There are right and wrong things to say at times like this. This is the wrong thing.

"Like you care."

"Is Kip inside? Let me talk to him."

She swallows hard, stares into the sky and juts her jaw. "I told you. He's not here."

"Okay. So. Where?"

"This is just like you. Drop by expecting people to be waiting."

"Will you please just tell me."

"He's at a fucking friend's house for the week. Christ fucking hell."

"What friend?"

"How should I know?"

"How should—What do you mean how should you know? You're his mother. He's a nine-year-old boy."

"And where the fuck are you? Oh, right. You're getting STDs and shipping HOP."

"Keep your voice down. I don't ship HOP."

"No comment on the STDs?"

"It's a school week."

"Is it? I thought it was summer."

"Ani."

"The kid's parents drive them to school, okay? He asked to stay and I said yes."

A wind rips through Jack. His only coat is a busted leather jacket. A rage rises in him. He just wanted to see Kip one last goddamn time. And here's his drunken ex-wife standing in his way, toying with him, no idea where the kid is. He should keep his mouth closed. She's miserable enough. And she could do a hell of a lot better, but has chosen not to. She is alone and knows it. Always has been. But he is mad like a little boy and he says it anyway.

"You know why a family would take in someone else's kid for a week, Ani? They do it because they feel bad. Because they can't stand the thought of what he must come home to. For example, just off the top of my head, a scumbag lawyer and a drunken bitch who can't keep track of her own son."

The glass wizzes past his head. Red wine splashes like blood over snow.

She slams the door.

He stands with his shoulders hunched, chin tucked against the cold.

Idiot.

He could have turned the conversation around, been patient, even kind. He might have slipped inside, checked Kip's room for a friend's name or number.

He knocks and waits, knocks and waits. Calls out apologies. A light in the front of the house goes out. He walks around the front and finds a window, taps on the glass. He could break in, but what then? Ani's already on the verge of calling the cops. That could seriously disrupt the timeline, not to mention alert the buyer that Jack has been planetside for several hours. He waddles back down the drive.

He has the car drive him around town in aimless circles. He glares into the bitter darkness. All these houses and their anonymous residents, dusky in the moonlight reflecting off the snow. This may be the closest he ever gets to his son again. And there is nothing left to do but leave.

CHAPTER 4

Dandy calls again.

Jack ignores it.

He books a pricey hotel in NYC, sure to confirm that it has a fully stocked bar. It's the last place he wants to go, but he needs a medical technician and he knows who to ask. Whether or not she'll hear his offer is another matter. He'll need more finesse than he had with Ani.

It takes fifty minutes to the reach the nearest hypertram.

Plenty of time for his failures to sink in.

How much will Kip remember of him? A vague presence, appearing and disappearing. Some tall guy buying him things. The voice that made his mother shout, turned her bitter. He always felt, foolishly, that being a parent was something that happened *to* you, like puberty. One day, he would wake up and find himself looking forward to time with his wife and child, and it would all be very comfortable, and the thought of leaving would turn his stomach. That day never came, and it's clear now that it never will. He was never going to be a worthy father, yet it sometimes feels that he could have been. That's the worst part.

He boards the hypertram in Syracuse, sits next to a pregnant woman with a cough. A handful of bum children move down the aisle asking for change. Angular faces smeared with snot and grime. He feels like crying. When the kids reach him, he transfers twenty bucks from his device. Three seats ahead of him a man looks back and smiles, and Jack is sure it is Barton Claiborne who died at Camp Gertrude when the guards found his homemade portable. They took turns jumping on his chest until it was flat except for the shards of rib. These are the memories Jack carries with him. The man in the seat turns away. It is not Barton Claiborne. Just one more ghost Jack sees now and then, especially in times of stress. The doctors say it's his mind trying to process traumatic events, but shouldn't the processing be done by now? The bum kids nod and thank him and tell him God will reward his generosity.

At the NYC station, he stumbles into the cold. The map on his portable steers him down the sidewalk. The streets are filthy with salt and brown snowbanks. They're old buildings in this part of town, made of brick and concrete and steel. Many with windows boarded up or busted. If small towns had it bad, the Space Boom turned big cities into wastelands. Corporations took their money and resources into the sky, resulting in a worldwide depression. As work in the rural areas dried up, the poor flocked to the cities and wandered the streets starving and calling out for water or dying on the pavement while onlookers snapped photos. This was all more than a hundred and fifty years ago. Not much has changed since. There were attempts to improve things, but the most substantial efforts got caught up in the nets of bureaucracy.

He comes to a wooden door wedged between two apartment buildings. The handle has fallen off, leaving a hole he sees the floor through. He pushes inside.

He finds himself in an entryway no larger than a portable toilet. The next door is solid steel with a camera lens in the frame. The eye goes green. A voice says from a hidden speaker, "You have a reservation?"

He gives his name.

"One moment."

There's a clank and thud, and the voice tells him to come in.

The lobby is a swanky affair with plush sofas in the corners and holograms replaying the day's best and worst sports moments. He checks in at the counter and makes for the bar and restaurant through a stone archway. He seats himself in a booth against the far wall beside what was once a window, now stuccoed over and poorly disguised with a tacky painting.

It's busy here. Men and women in dark suits crowd the bar and gesture at the holoscreens. He doesn't belong. A blue collar sweat-stain among the business class. They try not to glance in his direction and fail. Two men with buzz cuts swagger through the archway and find stools at the bar. Big dudes with tribal tats on their cheeks. They catch him watching and turn their backs. No comradery among misfits.

His waitress is a pretty young girl with dark skin and wide hips under a black apron. She probably admires all these suits around, wants to be them one day but never will. He orders a Belgian ale with a real-beef burger and fries. It's expensive but worth it.

While she's gone, he turns to the holoscreens. That same generic space feed from earlier plays on every one. There's a banner at the bottom of the screen but he can't read it this far away.

When the waitress returns, he points. "Something happen?"

Her face lights up, mischievous. "Just the first definitive proof of extraterrestrial life."

He grunts and takes his beer and swallows a gulp.

"My thoughts exactly," she says with a smirk.

"What are they saying this time? More microbes that'll turn out to be salt or whatever?"

"Supposedly, they found something big. Maybe a ship."

"Right."

"Mm-hmm. All hearsay, of course. Rumors and speculation."

Jack raises his glass. "To rumors and speculation."

"No official announcement yet." She pouts. It seems genuine, this hint of disappointment. Like maybe, despite the sarcasm, she's hoping for something big.

"I was holding out for another panel discussion," he says.

She winks, and that flash of sadness is replaced by her friendly-waitress act. She says the food should be out shortly and turns tail back to the kitchen.

His portable buzzes again. He doesn't have to look to know it's the Dandy.

The food sits in his gut deep and solid and he drinks six beers and a shot of tequila for the road and leaves a generous tip. The holoscreens move onto something else and the alcohol makes them blurry. He burps, shoves from the table and sways, a sour cloud above his head.

He spots their shadows in his peripheral before they're on him—two black shapes on either side. It's too cramped to spin and fight, so he lets the hands slap his back and grip his elbows.

Hot breath in his ear says, "Good to see you again, Jack. How long's it been?"

The buzzcut tough guys from the bar. He doesn't know them. They smell like aftershave and oil.

"We really oughtta catch up," the other says.

"Let's get some fresh air."

*

These are not your run-of-the-mill HOPheads. Of all the richies at the bar, a couple junkies would choose the best-dressed, not the worst. They targeted him. Waited while he finished his meal.

Out into the cold again.

His legs are unsteady. As they drag him, he subtly pats his pockets, hoping to find a weapon he forgot about. There's the small military can opener in his front hip pocket, a piece of metal about the size of a nail clipper, another object he depended on in the prison camp. He's been carrying it and the canteen every day since. It's still sharp, and the canteen heavy with water.

He stammers some halfhearted pleas. *Whatever this is, guys, we can work it out...*

They move him down the sidewalk, away from the hotel, into the shadows.

They shove him against a wall.

The first fist in his stomach sends the night's refreshments onto the pavement.

"The fuck," says the guy who hit him.

Doubled over, he fingers the can opener and snaps the canteen's holster free.

The guys lift him upright and fling him back.

His head hits the brick. He drops onto his ass. Warm pain bleeds into delirium. His half-assed plan goes fuzzy. It's hard to see. The camp is dark. The lights are out. He's supposed to be asleep. Blood in his mouth. He bit his tongue.

The guards must have caught him scrounging.

They'll kill him now.

He says, "I'll work harder."

"Damn right," they say.

Sting of vomit in his nostrils. "I'll choose. I can choose. I'll choose anyone."

"What's he talking about?"

"He's piss fucking drunk."

"I'm sorry," he says. He sobs. He doesn't need to fake it.

Other men refuse to beg. They fight back. Sometimes the guards respect this. Sometimes they hit back harder. Sometimes they cut off your head and leave it outside your hut for your friends to find.

"Christ," says one of the guards.

"This is just sad, bro."

"Yeah well. We got a job to do."

"I don't like it."

"You gonna tell that to Dandy?"

Dandy? Jim Dandy? In the camp? Was he here with Jack the whole damn time?

He's probably been bribing the guards.

One of the guys lifts him by the lapels and lands a hard right cross under his eye. Jack sees white, then the alley, then the buzzcut beefcakes. They aren't FROST guards in camp Gertrude. They're a couple of ugly Americans in a New York City back alley.

"God dammit," the guy says, and drops Jack onto the pavement. "I can't do it either."

Jack does not wait for them to change their minds. He pinches the can opener hard between the knuckle of his forefinger and his thumb and slashes upward, catching the fabric of one of their shirts. At the same time, he flings his canteen hard at the other guy's head, jumps upright and runs wild and crooked through the night.

"Tried to cut me!" one of them yells.

Jack laughs.

"Catch him!"

Something rises out of the night in front of him. A black shape looming. He sees it but his feet are slush from the drinks and the punches and he can't correct.

Whap.

He slams into a defunct USPS drop box. He flops to the ground, moaning.

The men catch up, their apprehension gone.

When they're done, when his mouth feels like pulp and he can't see from his left eye and there's nothing in his stomach to puke up, they tuck something down the front of his shirt. A piece of paper. They walk off, muttering and shaking their heads. He digs the paper out and holds it to his face, but the writing won't hold still. He tucks it back, rolls over and floats in the void.

CHAPTER 5

"God amighty," a familiar voice says. "Let's get him up."
Arms grab him and lift.
"He's covered in puke and blood."
"And piss."
"Are you sure he's alive?"
Jack moans to let them know he is. "Hotel," he says. "Room."
"Okay, big guy. Just take it slow."
He squints into the early dawn. Dino and Justin squint back.
"You could've froze," Dino says.
"Not frozen. Doin fine."
"Okay, man. No problem."
"Canteen," he says. "Can opener."
"We're on it. Just take it easy."
They limp toward the hotel.

*

He wakes again in an unfamiliar bed. The light from the window burns. New clothes lie beside him, including underwear. Everything hurts. Neck, ribs, kidneys, face. He checks each tooth with his tongue. Nothing loose. A small mercy.

"Careful who sees you in those clothes," Dino says from a nearby recliner. "The shops were all closed. We tested their window strength and they did not pass."

There's a nightstand by the bed. The holoclock reads nearly 8am.

"You tracked my portable?"

"You weren't answering my calls. I figured with all the shit we're in, better check."

"Well. Thanks."

"That's why you pay me the big bucks."

He can't help but smile. It re-splits his lips.

The crumpled up note lies beside the clock, stained with blood and snot and orange vomit. He smooths it out and tries to make sense of it. Scrawling black handwriting reads:

08 33 97
the barber needs a haircut

Dino stands and wanders to the kitchenette, returns and offers a glass of water. "Who was it? The buyer's men?"

Jack takes the water. "Dandy's, I think."

"All the way out here?"

"He's everywhere."

"So he knows."

"He knows."

"Those look like coordinates."

"Yeah."

"Any ideas what they correspond to?"

"Other than our deaths? No."

"The barber needs a haircut. The hell does that mean?"

"Well." Jack takes a big gulp of water. The glass hurts his mouth, but the water melts his throat. He sighs and drinks until its gone. "You know any shaggy barbers?"

The door swings open and in pops Justin with a bag of fast food breakfast.

"Thank the stars," Dino says. "I'm starving."

"You're looking pretty messed up, Uncle Jack."

"I hadn't realized."

"Sorry."

Jack throws the covers back. Streaks of blood here and there. The cleaning lady's going to love him. "I've been through worse," he says. A statement that will always be true.

*

There's time to rinse in the shower. Filth sloshes off and he keeps the water icy for his bruises. He holds himself against the wall, nearly falls as he towels off.

They stop at a pharmacy kiosk for hangover pills and painkillers. He swipes the front of his portable against the machine and makes his selection and a few tabs pop out of the dispenser. They help with the nausea but not much else. He calls for an autocar and they mill at an empty intersection. They breathe into their fists and hike their collars and bounce on the balls of their feet. The world seems very still. There are no people out, no cars. A typical winter morning in a crumbling Earth city.

"Back to the ship?" Dino says.

"We need a med tech."

Dino thinks. Realization hits. His face screws up. "Are you kidding me?"

"We've got barely eight hours. Can you think of anyone else?"

"We could ask around."

"It's too late."

"You've got a soft spot, Jack."

"She's good at what she does."

"And she hates your guts."

"So do you."

Dino grunts. "What if things go south? You really want her onboard?"

It's a valid point. Asking her back now might condemn her to death with the rest of them. Jack says, "If things get hairy, that's all the more reason to have a qualified tech we can trust. Besides. Like you said, she hates my guts. Chances are she won't even see me."

"Which raises another point. Where is she?"

"Long Island. I keep an ear to the ground."

"Christ. Starvation City?"

"She's always been an altruist."

"Are we thinking of the same person?"

"You didn't know her like I did."

"It's been five years."

"Four years. Four and a half."

"Whatever."

Justin has been following this exchange with darting eyes. Finally, he says, "Who the hell are we talking about?"

CHAPTER 6

Mr. Emcee Doyle has pneumonia. Lana can tell just looking at him. The labored breathing, the bags below his eyes, the wet cough like there's a sponge in his throat. She goes through the motions. Stethoscope here, there, breathe for me, deep breath, thank you, how long have you had that cough and you should have come in sooner. If he could sleep in a warm bed and rest and let the antibiotics do their work he would recover. But there is a good chance when he gets out of here he will trade his meds for HOP or some new addiction makings its rounds. There are the old standbys too. Heroin, HG, meth, crack, P-puff. He lied on his form, said he does not use, but she can see old track marks in the crooks of his arms and when she checks his feet for camp rot there are needle punctures between the toes. Her speech is rote and tired and she delivers it that way. *Do you really want to die in this place? You need to take care of yourself. No one can make these choices for you. They can only give you the means.* Nod, nod, yes, yes, Emcee Doyle avoiding her eyes and then looking into them all watery and guilty and sincere, but it will not last beyond the front door.

The morning has been slow for once. She lets the next patient wait five minutes while she slips into the back and fills a mug with the last dregs of coffee. She sits under the monitor, mutes the sound, and reads the captions with zero interest. More about that so-called "breaking story," no longer breaking, no longer a story worth reporting. Rumor control is in high gear. Media apologizing for their hasty conclusions. *No sign yet that the object is of extraterrestrial blah blah.* Same old. Everyone gets anxious at the mention of aliens. She is sick of them and sure they are not out there and it is time to stop waiting for a savior. They couldn't save us anymore than she can save Emcee Fucking Doyle.

She swirls her coffee. They are out of sugar again, overdue for a Red Cross shipment. Low on bread and clean water, low on antibiotics and antiseptics and ibuprofen.

Just plain low.

But that's typical.

The camp's official title is The Midland Housing and Medical Center for Those in Need, shortened simply to Midland, and later nicknamed Starvation City for obvious reasons. She hasn't seen a distended belly in a while, but ribcages often show though. It was supposed to be a temporary relief center, formed at the start of the Space Boom, shut down for a few years, then revamped in the aftermath of FROST's defeat. Still buzzing from victory, the newly re-named Star Nation (previously the Solar Alliance) felt it was high time to fix the solar system's most miserable cities. NYC and the surrounding areas had been in ruin for years. Finally the risen seas were fought back with levees and pumps and the city reclaimed, as if that would solve the economic realities. A few bankers returned, but not enough to make a genuine difference. She grew up around Saturn and worked there during the war, and it was the same story then. Some places never recovered. Some had been vaporized. Camps such as Midland kept the have-nots out of sight and out of the way of progress. They still do. Physicians like Lana help mop up.

She collects her next patient's paperwork and reads it on the walk down the hall.

It's definitely a false name. James Wankerfist.

Ha-ha. Big laugh.

The rest of the form is blank. She'll rip into the nurses for that later.

She spins inside the room. She says dryly, "Mr. Wankerfist, is it? Looks like you failed to complete your paperwork, so I'll just have to—"

A man she has not seen in years sits on the table with a bashful—if mangled—smile.

She is supposed to say something clever here. Have some emotional reaction like to guffaw and throw him out of the room or get all pissy about tricking her with a false name. She's too tired. Plus it looks like he could use some medical attention.

"Hello Jack," she says.

"Sorry about the name. Dino just blurted it to the receptionist."

"What happened?" He is clearly in pain. He holds himself crooked on the table, and his left eye has practically swollen shut. Another one of his barroom confrontations, no doubt.

"Had a run-in."

"Anyone I'd know?"

"A few of Dandy's guys."

Jim Dandy. She remembers him all right. Corrupt politician. Extremely rich and even more dangerous. They took jobs from him in the past. Always high priority.

"You're still running around for those idiots," she says.

"I run around only for myself."

"I recall."

That shuts him up.

"Take off your shirt," she says. She plucks a couple gloves from a box on the counter.

He blinks.

"You look like hell, Jack. I might as well write a prescription."

He does what he is told, reveals a torso covered in contusions. Some purple, some greenish yellow. He'll be pissing blood, judging from the damage around his kidneys.

"When did this happen?"

"Last night."

She feels over his ribs. He winces. "Can you move alright? Any trouble breathing?"

"I'm not here for medicine."

"What are you here for? Do you realize you're taking time from people that need help?"

"I need help," he says.

"No kidding."

"I want you on my crew. There's no one else."

Could he have planned this to be any more random? "What are you talking about?"

"It's not what you're thinking. I need a medic. We're in some trouble and once we're clear, I'm going legit. No more running around for Dandy or anyone else."

She feels herself rolling her eyes. "Should I write 'delusional' on my sheet here?"

"Probably."

"You're sitting funny. What's wrong with your leg?"

"Leg? Nothing. I twisted my ankle, I think. Ran into a mailbox."

She writes.

"Lana, you don't belong here."

"Jack, you have puke in your hair."

"I washed it this morning."

"Did you use shampoo?"

"I think so. I thought so. I don't know."

"Why would I come back?"

"You mean because you're doing so well for yourself?"

"That's not fair."

"I didn't mean it like that."

"Yes you did. These people are dying, Jack. I'm doing good work here."

She almost believes the words.

"I'll pay double," he says.

"It's not about money."

"I know that."

"Then why are you here?"

"I told you already."

"You think I'm not supposed to be here."

He shrugs.

"You're wrong," she says.

"Am I?"

"Yes."

"Okay. I guess I'll find some amateur medic to drag along. And when he programs my grav tank wrong I'll come outta the jump with my guts all over the walls."

"See? You've got it all planned out."

"I'm serious." He hops down, winces.

"You're seriously hurt. Rate your pain one to ten."

"Three when sitting. Six standing."

It feels just like old times. Wounded Jack Kind back from a fight, his loyal mistress ready to heal him. She hates herself for playing along, but keeps right on going. "I can see boot prints," she says.

"I won't rest till you're on my crew."

"Then you're going to be very tired."

"Anijira left me. Two years ago."

Another eye roll despite herself. "Took her long enough."

"I should have left her a long time ago."

"We are not having this conversation. It's about five years too late. Longer, actually."

"I just thought you'd want to know."

"Well, fine. I'm glad to hear it, I guess."

She writes a couple prescriptions. Painkillers and immuno-boosters.

"What are you doing?"

"Is the room still spinning?"

"A little."

She writes another, tears the sheets and offers them.

He recoils like she is holding out poison. "Remember where we used to park?" he says.

"Sure."

"We meet at the main terminal at 1800. I'll see you there."

"Jack," she says, waving the prescriptions, "save yourself."

"I'm trying." He takes the papers. "Your turn."

CHAPTER 7

Jack reenters the lobby.

Dino and Justin stand. "How'd it go?"

He takes his jacket from the chair. "She'll be there."

The autocar waits outside.

He watches the clinic through the rear window as they pull away. White snow on a flat gray roof, blank walls. The universal medical symbol on a small sign by the door. He cannot believe Lana has spent four years here. She's always been righteous, but she's not an idiot. Back when he hired her, she was disillusioned with the treatment of medical staff in the outer limits, working 20 hour days and barely able to feed herself. She sought him out. She knew she was better than all this back then. She must know it now.

A woman with a basket balanced on her head steps in front of the car. They lurch to a stop and she crosses. She is not wearing pants.

The roads are all unpaved, mud and slush. There are no borders or fences to mark where the camp begins or ends. Just tents everywhere, rusted out dumpsters turned on their sides, trash barrel fires. Men women and children gathered around the smoky rims.

They reach the paved roads and in minutes the camp is a smear of smoke behind them.

She only left because he could not do right by her. But things have changed.

Haven't they?

He doesn't know why he said that bit about going legit. It just came out.

They stop at another pharmacy kiosk which takes the prescriptions and spits out two half-filled bottles of pills. He washes the pills down with water from his canteen. He has kept it for 12 years, this canteen, a relic from his days in the camp, and today the water tastes the same but somehow foul. Old metal and oil. He drinks it anyway, staring out at the gray skies and the dirty snow. He should savor this ugly view. Earth. All her squandered potential. Despite all we've done, she still cannot get rid of us.

*

He sits on a bench at the hypertram station. Hunter and the others mill around in a cluster by the entrance ramp. It's not as busy as it was when they arrived. Maybe they hit holiday travel. He isn't sure what day it is. When you're off planet, you learn to ignore the clock, to nap when you're tired. It's disorienting at first, but he's come to prefer it to this night and day crap.

Hour 22 is winding down. He checks the time every thirty seconds as if it might slow. His head is clear and his limp is gone and Lana is not coming. They are out of time.

"Let's go."

Back at the landing site, crunching across fresh snow, Belinda stands tall under darkening clouds. He rarely gets to see her from the outside. She's bigger than she seems inside, all those cramped corridors. Eight hundred and fifty feet from end to end, six hundred feet tall, she's an older model with a retro-traditional look. The three grav drives on her back and sides look almost like jet engines, and her rear expands like the base of a rocket filled with holes, small thruster ports for maneuverability in docking. She has attitude. Always has. He respects that about her. He'll ask her to take him from this place, from his family, from Lana, never to see them again, and she will oblige.

He calls the loading tunnel down. It lowers with groan, hits the ground with a puff of powdery snow. The doors open and the lights wink on, stretching up and out of view. He takes his final footsteps on this planet and steps onto the ramp.

About halfway up, he freezes. He thought he spotted something on the landing, someone backlit by the chamber.

"What is it?" Hunter says.

"I'm not sure. I thought—"

And there it is again, a flicker, a shadow, a rising form.

"Hold it!" Dino slips the Luger from his shoulder holster and the barrel bucks in his hands as he squeezes off a round. Jack's ears go stuffed with cotton and he slams Dino's arms, pointing the gun to the ground.

"Hold it for fuck's sake!"

"It's a pirate!" Dino says.

"That's no goddamn pirate!" Jack screams, charging up the ramp.

CHAPTER 8

She went straight to the landing site from NYC, giddy with the recklessness of it. The clinic would be shorthanded and fully-booked, but there are a hundred excuses not to do something and only one reason to. Jack was right. She never belonged there. No one would make that decision for her.

She spotted the ship from the hypertram, in the same lot as always. Her old passcode got her into Bel's system. She lowered the ramp. She came out of the airlock into the cargo hold on the first level. It was dim and cold and stunk of mildew and always had. She hardly ever had reason to go down there, even when the others loaded and unloaded hauls. It was the work level. Like a basement or garage. Her boots echoed on metal. She climbed the central shaft—a ladder running from the high ceiling to the floor, housed in a cage with an opening like an arched gate at the bottom. There were two more shafts just like it running between the levels. It was an unfamiliar sensation, having to climb. In space, the shafts would be Zero-G, and she could float effortlessly up. Jack had modified the ship so he could add and reverse the gravity in the shafts, a defense mechanism in case they were ever boarded by hostiles. As far as she knew, that feature had never been tested.

She paused on the ladder at level two, looking through the open doors down the hallway. She'd always thought of this level as Bel's nervous system. Each room contained some vital machinery that kept the crew alive. Mainframe, life support, air filtration, water recycling and heating. The machines ran better in Zero-G, so the whole level free-floated most of the time. The grav tanks were toward the bow. They were her sole purpose for being on the ship. As complex as any medical equipment could be, they had to run smoothly to ensure no casualties during a jump. That meant keeping up with the crew's body mass and programming nutrient levels and double and triple checking the seals. She'd never seen a malfunction, but heard stories. Rooms coated in viscera. Whole crews starved to death when the nutrient lines froze. It's why med techs were required on ships with gravity drives. Too many people turned to jelly. She skipped the tanks for now. She'd get her fill of them later, no doubt.

The third level was where the crew spent most of their time. The kitchen and dining area to the rear along with food storage, crew quarters in the middle, the bridge at the very tip of the bow. As with the second level, it was really one long hallway sectioned off at the landings where the shafts came through.

She made for her old quarters and wiggled the handle. Unlocked. The only personal effects were a rumpled bedspread and a few cabinets full of stationary. She could tell from the legal pads and the med kit on the wall that this was the previous tech's room. Toward the end of her stay, she'd spent more time in Jack's quarters than her own. So much could change in four years. She'd been a foolish little girl who believed she could fix a seriously damaged man. Only managed to damage herself in the process. Go figure.

She shut the door and continued down the hall, running a hand along the white walls. These walls used to make her feel trapped, like she'd gone from working in a hospital to living in one. But now there was something calming about them. Today they felt like a break from the noise, the garbage stink and mud of Starvation City.

The only room she did not recognize was off the corridor near the observation deck. It was a little shocking to find, this renovation, and she wondered for a moment if she'd boarded the wrong ship. She was about to step inside when Bel told her someone had remotely lowered the loading tunnel.

The crew.

She rushed back the way she came, sliding down the shaft, palms squeaking on the metal, then back through the cargo hold and to the airlock chamber.

A cold breeze blew up through the tunnel. She leaned forward to see. Heard footsteps.

Whispers.

Distant forms.

She hung back. Jack had mentioned trouble. *What if it's not the crew?*

She poked her head out.

A muzzle flash and bang.

Something went *crunch*.

She fell backward, darkness all around.

CHAPTER 9

"Lana!"

He finds her lying on her back, blinking at the ceiling. Above, one of the lighting strips has blown out. There's a big hole in it. He kneels and checks her vitals, pats her down and inspects his hands for blood, whispering over and over, "You're alright." Her pupils are dilated. She's in shock. He cannot find a wound. Strong pulse. Fast pulse. Rising pulse. Face getting red.

"You fucking shot at me?" she says.

Dino's voice comes from behind him. "That was me. Sorry."

"Sorry? You're sorry?"

She looks like she might bite someone.

She drops her head, arches her back, and laughs until she runs out of breath.

The others stand with nervous smiles.

Finally she says, "It's good to see you too, Dino."

Jack helps her to her feet.

She brushes herself off and runs her hands through her hair and points at the busted light. "That's some welcome."

CHAPTER 10

Apart from being shot at, it really is good to see everyone. Dino takes her into a bear hug and apologizes endlessly. She promises to never let him live it down. Stetson grins and slaps her shoulder and Hunter shakes her hand in a steely grip. It's a type of reunion and feels like it. She's supposed to be here. She's sure of it. Attempted murder and everything. She wants to ask how they are, what they've been up to, what she has missed, but there will be time for that later. She introduces herself to the new guy, Justin, Jack's nephew, blonde kid with big dark eyes. She can see the resemblance. He nods awkwardly and mumbles something she can't quite hear. And then she is face to face with Jack, who has not recovered from nearly finding her dead.

"I'm not sure who's more shook up," she says.

He touches her elbow. "You're sure you're okay."

"I'm fine. I swear."

He stares at her, eyes welling up.

The crew looks on, embarrassed. It's a private moment in full view. He wants to say a whole lot more.

Not now, Jack.

She slaps him lightly on the cheek and successfully breaks the moment. "Come on, bud. We've got work to do, yes?"

She walks with him for pre-takeoff inspection, checking for anything loose that might cause problems in Zero-G or during the subsequent grav jump. He fills her in on the details. The pirates, the stolen loot, the confrontation at the hotel and the strange note. This was the first job he'd taken with the Dandy in a while. It started out normal enough.

"You think you're being set up?" she says. She's voiced concern about the Dandy's trustworthiness in the past. Something about him always felt off.

"With Dandy?" Jack says. "Absolutely. Maybe you shouldn't have come back."

"A little late for that."

"We're still on the ground," he says. There's no irony in his voice.

"Wait a minute. You barge into my clinic and beg me to follow you, and like an idiot, I do. Then your personal security nearly blows my head off, and you want me to leave?"

"Want? No."

"You never knew what you wanted." The words surprise her. "Sorry. I didn't mean—"

"It's fine. You're right, anyway."

Old puppy dog Jack already feeling sorry for himself.

Still. She can't help feeling sympathetic. He's got problems.

Back in the cargo bay airlock, they check that the shovers are secured and find three loose tie down straps. They either came off during landing or someone forgot to secure them after unloading the shipment. Justin has been shirking his duties, Jack says. Half-assing things. Little chores, mostly. Changing the garbage, sweeping the bay, cleaning the toilet. But a loose shover careening around an airlock could cause a hell of a lot of damage. He'll talk to him.

They walk the new room, the addition by the observation deck. There are square seals arranged in a pattern on the tile floor. Jack says these are the hideaway seats. Against the far wall, a holo monitor. She counts seven EVA helmets plugged firmly on their holders, several lockers that must contain the rest of the suits. Straight ahead of the main doors, a narrow hallway leads farther in. Halfway down, a door on the left opens into a storage room. Looks like food and water, mostly. At the end of the hall on the right, a cramped lavatory.

All at once, she knows what this is. "An escape pod," she says.

Jack nods. "We call it the panic pod. Anything goes wrong, you get here fast and shut the doors. There's no other way inside. She's sealed off from Belinda completely. O2 and water filtration can last up to two years. There's enough food for about half that right now, but space for more. Six suits for the crew, plus one spare."

There are no grav tanks, she notes.

Jack says, "It's just a life boat, not a getaway vehicle. Has basic propulsion but there's no grav drive. Say you're a few miles from the nearest lunar outpost and Bel has critical damage. Take this baby out to a safe distance and wait for rescue."

"There's no airlock either. Opening the doors would depressurize the whole thing. That doesn't seem like much of a rescue."

"That's what the suits are for."

This all makes logical sense, but it's not like Jack to think so far ahead. He's more of a fly-by-the-seat-of-your-pants kind of guy. At least he used to be. "Why?" she says.

"Why what?"

"Why'd you get it?"

He shows her the pink circle in the center of his right palm. Scar tissue about the diameter of a grape.

"Laser rifle?"

"Yep. Some jumpy cop. I went to shake his hand. He thought I was pulling a gun. After that I thought, you know, in this line of business, a safe room might not be a bad idea. I didn't like paying for it, but it makes the rest of the crew feel better."

"You're lucky you didn't lose the hand."

When they're finished with their rounds and the others report clean diagnostics, they head to the bridge. The third-level ceiling transitions to transparent materials. She sees dark gray sky through a light dusting of snow. This is the observation deck. It gives her vertigo. A knot of nerves has been building in her stomach since she got here. She's managed to ignore it until now.

The doors to the bridge open automatically. A set of steps leads them down to the deck. Storage compartments and straps cover the walls. The ceiling, half transparent, is peppered with handholds in case the gravity goes out. Grooves in the floor serve the same purpose.

There are two command monitors in the nose. Hunter and Stetson have already taken their places at them. Jack stomps a black switch on the floor and six shutters slide back. Chairs rise and unfold. Behind them stands the interactive mapping module, the same size and shape as a billiards table. And beside it, there's an emergency hatch in the floor, a slight depression that opens to a vertical shaft leading to the forward airlock prep chamber.

She straps into a seat and focuses on these familiar features, reminds herself how routine all of this is. Because the thing is, no matter how many times she takes off and lands and pretends she is safe, and though she was born and raised on a space station orbiting a gas giant, she has never been comfortable in space. The first time her father took her to the observation park looking out on Saturn with its soupy bands of cloud and those mystifying rings, Lana burst into tears and wouldn't stop crying until she was back in their apartment and her parents told her it was a holograph. That was the other reason she left Jack's ship. The one she tended not to acknowledge. She'd been afraid. She always would be. Like a sailor with a fear of drowning. And Jack keeps glancing in her direction, a half-concerned look on his face. In another time, he might have reached out and grabbed her hand, told her everything would be alright. More likely he would have made fun of her. Not now. He leaves her alone with her deep inhalations, her silent refrain of, *It's safer than taking the tram.* Takeoffs bother her most. Even docking isn't so bad. Something about the transition from solid ground—or any ground—to the great void. And even though she knows space is not really empty, its size gets to her. Its foreverness. Unquantifiable. Every run around the sun flirts with our vague understanding of physics. Faith alone tells us gravity will not fling us into the darkness.

As the gravity engines kick on, the ship begins its humming shake. She feels it in her teeth. She grips the arms of her chair.

"We're golden," Hunter says. "UAFA has cleared us for takeoff."

Jack says, "Hit the gas."

The shaking stops as the ship lifts. She makes the mistake of looking up. The clouds shift and seem to boil downward. Gravity fields cause distortions in spacetime, bending light. She glances to Jack, expecting his cocky half-smirk or a reassuring smile, but sees instead that his own head is thrust back and his eyes are closed and his hands are white-knuckled on the arms of his seat. There's nothing she can do or say. She leans back and shuts her eyes and gives herself over to what might come, hoping she made the right decision.

CHAPTER 11

Once they're out of the upper atmosphere, Hunter sets course for safe jumping distance and Jack retreats to his room. He lies on his bunk and swallows more pills. His thoughts race.

There is nothing good about this run. Dandy's mystery coordinates are way off the standard axis, in a realm where FROST fleets used to hide before an attack, an area so vast that trying to spot and armada was like searching for a needle in an ocean. Jack is wary of such places. Twelve years may have passed since the war's end, and he has traveled the solar system countless times, but anything beyond Mars still feels like enemy territory. Sure, FROST was disbanded, but that doesn't make up for their atrocities. Reminders still litter the systems. Five years after the Alliance's victory, a crew of freelancers in the asteroid belt approached what they thought was a small, slow-moving comet. Upon closer inspection, they found a mass of bodies compressed into some kind of meteoroid from Hell. Hundreds of thousands of dead, their bones snapped, contorted, faces staring frozen and irradiated. Civilians, probably. Unclaimed.

The war had been a brutal conflict from the start, though you wouldn't have known it from the way people talked. Like it was some romantic adventure. The Great Solar War. They signed up by the millions, wanting to be heroes—whatever that means—men and women both, buying into the myth of honorable warfare. Maybe they imagined stringed instruments playing in the background as they marched to their ships. Probably saw themselves returning as hardened veterans with stories to tell of patriotism and valor, weeping softly when speaking of fallen comrades. It would be a respectable pain. Somehow modest. Cause for reverence in the hearts of their children and grandchildren.

Horseshit.

Even at 18, Jack knew better. He signed up to escape his life on Earth, but volunteered for mess duty to keep out of the fighting, and for a long time, it worked. COs valued talented cooks. They laughed with him, made special requests which he obliged, assured him he deserved a promotion. Then one day he found himself face-down in the barracks, FROST fighters kicking his ribs and laughing. He was marched with the other survivors into the cargo holds of ancient freighters, rickety grav tanks lined up in rows. They crawled inside at gunpoint.

The likelihood of surviving that first gravity jump was one in three. The tanks had not been adjusted. Some leaked. For every prisoner that woke up on the other side, two had been liquefied. Those early dead would later be thought of as the lucky ones.

Well before the rebels deemed themselves The Free Republic of Outer Solar Territories and went on the offensive, they established their own mythos. They believed that all people from the inner territories—any systems within the orbit of Mars—were weaklings, crowded around Earth and the Sun because they couldn't handle the bleakness of life beyond the snow line. This mindset had its roots in a philosophy known as New Darwinism, sometimes referred to as Supreme Selection, which stated not only that the strong overcome the weak, but it was the duty of a superior entity to dominate all inferiors. Any sane person would recognize this as bat-shit crazy, but politicians exploited it quite effectively. It became something of a rallying point, providing a deeper reason to deride the inner colonies. In time, it found its natural apex in the form of rebellion and war.

There were legitimate reasons the outer colonies were pissed off. High taxes and trade laws were created and maintained entirely by the inner systems. So, like most wars, the Great Solar War was about allocation of resources as much as it was about racial prejudice.

FROST was eager to put New Darwinism into action, enslaving and destroying anyone in their way. Because the life of a prisoner was deemed worthless, they tended not to care much about things like food, water, or sanitation in the camps. Prisoners became slaves forced to build new colonies for their masters. They died from malnutrition and dysentery and cultivated new diseases that no one had ever seen before—the most famous being a mutated form of herpes that began as an ulcer on the tongue and slowly ate the flesh of the mouth: gums, lips, cheeks, turning faces into skulls before the body gave out. Infected men might take weeks to die. Such hardships were less common than the daily beatings and public executions to keep prisoners fearful, as if they weren't already on the verge of madness.

The war escalated while Jack wasted away in a prison camp on Ganymede. Some POWs made makeshift portables and hacked into FROST's network, accessing news about the fighting, but by the time it diffused through the camp it was all rumors and hearsay. FROST had destroyed Earth. Or it was the Moon. Or it was Mars. The Alliance had won and the camps would be liberated in a week. Or two weeks. Or two days. Or FROST had won and they were all going to be executed. Or the Alliance was gaining, or the Alliance was falling back. On and on. Jack learned the truth later, by the time it was already considered history. As FROST gained territory near Earth, they spread themselves too thin and ultimately ran out of fighting forces, but not before they developed a new WMD—something called a grav bomb—which put the hydrogen bomb to shame. They detonated two on Earth, destroying most of Europe and Africa, and one on Mars. The Solar Alliance refused to surrender. Luckily, FROST had a limited supply of these bombs. And the Alliance had been making their own advancements, building faster ships and more accurate weapons. Their hardware outmaneuvered anything FROST produced. Once the Alliance had a stronghold on Jupiter, they pummeled FROST's defenses until there was virtually nothing and nobody left. After the grav bombs, the Alliance had no interest in mercy, either.

All in all, it was a rehash of what *homo sapiens* had been doing for millennia, just on a much grander scale. Although there has never been an official death count since both sides were so shoddy at documenting their war crimes, estimates put the figures around 2.5 billion dead all told, civilians accounting for roughly 2 billion, soldiers 450 million, and POWs 150 million.

And yet, when peace came and the vets and survivors went home, the Great Solar War was treated like a minor pit stop on the road toward progress. The Alliance saw an opportunity to strengthen itself, shifted some resources around, and rechristened itself the Star Nation, a singular governing body to encompass the entire solar system. No more colonies. No more countries. Just states within the Nation. Some perpetrators of war crimes were executed or jailed, but most of FROST's leaders—politicians and generals—were pardoned and made into trading partners. Within ten years, anyone jailed was released. All in the spirit of moving forward. They turned a blind eye to corruption. Made new laws. Invented fines. People like Jim Dandy rose to power by rigging elections and then shutting down the democratic process. And people like Jack found ways to get by. Tooth and nail.

He sometimes wonders if the outcome of the war proved FROST right. The Solar Alliance really had been unjust, greedy and imperialistic. The strong obliterating the weak. Just like in the camp.

CHAPTER 12

"Attention. Minimum safe distance has been reached. Jump drives may now be activated."

"Shit." Lana is crouched down by the last tank, wires dangling from a side panel. She flicks through them one at a time, rolls them in her fingers, checking for crimps or frays. She shines a flashlight in the panel to check for rust or residue, that blue shit that builds up around the plugs. She found and replaced three corroded lines on three different tanks. A few more jumps and bye-bye Dino, bye-bye Jack, bye-bye Hunter. Whoever they found to replace her was either a fraud or an idiot and deserves a good smacking around.

Jack's voice is static in her portable: "You know what to do, people. Be at your tank in two minutes. Lana will assist."

The tanks are arranged in a line, cordoned off by privacy stalls like in a public lavatory. There's a scale just inside the main door. As the crew come in, she measures them and records everything in her portable. They've all changed into their grav suits except her. Form-fitting bodysuits that do nothing to flatter the average body type. As Stetson steps into the scale, he grabs his love handles and jiggles. "Don't lie, girl," he says. "You missed all this."

She laughs.

She helps them down one at a time. Into the lukewarm gel of the tank, watching her with drowsy eyes as their masks feed them sedatives. Jack goes last. Something is wrong, but she knows better than to ask. His suit fits him a little too well. When he was shirtless in her clinic, she was too exhausted to care. Now in the claustrophobic grav tank stall, as he slips down to the neck in plasma, she remembers the desperate loneliness of these runs and the comfort of a warm body to curl against. She had her share of partners on Earth. One lasted two and a half years before she broke it off. Just a gut feeling. Nothing rational. Haunted, of course, by the memory of a man she had come to loathe. And for some reason she came back.

It was all a sham, of course. The whole romance-on-a-spaceship thing. A symptom of fear and isolation. She could just as easily have slept with Stetson if the timing had been different. Or Dino if he was straight. Infatuation, she always believed, is pure circumstance.

Probably.

"What is it?" Jack says.

"What's what?"

"You've got a look."

"I don't know. This is just how I look."

"Do I stink?"

"You do."

"I got the puke out of my hair, at least."

"I saw."

"Seriously. Are you alright?"

"Seriously stop asking me that."

"Sorry."

"Lie back," she says.

He lies back. She pulls down the mask and snaps it over his head.

"Breathe in," she says.

"I have nightmares."

"What?"

"Every jump. The whole way."

She doesn't know what to say. Nobody dreams in the tanks. The mind shuts down completely. She tells him to relax.

"Nnnng," he says. His eyelids droop. He seems to shrug, making the gel shimmy, then his face sinks below the surface and he is out.

She sits on the edge of the tank a while, watching him sleep and wondering why he decided to share this now, after so many years. Except she already knows. This opening up. Stopping by the clinic. Bearing his soul. Somber Jack. He hasn't changed at all. He just thinks they're all about to die.

CHAPTER 13

The floor of the hut is so cold it will rip the flesh from your soles. They use what little cloth they can scrounge for extra warmth. Jack wraps his feet and stuffs his pant legs with the fabric of dead men's coats. When the guards burst in, he is not fast enough from his bunk, so the one they call Blunderbuss whaps a baton across his temple, laying him out. He rises slower than they'd like, so Blunderbuss whaps him again. The other prisoners keep their eyes ahead. He knows what they feel because he always feels the same: *thank God it's not me this morning.* Blunderbuss gets bored and leaves him to spit blood. He claws along a bunk to right himself. His ears ring over whatever announcement the guards have come here to make. Judging from the sinking expressions around him, it's another work detail.

Perhaps the most surprising feature of the camps is how military rank has not vanished. In many ways, it has amplified. The CO's live in huts away from the other prisoners and are rarely forced to work. Jack has puzzled over why the guards allow this. Perhaps it's psychological. They fear their own superiors so much that they respect the indignant shouts of their enemy officers by proxy. Jack once witnessed Ltd. Davis, a 5'2" bespectacled redhead, scream down a guard twice his size who tried to steal his morning rations. Davis's head looked like it would pop, and the guard seemed to shrink the more those veins stood out. Finally the guard handed Davis's bowl back and walked away cursing. Whatever the cause of these odd mercies, the officers lived in slightly improved conditions compared to the rest. They were fed bigger portions, slept on wider bunks, had sturdier shelters, and at one point even convinced a guard to bring them a space heater, though it was stolen a short while later.

Jack is no officer, but he cooked for several of them on the ship. During the early days in camp, he convinced them he could improve their camp food if they let him bunk with them. Now he spends all of his time and energy worrying over how to stay valuable. Finding ways to add spice to tasteless rice and protein blends, stretching meager rations, combining swill to make a stew or rubbery pie. He has good relationships with one or two guards, and on rare occasions, successfully barters for an egg or some grain. There are always prisoners willing to steal from the guards' quarters—a dangerous but rewarding affair. A sack of flour, a cupful of sugar. He whips up flat cakes, sells some on the side in secret. It's amazing what a starving man will give for a palm-sized treat, a reminder that somewhere out there, pleasure still exists in the universe.

When the guards leave, the men mill, their expressions sinking further. It is not unheard of for officers to go on work detail. When the number of able-bodied men dwindles (ie: an outbreak or a collapse of ice or an eruption of toxic fumes), the guards do away with their minor mercies and club any officers who protest, no matter their indignation. But if it were a work detail they'd be gathering their shit and heading for the door right now. Instead, they stand or sit with shocked looks on their faces.

They explain it to Jack when his hearing returns. It is much worse than a work detail.

The dream skips ahead.

He is holding a pickaxe and swinging it down into a sick man's skull. The man's eyes are wide open, staring. They cross as the axe plunges.

They have to restrain the doctor. He took an oath, he says. They cannot do this.

A splash of brains on concrete, frozen in pinkish clots. Jack twists the axe head free.

The dream skips again. Memory melds with the abstract.

Jack is inside a vacuum-sealed bulldozer, shoving a mound of frozen corpses into a blast crater, and at the bottom of the crater is Jack's enormous gaping mouth. The bodies roll down the side of the crater and the mouth licks its lips and opens wide and Jack is careful not to leave any bodies behind. He is so hungry. Guards stand watch and clap and when the last of the corpses are gone, they bring out Lana, who has been stripped naked. They hold her arms out. Blood trickles between her legs. It is the same with all female prisoners. She wails but there is no sound. Jack swings the bulldozer to face her. The guards let go. She runs toward Jack like he will help. He aims the bottom edge of the dozer's bucket for her waist, catches her in mid-run. The force pins her there and her intestines plop out of her mouth. Jack raises the bucket and rams her against the side of the compound, slicing her in half. Her legs drop to the ground and Jack is a hundred feet tall and leans down and picks them up and cracks them like chicken wings and dips them one at a time into his mouth, sucking the flesh from the bones.

CHAPTER 14

The ceiling undulates, bubbles and ripples and shifts. The plasma has already drained, leaving him slimy as a newborn. The lid lifts from the tank. He waits for the disorientation to pass. The walls quit wavering after a while. Grav jump aftereffects. Worse than any hangover. It used to take a full day, maybe two, before his feet were steady enough to stand.

He hears bare feet approaching. They stop outside the stall. "How we doing?" Lana says.

He teeters on the edge of the tank and carefully slides his feet to the floor. "Peachy," he says as he opens the stall door.

It's clear she's been up for a while, standard procedure for med techs. She's back in her street clothes, looking fresh and clean. She fiddles with her portable, studying data. Her eyes flick along his body, then back to her work. He can still taste the meat of her flesh, feel the warm blanket of her skin sliding down his throat.

She types and reads. "Your vitals look good." She's all professionalism, falling into her old role with ease. He wonders if this is intentional, that she is setting boundaries.

He's immediately annoyed with himself. What a stupid thing to be thinking with everything else going on.

"I'm going to wake the others," she says. "Why don't you go on and take a nice hot shower."

"Yeah right." Of course it was a joke. Water is far too precious to waste on bathing. It's a nice thought, though. Would beat standing in his quarters sluicing the grav juice off with citrus-stinking chemical wipes. They leave him clean but sticky in the crevices. It takes a while to get the gunk out of his hair, and if it dries there it forms a white crust that itches like hell.

He dresses and pulls bedding from the footlockers. He gets the bed halfway made before he stops to wonder what the hell he's doing. He strips the sheets and folds them and tucks them right back where he got them. They aren't here for the long haul. For all he knows, they'll need to make a last-minute jump. Few things are more irritating than waking on the far side of a jump and realizing you forgot to tuck your shit away. Loose sheets tend to tangle and knot as if they've tumbled for years in an overpowered washing machine. Anything else is bound to shatter.

He retrieves his can opener and canteen from kitchen storage and chugs till the canteen is empty and refills it. Feeling somewhat human again, he heads for the bridge.

Hunter and Stetson are already there, leaning over a holo map, a grid of stars with a few glowing bulbs. They don't look happy.

"How we doing?" Jack says.

"Well," Stetson says, "we missed our mark by about a million clicks."

"Oh goody."

"Yeah."

When Stetson concentrates, his eyes get narrow and those gray irises seem to glow. He's the best engineer Jack ever met and has no patience for mincing words. Jack appreciates that. They don't talk much unless it's work-related, but over the years bits of information have trickled out. Stets was in the military, too, and operates with the same protective emotional shell so common among servicemen. He had it before he joined up, though. An albino black man, he'd fought off bullies from a young age, and this stigma led him away from social games and toward a lifelong fascination with machines—computers, hypertrams, antique automobiles, propulsion systems of all kinds. He wanted to crack open the world and examine its moving parts. He'll talk for days about the mysterious physics of grav drives and the software that regulates them. People say it's mostly guesswork, based on half-formed theories about the underlying nature of time and space, but Stetson disagrees. It just takes finesse. And he's got that, he'll say with a wink. After the war, he worked for a resource collection agency. Asteroid mining and comet capture and the like. He was caught stealing some of the more valuable hardware and went on the run with a price on his head. The funny part is, he only stole the hardware to experiment with more effective surveying equipment, but it violated some contract or another with a manufacturer. He started selling modified super-computers on the black market, paid off his own bounty, and lingered around various spaceports looking for work as an engineer at a time when Jack needed one.

"A software glitch, or hardware?" Jack says.

The last thing they need right now is a malfunctioning ship.

"Neither," Stets says. "I've been combing it over and nothing pops out. Hunter's with me, yeah?"

"Yep," Hunter says. "For once."

"So? What happened?"

Stetson's eyes sparkle. "Someone knocked us out of the jump."

"Is that possible?"

"Apparently. It's kinda like we hit an electric fence. Some kind of security system. I've never heard of such a thing. Highly advanced."

"What are you saying?"

"Buddy boy," Hunter says, "Dandy has his hands anywhere there's money, right?"

"That's a good way of putting it."

"What if those rumors about the alien ship or whatever are true?"

"You're kidding."

She is not kidding.

Stetson has the same look of nervous excitement.

Jack says, "Even for the Dandy, stealing an alien spaceship seems ambitious."

"Come on," Hunter says. "It's the wild west out here."

"This could be big. Like, really big."

"Let's focus," Jack says. "Technology to cut a jump can't be that complex. Are we talking military?"

"Military or something *other*," Stetson says.

"How long before we reach our destination?"

"Three hours. But Jack. There's nothing on the map out here."

"And that surprises you? Nothing's mapped this far out."

"No, I mean something's jamming our systems. But check this out." He points up at the transparent roof.

At first, Jack sees nothing out of the ordinary, just the same old faint field of stars, but one hangs brighter than the rest, and Stetson assures him it should not be there and it is no star.

*

It's like approaching a city on a desert plane at night. As the hours draw down and they draw near, the object reveals itself to be not a single point of light, but a network of thousands. It is roughly cube-shaped and does not appear to rotate, probably anchored by grav drives, a trend among newer stations to make docking easier. Physically, there's nothing unusual about it.

"That look alien to anybody?" Jack says.

They say nothing. They may be disappointed, but he's relieved.

"Is it military?" Lana says from behind him. She stares upward, too, trying to make sense of the bright grid. He didn't realize she'd entered the room.

"Hard to say."

Dino and Justin came in at some point, too, and have since taken seats. Dino appears on edge, leaning forward and rubbing his chin. Justin slouches, sucking on a vaporizer and playing a game on his portable. Jack recalls the unsecured shover in the airlock and a ripple of anger runs along his scalp.

"Justin," Jack says.

"Yeah."

"I thought I told you to complete a full inspection."

"I did. I double-checked everything an hour ago."

"So triple-check."

Justin turns halfway in his chair. He shoots a pleading look to Dino, who shrugs.

"Now," Jack says.

"Going." He shoves out of his seat and plugs the vaporizer in his mouth.

When he's at the door, Jack calls to him, "Hey."

He half turns.

"If I ever find that you've failed to secure another shover, I'll dump you at the nearest outpost. You either pull your weight or get off my ship."

Justin starts to say something, thinks better of it, and continues through the doors.

Awkward tension settles over the room.

He hates playing disciplinarian, but better to be a living asshole than a dead saint.

Soon the station grows in size to fill the window, and they can make out the shadowed structures between the points of light. The station hails them. A low male voice in their portables: "Attention crew of B-class freighter Belinda, you are entering restricted space. You have thirty seconds to clear the area or be subject to deadly force." Stetson runs a diagnostic and confirms that they are being targeted by two very large plasma cannons. Military, then.

"What do we do?" Hunter says.

"Are we linked for two-way communication?"

"I don't know. Our comms are still down."

Dandy sent them here for a reason, and that reason was probably not to be blown up before anything interesting happens. Jack clicks his portable and holds it to his mouth. He takes a deep breath. Counting down, they've already lost fifteen seconds. It's this or it's nothing.

"The barber needs a haircut," he says.

Nobody moves.

"They're still targeting us," Stetson says.

"I repeat. The barber needs a haircut. Do you copy?"

Nothing. Not so much as a confused reply.

"The barber needs a—"

"Copy," The voice says. "Standby for docking procedures."

"Holy shit," Hunter says.

Stetson says, "They've lowered their defenses."

Jack feels like a leaky balloon. Despite not knowing what this place is or why it's out here, this is otherwise familiar territory. They're here to pick up a package.

CHAPTER 15

The station appears to be a giant storage unit, a warehouse, each area color-coded. They follow a strobing green light to their dock on the opposite side of the cube. All around, ships flit from one area to the next, some nearly invisible but for the occasional glint of light across their hulls. Most are combat vessels decked out with plasma cannons. Jack keeps expecting one to swing around and blast them into dust.

They find their assigned dock and attach the cargo ramp. Forty minutes later, Jack and Dino pull themselves along the railings of the tunnel. Bel sensed a pressurized atmosphere and the linkup confirmed clean air, so they go without suits. The outer door slides open with a hiss and a thump, popping Jack's ears. The station's airlock is about the size of a two-car garage. It seals them in. A female voice tells them to prepare for gravity. Red arrows marked "floor" point at what Jack mistook for the ceiling. They resituate and grip handles while the gravity amps up. He feels it in his chest first. Then the floor pushes against his feet. A green light flashes, warning that the inner door is about to open. Jack attempts to erase all thoughts from his mind. It is easier to face the unknown with no presumptions. Yet he can't help imagining a line of soldiers on the other side. *Zip-zap.* He will fall limbless to the floor.

The door rises. The gap widens, widens, until Jack and Dino find themselves staring into an abandoned cargo bay. It is at least 500 feet long, 300 wide. Mesh floors, concrete walls, harsh lighting. No soldiers, no guards, no nothing. Abandoned. It must be a mistake. They were given the wrong dock number. Or—

"There," Dino says, pointing.

"There." The word bounces back, startling them both.

"There what?" Jack says.

"Air what?" says Jack's echo.

Dino points. Way down, across the cavern, a large object.

Jack squints, struggling to distinguish its silver surface from the wall behind it.

"Let's go see," he says.

"Oh see," the room responds.

They search everywhere for signs of life but find none. No scraps of paper, no candy wrappers, no spent vaporizer cartridges, not even any dust. Weirder still, the security turrets are turned off, the camera lenses beside them dead black circles. Seems odd to point a plasma cannon at visitors and then give them free reign once they're inside. Whatever strings Dandy pulled to get this done must have cost a fortune.

The object is a suspension cube, ten feet tall and wide, a fancy shipping container designed for fragile cargo. The surface is grooved metal, the corners slightly rounded and coated in a rubbery material. It appears fresh from the factory, but that's not surprising given the high-profile nature of the facility. There's a single control panel on one side, but without the access code, it might as well be a bank vault. Jack flips the lid to the panel, regardless.

"Huh," he says.

A bit of white tape holds a small black rectangle against the display.

"What is it?"

"A memory stick." Jack peels the tape away and folds the stick in his palm.

"From Dandy?"

Jack ignores him, calls Justin on his portable. "Get in here with a shover. Bring Stetson. Tell him we need his computer skills."

*

Stetson keeps an extensive collection of Frankensteinian portable communicators, most of which are no good for communicating and hardly qualify as portable. The one he brings with him to the bay is about the size of a vacuum cleaner and weighs nearly 80 pounds. The Nation declared it illegal to modify portables ten years ago, so he builds them all from scrap. He calls this particular device Mr. Crackerjack, and talks to it as some people talk to their pets. He turns it on and plugs the data stick into one of its many ports. Jack stands over his shoulder and watches, as if it will make any sense to him. The tech is so old there's a physical keyboard. The symbols have all worn off, but Stetson goes by feel, typing away with a series of pleasant clicks. A small square lights up on the device's back, black text on a white screen. A word processor.

Across the bay, Justin sits at the wheel of a shover, guiding the cube into the airlock. Dino follows and directs, shouting occasional commands. "Hold on a minute!" and "I said slow down, man!"

"Hmm," Stetson says.

"Good or bad?"

"Neither. Give me a minute."

Inscrutable symbols flash onscreen. Row upon row.

"Weird."

"What?" Jack says.

"Okay," Stetson says. "Alright, so, it's no virus, so that's a plus. I'm seeing one file, and it's an old format."

"Go on."

"I mean old. I haven't seen anything like it in years." He pauses to grin up at Jack.

Jack is unamused.

"Nevermind. You know how they talk about the digital dark ages?"

Jack knows the term, but can't place it.

"It's something only museums and hackers care about. See, like, when you want to store a secure message, you've only got a couple of options. Find a good hiding place for your data stick, encrypt the file and hope it's uncrackable—except nothing is truly uncrackable—or store it in an obsolete format. So even if someone steals it, they can't open the thing, right? Okay. So, the bad news is Bel's software can't read it. The good news is, Mr. Crackerjack is old as a dinosaur turd." He grins again.

"Is that your way of saying you can read it?"

"Yes."

"Great. And what's it tell us about our cargo?"

"Nothing. But it does tell us where to take it."

"Coordinates."

"Yep. And one more thing. A very short message."

"Yeah?"

"Okay, so. It lists the coordinates, then it says, um. Well, I don't think you're gonna like it."

"What does it say, Stets."

"It says, *Or your family*."

"Or your family."

"Yeah. I'm thinking as in, like, take this box to these coordinates, or, you know..."

Jack stands upright, wipes his forehead with a sleeve. "Let's get the hell out of here."

CHAPTER 16

Stetson leans over the billiards table and eyes his shot. Lana looks on from the corner sofa. The stick makes an artificial clicking sound when he strikes. The holographic ball hits another and the table speakers seem to clap. The spheres bounce around the bumpers but none hit the pockets. Stetson stands back and curses. Hunter clucks her tongue and sets up for her next shot. She sinks two. Sets up again. Sinks one. Sets up again. "Eight-ball, side pocket." A near miss.

"You get overzealous," Stetson says.

"Count the solids, grasshopper."

"I'm saying. You always choke with the eight-ball."

"Keep talking and you'll be choking on it."

He sinks three in a row.

Next shot, Hunter calls eight-ball corner pocket. Misses.

"Son of a bitch."

"Told you."

They've been holding at the new coordinates, an area deep within the sun's corona, for three full days as of this morning. They couldn't have picked a more dangerous spot in the solar system. If they aren't gone within fourteen days, Bel's mag shield will run out of juice and the radiation will flash-fry them. Perhaps more telling is that being this close to the sun means nobody without their exact coordinates could find them if they wanted to. Distant broadcasts would be lost in the interference, including an SOS. The first thing they did when they woke from grav sleep was shutter the observation windows. If they could have looked without destroying their retinas, they'd have seen a white sun about six and a half feet in diameter burning insanely close. Even with Bel's shielding, the radiation bleached a patch of the front hallway yellowish-white. It also fried their exterior cameras and most of their sensors. So until they get to a safer distance and replace the parts, they're essentially flying blind. In the meantime, Lana wastes the days with Hunter and Stetson in the rec room. They don't mind that she sits in. Their sniping flourishes with an audience present.

"We should start taking bets," Stetson says.

"Maybe if you didn't cheat."

"I don't cheat."

"You programmed a tilt into table. What? You thought I couldn't spot it?"

"That's just your short left leg, Gimpy. I wasn't talking about the game, anyway. I'm saying about the mystery box."

That's what they're calling the suspension cube in their cargo hold.

Hunter says, "What's the bet?"

"What it is. My guess is a bomb. When Dandy's people get here, we all go boom."

"They wouldn't bring us all the way out here to detonate a bomb."

It makes enough sense to Lana, actually. "If it's a prototype, maybe," she says, and feels immediately guilty. The undertone of this conversation is that Jack is going to get them all killed.

"That's right," Stetson says. "We're in the perfect place to test a weapon. It wouldn't register on any sensors."

"You know what?" Hunter says. "I'll take that bet. I can't lose."

"How's that?"

"If you're right, and it is a bomb, we'll be dead before I have to pay up."

Stetson grunts. "You always find a way to weasel out."

Hunter frowns and glances at Lana, goes back to the game.

Lana pretends not to notice the implications of Stetson's remark. He and Hunter have always acted like rivals. Lana never thought to ask if they'd been romantically involved, though if they had been, romance would have had little to do with it. She used to maintain psychological profiles on the crew. They were unofficial, and she did it more for her own peace of mind than theirs. When you're stuck in a tin can with five other people for months at a time, it helps to know what makes them tick. And what sets them off. Stetson has a mean streak, especially when threatened. He lashes out because he's insecure. Hunter's not exactly a saint, either. According to Jack, she fought in the war when she was just fifteen, but not for the Star Nation. She was a pilot for a rebel faction loosely affiliated with FROST. In a very real way, she could have wounded the same soldiers Lana treated. Once it became clear FROST would lose, Hunter abandoned and went underground. It probably saved her life. She comes from a large family, but most of her siblings didn't make it through the conflict. She's always been closed off. If she and Stetson did have a tryst in the past, it could only end in fireworks. Then again, supposing they did, it's impressive they've remained as civil as they have. Lana didn't manage as well with Jack.

Speaking of Jack, she's seen little of him since their arrival. When something's on his mind, he hibernates. Last she knew, he went to make a late breakfast, which means he'll be in the kitchen or his bunk.

She stands and heads for the door. "Gonna check on the food."

Stetson says, "You didn't place your bet."

She thinks a moment. "Something bad," she says, and ducks out.

*

Eggs are pretty much impossible to store on a spaceship. Even in suspension, they crack and lose their innards, end up congealed. Something about micro-pressure changes. The only way to guarantee their safety is to plop them into a grav tank typically reserved for human beings, which would be a waste of resources. Powdered eggs, on the other hand, may be artificially colored and taste like rubber, but they last. Jack combines the powder with water in a large bowl, stirs it with a spatula, pours it out on the grill beside a row of sausages. He should have had a real egg or two on Earth. He'd have settled for hardboiled. And he hates hardboiled eggs. Why is it that even something loathed becomes an indulgence when rare? He folds the eggs and sausage and onions into a tortilla and leans over the counter and eats. He leaves the rest out in the dining room and heads back to his quarters. He lies on the bunk and tries to get his head on straight.

He knows the others are on edge, wondering what they're walking into, the lovely little note, what Dandy's intentions may be in all of this, and just what kind of clown might pop out of the mystery box. Personally, Jack couldn't care less about its contents. It doesn't matter why they've gone through all of this trouble, why they have to make the handoff in the astronomical equivalent of a shady back alley. He cares only about the fact that they have been given a task and they have to complete it. They've done their part. It's up to Dandy to follow through. If Jack can make good with him, maybe he can make good with the second party, the buyer, back on Earth. He'll go legitimate like he said, jump through the Star Nation's hoops and scrape by with a penny here and a penny there.

Except the more he thinks about it the less appealing it sounds. He doesn't owe the Star Nation. Did they compensate him for his time as a POW? Did they help with his medical bills? Did they do anything to end the nightmares when he got home? Did they pay for his therapy sessions with the quack doctor who, after all his diagnosing, calmly told him to "put it out of his mind and move on"? The Nation left them to their own devices. It took a solid month after the war ended for the camps to be rescued. There were food drops, but no evacuations, no medical experts pouring in. The sick were still sick, and anyone who was seriously starved overate and burst their guts and died. FROST's prison guards had different reactions to defeat, depending on the camps. On Enceladus, they let the air out. Killed over 15,000 prisoners. Europa's entire prison population was supposed to have been ordered into hand-dug pits and then sliced up with laser rifles. A handful of the camp commanders refused, knowing that the war was over and they'd been defeated. Most were not so merciful.

At Gertrude on Ganymede, where Jack was held, the guards went skittish. Turned tail. Some abandoned. Suddenly the prisoners ran the prison. It was a strange and immediate switch. Jack watched ten prisoners take turns beating a guard to death with his own baton. Blunderbuss, the one who beat him so bad the day of the big announcement, vanished from the camp, but was eventually arrested. He was never executed, though. Within ten years, the new prisons housing war criminals were deemed too costly, so they were shut down and the serial murderers released. The show of so-called justice had ended.

Anyway, profit and justice are the same thing in the eyes of corporations, and the Star Nation is little more than that. Today they let men like Jim Dandy corner the weak because it works for their system. They add new laws and regulations to the shipping industry so they can collect heftier fees. A new tax here, a new fine there. All in the name of controlling the flow of cash. Petty criminals scraping by are punished, but billionaire murderers and thieves will never see the inside of a jail cell. As for the everyman, the hardworking blue collar asshole who abides by the law because he's either scared or believes himself loyal, he belongs at the bottom of the food chain. Scraps for the suckerfish. It has always been this way. Nothing to get upset about. Just keep your head down till the guillotine drops.

His thoughts are interrupted by a knock at the door, followed by Lana's voice. "You in there?"

He swings his legs over the bunk and sits up. "Come in."

She holds out two steaming mugs, offers one, and he takes it and inhales the coffee steam and carefully tips it to his lips. It burns his tongue, waking him.

"Careful. It's hot," she says.

"Thanks."

He pats the bed. She hesitates, then drops beside him, leaving a noticeable gap. He feels the shadow of an urge to wrap his arm around her. Funny how years of separation can't erase that fondness.

"You okay?" she says.

"Yeah. Healed up after the last jump." He slaps his belly where the bruises used to be. Grav tanks are great for the wounded.

"That's not what I meant."

He sips his drink. She wants him to say that he's scared, that it's unrealistic to think Jim Dandy will forgive his debt, that this hole can only get deeper, that maybe he saw it coming when he first got into this business, that it was all a self-fulfilling death wish, punishment for his unforgivable sins. But none of this is true. He feels like a cornered animal, ready to claw out the eyes of whoever's responsible for all this shit. Except "all this shit" is indefinable, and there is no one to blame but himself.

He laughs.

"What's funny?" she says.

"New Darwinism."

"What about it?"

He almost tells her about Keshawn. His dark eyes set in that leathered face. How they used to sneak out onto the barracks roof and watch the camp. Smell the stink of piss and shit in the troughs, the scrubbers struggling to keep up with all the pollutants in the atmosphere, such expansive human filth. Keshawn was a teacher. Jack never knew of what, exactly, but everyone called him Professor. He knew all about New Darwinism, understood its philosophies and said that although it was insane and brutal, it should not be disregarded. *Our minds,* he would say, *are mirrors of the world around us. Sometimes the glass gets distorted or cracked, but the causes are very real.* Jack never knew if he was reiterating classroom hokum or actually sympathizing with the men who beat helpless prisoners to death.

One night in particular sticks out. The enclosure lights were down, which was unusual, leaving the entire camp dark. They found their way outside and onto the roof by feel, and they could hear others rustling through the camp, and they could smell tobacco smoke that made them sick with envy. There were only a handful of guards doing their rounds, flashlight beams cutting through the rows of huts. Every time a beam fell on empty ground, someone hidden nearby would giggle, and the guard would shout threats, and the hidden man would giggle more. If it weren't for his bruises and strained muscles and empty stomach, it might have brought Jack a momentary sense of joy. Here in the dark, no one could see them, so no one could hurt them. Keshawn felt it too. He took a deep breath and said, out of nowhere, *If there is no escape from horror, then it is our responsibility to endure it, even enjoy it. Acceptance is the only freedom. It must be digested. That's why I will survive and so many others will die.* Jack said nothing. It sounded like bullshit. He assumed Keshawn was talking to himself the way starved men do, having forgotten there were others around. So when Keshawn gripped his shoulder, he startled so hard he nearly fell off the roof. He left the hand there, just squeezing for a while. A year and a half later, Keshawn was the first volunteer to help with the killings. A week after that, he used the lid of a tin can to slit his own throat.

Jack does not tell this story to Lana. He just drops his eyes and drinks his coffee. "Just thinking."

Lana says, "I came here to apologize."

"Apologize for what?"

She does that thing where she crinkles her nose like she's about to sneeze. "When you came to me, you said Ani left you. And I said something pretty cold."

He remembers. She had said it took Ani long enough. Which is fairly accurate.

"I just wanted to say that I'm sorry. I was running on very little sleep, and I didn't expect to see you."

"You thought I was trying to get laid."

"Please let me finish. I'm trying to—" She slaps a piece of hair from her forehead.

"Sorry."

"I just wanted to say that I didn't mean what I said. I know that despite everything, Ani means a lot to you. I'm sure it hurt when she left."

"It didn't."

"No?"

"It was a relief. I was the one who should've left. I was in no shape to be a husband. Or a father. I'm still not."

"Jack…"

"You think I'm just feeling sorry for myself, but I'm not. Acceptance is freedom, right?"

"Um. I guess."

"I never told you how I got this," he says, pulling down his collar. He rarely looks at the tattoo himself, but thinks about it every day and sees it clearly when he closes his eyes. It was crudely rendered with a crooked needle and blotchy ink. A jagged four-point star—the image on FROST'S flag—and the words *Killer* and *Coward* arranged vertically on either side.

She looks at it for only a moment, then flicks her eyes away. "No," she says. "You never did."

"Food was scarce. The guards came to our hut with new orders. What they considered a solution to the rationing problem."

She looks into the surface of her coffee.

Belinda's inflectionless voice erupts through both of their portables: "Warning. Approaching vessel will make contact in one minute and fifty-nine seconds."

The proximity alert.

Then Jack is out of his room and in the hallway, sprinting to the bridge.

CHAPTER 17

"What do we see?" Jack says.

Hunter beat him there somehow, a bite of breakfast tucked in one cheek. She taps at the monitor and a series of numbers and symbols pops up on the display. She skims the text and says, "Combat ship. Moving fast."

He almost asks her to put it on the monitor, but the outer cameras are burned up.

"It's gotta be our guy."

"Hang on."

"Transmission?"

"Not yet."

"Hail them."

"Already did. No response."

"Lost in the noise?"

"I don't think so."

"They're ignoring us?"

"Looks that way."

The others come through the doors and down the steps. Stetson rushes to his console. Lana looks Jack over and frowns and gestures at her stomach. He isn't sure what she means until he looks down. In his haste to reach the bridge, he forgot about his drink. He's still holding the mug, but it's empty. Hot coffee has splashed down his front, soaking his shirt and most of his right leg. He hadn't noticed. He drops the mug harder than he means to and the handle snaps off.

"Oh shit," Hunter says.

"What?"

"Stetson, are you seeing what I'm seeing?"

"I don't fucking believe it."

Jack says, "Talk to me, people."

Hunter says, "You're not gonna be happy."

He comes forward to see, but he can't read the data. Squiggles and text and numbers. He's never been good at this techy coded shit. "What am I looking at?"

She highlights two sets of numbers, one at the bottom of the display, the other at the top. She points to the bottom number. "This is the ship approaching us now." She points to the top number. "And this is the ship that approached us about two months ago." The numbers are identical.

"Two months," he repeats.

She waits for him to realize the implication, but he already has.

"How long before they reach us?"

"Thirty-eight seconds."

He whips around. He's about to order them all to the panic pod when his portable rings.

The room gets very quiet.

He already knows who it is. He lifts it to his ear.

"Hello, Dandy," he says.

"Good afternoon, *Jaaack*." The voice is nasally, his name drawn out into a whine. "I had a feeling you would pick up this time."

"Good guess."

His crew stares. They knew it was a trap. They just didn't realize how extensive.

"You should know, Jackie, before you try to run, that my ship is three times as fast as yours, and armed with a very powerful plasma cannon. So here is what's going to happen. You and your crew will meet my men at your forward airlock. And don't try sealing anyone in that little escape pod of yours. I know how to count. We're attaching to your airlock now, so I'd head on down ASAP if I were you. Toodles."

Toodles. Really.

"Dandy's with the pirates now?" Stetson says.

Hunter answers, "They were never pirates, Stets. It was a setup from the start."

Jack lowers the portable and stares into the faces around him, knowing and feeling and accepting that this may be one of the last times they are all alive in the same room.

He has an idea. It's reckless and desperate, but it's something. "Dino," he says, "come with me. Everyone else, forward airlock. We'll be there soon."

Moments later, Jack and Dino are on the other side of the third level, inside food storage, sweating from a hard sprint. Dino props one of the suspension cases open while Jack hangs in above the waist to dig through several hundred pounds of cans. He tosses them over his shoulder. A few smash open and leak on the floor. He empties half the container before he finds what he's looking for. The rifles are in hard plastic cases, protected from the weight of the cans. He hands one to Dino and opens the other. Glossy lightweight barrels and wooden stocks. They feel more like toys than deadly weapons. Both are early-model laser rifles, the kind infamous for overheating and blowing up, not the best choice, but even with his connections they were expensive and hard to secure.

Jack says, "Alright. Let's hurry."

They charge across the third level and practically dive into the forward Zero-G shaft, shoving off the walls and soaring downward. As he drops out of the first floor ceiling, he grips one of the handles and swings his body into the hall and back to gravity like a practiced gymnast. He hits the floor in midstride, Dino right behind him. The prep chamber door whips open and they raise their rifles as the pirates—soldiers, mercenaries, bounty hunters, whatever they are—come through the airlock. Caught in the middle are Lana, Justin, Stetson, and Hunter.

"Down!" Jack shouts.

The crew hits the deck.

The pirates aim their rifles at Dino and Jack. As before, there are five. They wear no helmets this time. Jack recognizes the leader with the facial scar. They are calm, stone-faced.

"Lower your weapons!" Jack says. "Now! Put them down! I said down!"

The pirates don't move.

Jack is vaguely aware of someone touching the center of his chest.

The pirates haven't budged or said a word. The one with the scar smirks.

No one is touching his chest. His portable is vibrating.

Careful to keep his rifle pointed at the leader's heart, he clicks the portable with his left hand.

"What are we doing here, Jackie?" Dandy says.

"Tell your men to back off."

"Don't be silly. You're going to get yourself hurt."

"You're on that ship. I want you here."

"That's sweet, pal, but I'm very comfortable."

"If you were going to kill us, your men would've done it already."

"Jackie, that's nutso. You're being nutso."

"Come aboard. Or I cut these people in half. They won't know what happened, but you and I will."

The leader is no longer smirking. His stance is a little stiffer.

"Call my bluff, Dandy. I dare you."

"Jackie. If you kill anyone, I will pull to a safe distance and blow your ship to smithereens."

"Yeah. And you'll destroy that thing in my cargo hold."

"You don't even know what it is." His voice takes an impatient edge.

"That's true. But you do. And I want answers."

"We all want answers, Jackie. But sometimes there just aren't any."

"Why don't you come aboard and we'll chat about it. Before I lose my patience."

"Are you going to count backwards now, Jack?"

"No, Dandy. I'm not."

"This is very foolish." His voice is flat now. Humorless.

There's a long pause.

Finally Dandy sighs and says something Jack can't quite make out. It sounds a little like *Orion.*

Then Jack is on his back and there is blood in his eyes. Dino lies beside him on the floor, and there's blood on Dino too. Someone pulls Jack upright by the lapels. The leader. Jack wobbles. He takes a step, nearly falls, tripping on bits of debris. He throws a hand forward and notices shards of shrapnel protruding from his palms. Sound comes back, and he sees his friends crouched on the ground, men standing over them with rifles to their temples.

How'd he get on the floor?

The men pull Dino upright. He and Jack stand there, swaying, fighting for consciousness.

Someone else is in the room. Someone in colorful clothes. Bright red hair.

Jack plucks a few splinters from his hands.

Where did this wood come from? There's no wood onboard.

The rifle.

Did he fire? Did his rifle backfire?

"Jackie," someone says.

Jack blinks.

His name is Jack, not Jackie. He hates that fucking nickname.

They shot first.

Someone pinches his cheeks. "Wake up, sonny boy!"

He coughs, takes a deep breath, coughs again.

They shot me.

I'm shot?

I'm dead.

No. Not yet.

Not shot.

Not dead.

They shot his rifle and it exploded. So fast he was on his ass before he knew what happened. Dino's too.

"Amateurish," a high voice says. And Dandy holds up what appears to be a melted barrel. He laughs, hot sour breath in Jack's face. "That was lucky. I told him to kill you."

CHAPTER 18

The effects of the blast recede in waves. Pain rushes in. A burning up and down his arms. He misjudged. A stupid move. He thought Dandy wanted the crew alive, but why would he need the entire crew? Dandy called his bluff.

Lana checks their wounds. Some third-degree burn patches on their inner arms, plus a series of lacerations. Nothing life-threatening, at least. The front of Dino's hair has burned completely off, including his eyebrows. Their jackets helped protect their arms, the sleeves shredded into tassels.

Dandy leads them to the cargo hold, his mercenaries walking behind with rifles aimed. He stays in front and orates. "Answers," he says. "You want answers." His wrists flip this way and that and Jack tries to focus on the words. "Try this. Aliens exist. Mind blowing, yes?" His getup is theatrical as always, a mix of antiquated French and Japanese with a dash of American showgirl glitz. He wears a green sort of kimono with long sleeves, a red cape, and puffy white cuffs, and his hair has been made into an intricate nest of shining orange braids. "And you, Jackie, have a piece of extraterrestrial technology sitting in your cargo hold." Fake purple eyelashes, painted white cheeks, lips a glossy smear the same color as his hair. Jack wonders if he does this all himself or if one of his grunts went to beauty school.

What did he just say? *Extraterrestrial technology?*

So the story on the news was true.

The hallway lights seem to be shaking.

He works very hard at putting one foot in front of the other.

"Crazy, yes?" Dandy says. "What's crazier is how you managed to steal it from a top secret military station. Not before murdering a handful of workers, I might add. You've got a lot to answer for, Jackie."

They enter the cargo hold. The box seems large and small at the same time, an obelisk in an empty cathedral. Its surface appears almost liquid in the lighting.

"Why?" Jack says.

"How's that?" Dandy says.

"Why steal it? You'll never find a buyer."

Dandy laughs. "Sell it? Oh no. We're going to turn it on."

"You're insane," Lana says.

"Genius is often mistaken as such," Dandy says, grinning.

He forces them to stand before the box while one of his men punches numbers into the security panel. There's a high-pitched beep and a series of clicks from unseen locks. Jack steps back as the box unfolds. The top lifts free like a swinging door, then all four sides lower flat to the ground. Fully opened, the pattern of insulation on the inner walls forms a series of straight lines that meets in the center, where the alien object stands.

A sphere. Ten feet in diameter, pulsating with a redness from within, like a heartbeat, slow build and fade, constant and evenly spaced. The surface is cloudy but at least partially translucent. Pale blue gems have been embedded in a deliberate pattern. Jack finds himself circling clockwise, following the design. The blue gems or stones or diamonds or whatever have been arranged in neat vertical columns. Consecutively, the columns become smaller in this direction, narrowing to a single point ending at a bright red stone. It could be a message or it could be decoration. To Jack, the red gem seems like a point of origin, spraying blue stones sideways. Like rows of soldiers exiting a building. He almost doesn't notice the other markings. Two squiggly lines that come out of the top and bottom of the red gem and curve around the blue ones like brackets or parentheses, as if to contain them. Just to the left of the red gem there is a deep indentation about six inches in diameter, black inside. An opening. It might run to the center of the sphere, or just a foot deep.

"The fuck is it?" Dino says.

"A bomb," Hunter says.

The Dandy laughs. "Why would you put jewels on a bomb?"

"We can't know," Stetson cuts in. "It's alien. That's the point."

"But you will know," Dandy says.

A few years after the war, stories of especially heinous atrocities began to trickle into the mainstream. Tales of experimentation by FROST scientists. Similar sadism had occurred during Earth's great wars. Doctors wondering how long a person could survive with his intestines pulled out. Babies put into pressure chambers. People dropped in boiling vats of whatever the fuck. These so-called medical experiments vastly improved humanity's understanding of the human body. So much so that the perpetrators who brought these nightmares to reality for thousands of innocent men and women and children would not be charged if they turned their data over to the western world, which they happily did. FROST followed this centuries-old lead, experimenting with prisoners to better understand the body's limits in outer space. People exposed to ammonium rains, dangled naked on cables into Jupiter's atmosphere, skinned alive and rubbed with Martian soil, crushed slowly by artificial gravity, and a number of Zero-G experiments: dismemberment, live vivisection, pain thresholds, immolation, etc.

And that is Dandy's plan. He'll retreat to his ship while one of his men stays to activate the sphere. If they can't turn it on—if it's not a device at all—they'll just shoot it or hit it till it cracks. Whatever happens, he will be the first to experiment with this technology. If it doesn't pan out, he'll just blast Belinda away, along with everyone aboard.

"Don't be an idiot," Stetson says.

"You know what I think it is?" Dandy says.

"If it is a bomb, you don't know the size of the blast radius."

"Look at the gems on its surface. That red jewel in the center. It's a generator. This, ladies and gentlemen, manufactures wealth. Diamonds and gold. Anything you can imagine."

"That's fucking crazy!"

"Oh, calm down. Gregorian, pick a volunteer. We're out of here." He spins on his heel.

The head mercenary nods and speaks rapidly in Saturnese. A thin youthful man with red hair steps forward and raises his hand. There is always some young fool ready to die first.

The others follow Dandy toward the exit.

There is nothing they can do. Lana gapes. He knows that look. People get it while trying and failing to comprehend their imminent death. Lining up with blindfolds on.

He has to think of something.

"You can't leave," he calls.

What is there? What logic?

"I'll be watching, so make it a good show."

Something real. Something plausible.

"No," Jack says. "I mean you can't leave. My ship won't let you."

Yes. No way to confirm or deny. A solid bluff.

He tries to put on a confident air, an imitation of Dandy's knowing snideness. It's difficult to maintain with the burning sensation up and down his arms and the pressure in his head.

"I wouldn't step foot outside this room if I were you."

Dandy pauses at the doorway. "Oh? Do go on."

"My ship has been listening to every word. Didn't you notice the turret when you came in? The one above us now? I told her if you come aboard, she can't let you leave. The moment you step outside the hold, she'll mow you down. And if you kill us first, she'll do it anyway."

Dandy smirks. "That sounds like a big fat lie to me, Jackie." He says this, yet he takes a tentative step away from the door. "Why wouldn't she just kill me now?" He points at the turret above. The camera lens is blank, dark.

"Because," Jack says. He licks his lips. He can hear the blood pulsing in his ears. "Because you still have your rifles pointed. Our safety is her number one priority. But if you leave you'll turn around and kill us. You said it yourself. As long as we're in this room together, we're all safe."

Dandy seems taken aback. His showmanship failing. He must realize there's only a small chance Jack is telling the truth, but with a guy like Dandy, that's chance enough. He'll put himself before everything. "Is that possible?" he says to the leader. *Gregorian.* The name Jack thought sounded like *Orion* before his rifle exploded.

Gregorian shrugs and mutters something.

It could very well be true. If Jack had thought things through beforehand, he could have programmed Bel in just this way.

Dandy considers the door. He says, "Tell her to speak."

"What?"

"Your ship. Her AI. Tell her I want to talk to her."

"She won't."

"No? Why?"

He glances at Stetson and Hunter, who ask with their eyes what the hell he is doing.

"We're under attack," he says. "She's in lockout mode."

"Lockout mode. That's very clever."

"Not clever, Jim. Dangerous. For you."

Dandy's eyes flash at the use of his first name. He puffs his chest, and then he rubs a hand over his lips and composes himself. He takes a breath. "So we are at a standstill."

Jack considers bargaining. He could say Bel will let them leave if no harm comes, but Dandy's word counts for nothing. If he escapes this ship, he will kill them. Guaranteed.

"Jackie." He's back to cooing in that theatrical tone. "Do you remember my note?"

He remembers. *Or your family.*

"I wasn't just talking about the shipment. See, if I'm not back in range of my people within two weeks, my men are going to kill your ex-wife and child. If I die, they die."

"Bullshit," Jack says. He feels flush. Sweat beads down his cheeks.

Please let it be a lie.

"I have a strict policy of covering my own ass on things like this."

There are only wrong choices to be made. Die with his crew and let Ani and Kip live, or take his chances with Dandy and his trigger-happy mercenaries, and maybe get his boy and his ex-wife killed in the process. Certain death vs. terrible odds.

Self-sacrifice would be most heroic, but it doesn't say "hero" on his neck.

"Fuck you," he says.

Dandy grins. "Looks like we're stuck then, Jackie. You won't let me leave, and I won't let you live. What ever shall we do?" His men are poised for something, their attention drawn behind Jack. Jack follows their eyes, which have settled on the sphere and the young man slowly approaching the hole in its center.

CHAPTER 19

It is surreal. This young man with his buzzcut hairdo hiking up his sleeve and looking out at the Dandy. The Dandy nodding.

Don't. This is the word stuck on Lana's tongue, a sane word. They should all say it together. Let it resound across the solar system, all mouths accepting its common sense. A nice thought, but impossible. Because here is the Dandy grinning like a demented circus clown, and here is Jack sweating and bracing for a sprint and mouthing something in her direction—*panic*, it seems to be—and here is Lana Weir with her own mouth half-open and her shoulders slumped forward, silent witness to a collective psychosis. This is how all wars are waged and repeated. Idiots locked into their forward momentum. *Don't.* The word does not exist to them.

"Do it," Dandy says.

The young man has to bend slightly at the knees. He bites his lip and pushes his arm inside. Hand, wrist, elbow, bicep. His cheek presses against the sphere.

What does he feel? Is it cold or warm, rough or pearl-smooth?

This is Jack's doing as much as it is the Dandy's. His quick thinking brought them this. Activation of an alien device, which is what they were meant for all along. If nothing else, maybe Dandy will die alongside them. When there are no sensible choices, chaos reigns.

The young man grimaces.

Everyone backs away. Lana positions herself in line with the far door, though it is blocked by Dandy. The rest of his men spread out, making to circle the sphere, raising their rifles.

"Mmf," the young man says.

The object's glow grows more intense. The blue gems light up vertically in sequence, a column that swings clockwise around the sphere. She notes how this flashing makes the blue jewels appear drawn toward the red stone, which pulses rapidly.

"There's something…" the young man says. "Got it!"

The light goes out. The sphere becomes a cloudy ball.

Nothing happens. Palpable disappointment settles over the hold. Even Lana feels it, however absurd. She didn't know what to expect. Just something.

The young man pulls his arm free. He stands upright, unharmed. He turns to the group and shrugs. "I guess—"

Behind him, the sphere explodes.

CHAPTER 20

Jack ducks. Shards of debris smash to the floor around him, thick and heavy. When he looks up, a great deal of dust lingers where the top of the sphere used to be. The bottom portion forms a jagged bowl. The boy is still there, but he's acting strange. He leans forward and slaps at his neck. He jerks upright and pulls his hair. He opens his mouth to scream but no sound comes out. Something has wrapped around his throat. A long tendril extending from the remains of the sphere. It resembles a thin electrical cord. The flesh of his neck ripples. He hops from foot to foot. The rippling passes through his face, his arms, and somehow through the fabric of his uniform.

Jack should be running now. He has been edging toward the nearest Zero-G shaft, but freezes in place. Any time now his feet will carry him away from this terrible sight.

The boy splits open with a tearing sound. For a moment, he remains standing, a skeleton in shredded clothes. Glistening muscle over pink knobs of bone. Fibers or cords wind around his limbs, stitch through his ribcage, wrap his jaw. They ascend from the gore, reach for a sky that isn't there. The bones rise and separate all at once, disjointing and folding wrong. Impossibly, they dissolve. Like sugar in hot water. Like a magic trick, the boy is gone, replaced by a waggling knot of pale fibers that retract into the base of the sphere where a central mass rises.

Jack's feet come unglued.

He spins and sprints. Everything is movement and color. The Zero-G shaft is only 15 feet away. One of Dandy's men has gotten in front of it. He raises his rifle. Jack throws up his hands. A faint light slices the air and he smells burning dust. The laser zips over his head, targeting the thing behind him. The thing he can hear bounding closer on heavy legs.

No time to look.

Jack passes Dandy's man and glances to where the others should be.

They are gone.

No, not gone.

There by the door. They crowd through the exit, bottlenecked. No one looks in his direction. He does not blame them. Instinct takes over. You forget the world, your buddies, your orders. You run your fucking ass off.

He ducks through the grated archway of the Zero-G shaft. Gravity goes. He catches the central ladder with his left hand. Momentum swings him around to the other side and he faces the way he came in time to see a bear composed of wrinkled brain matter smashing into Dandy's man. Except it is not a bear and it is not made of brain. It is a mass of tentacles compressed into the shape of a beast without features. No fur, no head, no tail, no paws or claws that Jack can see, just stumpy bundles of rope. An imitation of what an animal should look like. And when it connects with the man wielding his useless rifle, the tentacles come apart and wrap him and drag him across the floor beside it. He screams and fights but the cords lash out. They enter him. His skin shakes, and then his skin is gone, and then he is filled with snakes, and the snakes reattach to the animal form and the man is gone, the animal nearly twice its original size. But just as fast.

It charges for Jack.

He kicks off and up, rocketing toward the ceiling as the creature smashes into the base of the ladder. The metal vibrates like a tuning fork. When he looks down the animal seems to have exploded. Disembodied sinew swirls around the ladder like webbing. The strands flash to the sides of the enclosure and all it once it spirals up at him, a churning cluster. It is too fast. He kicks another rung to increase speed. He enters the ceiling. Dim lights set in the walls, a cramped tunnel. Sound is amplified in here. He hears wet squishing like a vat of meat. It enters the tunnel after him, swallows the light, filters it orange-red-brown, inches behind.

The tunnel ends five or six feet ahead. White hallway of the second floor.

Jack doesn't think. He screams: "Belinda increase shaft three gravity twenty Gs now!"

Nothing happens.

He floats out of the tunnel and up into the corridor. The shaft continues overhead, forming another tunnel that extends to the third level, but there is no time to continue up. He kicks against the ladder, floating sideways into the second floor hallway as tendrils spill from below, winding the ladder, gripping the floor, shooting toward him and—

"Bel!"

The shaft's gravity kicks on.

The force slams the creature down the hole. The ladder twists and rends under this new weight, snaps with a series of cracks and bangs and whines. There's an incredible clatter as the base of the enclosure falls away, yanked apart by that thing's strength and 20 Gs of force.

He floats in midair. He pats himself down to check that he's intact.

What just happened?

He wipes beads of sticky sweat from his eyes.

The crew is probably to the pod by now.

He calls Lana. She doesn't answer.

"Bel," he says, "where are the others?"

"I cannot be certain, Jack."

"What do you mean you can't be certain!"

"Communication between my systems is incomplete."

"Where's the creature now? Is it still in the cargo hold?"

"Communication between my systems is incomplete."

"The hell does that mean!"

"My surveillance capabilities are functional, but cannot exchange data with my verbal relay system while my neural network is deactivated."

He remembers, vaguely. Stetson used the analogy of two sides of the brain. When the bridge between the sides is damaged, simple systems go haywire. You might show someone a picture and they can't say what it is, but they can write it on a piece of paper. It's convoluted and strange and whoever modeled Belinda after the human brain was a fucking moron.

Bel says, "If you'd like, I can direct you to the nearest video terminal to access my surveillance feed directly."

The nearest video terminal is on the floor above. The creature might already be heading there in one of the other shafts. How much time has he wasted just floating here? Thirty seconds? Ten minutes? He almost tells Bel to increase the gravity in shafts one and two, but stops himself. The crew will need the shafts in order to reach the panic pod, if they aren't already there. Or already dead.

He calls everyone. Even the Dandy. Nothing.

There are few options, and the longer he stands here paralyzed, the longer the creature has to move freely around the ship. He can make for the pod, but if the thing sees him, he's done.

Never sneak around camp before you know the guards' rounds.

He is not in the camp. He needs to stop thinking about the goddamn camp.

He needs to get his bearings. Concentrate.

He is on level two, at the rear of the ship. What else is back here?

Computer mainframe.

Belinda's mind.

"Bel. If I reactivate your AI, will your systems realign?"

"Yes, Jack."

"And you can tell me where the crew is?"

"If they are in view of surveillance systems, yes, Jack."

"Can you walk me through the process?"

"Of course, Jack."

Any relief he feels vanishes at the sound of a muffled explosion from the front of the ship.

CHAPTER 21

Lana has been told that moments of terror feel unreal. When she was a girl, she wanted to be a teacher. Then she became a nurse. She sewed wounded soldiers back together, or tried to. Then she became something of an outlaw working for Jack Kind. That does not feel entirely real, either, she has always felt. As she sprints across the first floor hallway with Hunter in front of her and the Dandy behind, something about the size of a dog in chase, she realizes just how inadequate her understanding of moments like this has been. It is not an intellectual surrealism, but physical. She sees herself from outside. A rat trapped inside a human body, consciousness relegated to some back room with a small window. Death probably feels like this.

They burst through hallway doors and close them. She hears the doors erupt again as the creature—dog, wolf, coyote, something—smashes through. This buys them enough time to reach the forward Zero-G shaft. Hunter leaps and swings around the ladder with grace, and Lana jumps and throws her arms out and crashes into the ladder and knocks the wind out of herself. Hunter grips her by the shirt and screams, "Up!" Someone climbs over her body. Green and orange color. The Dandy, crab-walking up the ladder. Someone else grabs her from behind. Dino. She struggles to jump but can't get a foothold. Dino and Hunter lift her. She can do nothing but be carried and watch her feet make swimming motions below.

Justin is down there still. Blonde head bobbing, hands reaching out.

Two of Dandy's men come with him. They turn and scream and one of them jumps with Justin up the shaft. The second stays below, grips the ladder and turns his rifle to the hallway and pulls something from his belt. "Fire in the hole!" someone screams. A brownish-yellowish streak of motion erupts out of the hallway and tackles the man, followed by an explosion that seems to go off more inside Lana's head than in the shaft. She feels it in her chest. A compression. The air gone. She sees white, then black, then smoke and faces and a fire alarm shrieks and nearby vents suck in the smoke. Somehow she has made it to the third level, just outside the open doors of the panic pod.

Dino and Hunter drag her inside.

Dandy runs past, down the hallway. He comes back.

Two of his men follow. The one with the scar on his cheek, and one with silver hair.

Where is Jack?

She collapses on the floor. She pushes on her chest.

This is called shock. She is hyperventilating.

"Close the door!" someone screams.

"Justin and Jack!"

"They're gone!"

"Shut the fucking door!"

"It's coming!"

Hunter does it. Cranks the red lever beside the door, sealing them in just as something clangs against the other side.

Lana counts her breaths. *One-two-three-four.* Too fast.

Slow down. Calm down. Start again. *One. Two. Three.*

Her portable vibrates. She reaches for it and then there is a rifle in her face and the man with the silver hair tells her not to move or he will slice her up real real good.

CHAPTER 22

Bel guides him into a room covered in reflective metal panels. They look like tinfoil. A single word has been scrawled across the central panel: *MAINFRAME*. He touches this panel and it springs open to reveal a crawlspace of twinkling colored light.

He floats inside.

Her mind is a labyrinth. The layout was designed to conserve space, not for ease of access. Endless rows of consoles house vital electronics, all thrumming and hot, which accounts for the steady stream of air blowing across his face. She guides him past the first intersection and through an opening in the ceiling. The thrumming grows in volume. He turns his portable up to hear her voice.

She tells him someone is trying to call him, but this area is blocking the signal. She'll need to relay any message. He says to do it immediately.

A panicked whisper, full of static: "Where—hell is anyone? Hunter? Unc— Jack? Can anyone f—hear—e?"

It's Justin.

"Bel, can I respond?"

"Not live. I can relay a recorded message."

He records one.

A moment later, Justin's reply comes in. On their way to the pod, Justin got separated from the others. Most of Dandy's men are dead. Justin is in his quarters, hiding under his bunk. He hears something moving in the hall. He believes he is probably dead too and that he is a ghost and he wants to go home and tell his mother and father that he is sorry, but they were never very easy to get along with, and if they weren't such hard asses maybe he would have tried harder, but they did the best they could and he forgives them.

Babble of the hopeless.

Jack floats into the final room. He has no idea what he is seeing. Blinking lights and what appear to be motherboards stick sideways out of the walls. He has never been here. This is Stetson's realm.

Jack sends his last reply, telling Justin to hold tight. He's not a ghost and everything is going to be alright as soon as Jack fixes things up. It almost sounds true.

"Bel," he says, "tell me what to do here. And hurry."

*

Shouting fills the panic pod. The silver-haired man keeps his rifle pointed at Lana's head and tells her to press against the wall. Dandy's makeup runs. White droplets of sweat rain off his chin. Hunter screams for them to all just calm the hell down and put the rifles away. The scarred guy aims at her with less conviction. They are outgunned. They comply. Place their hands on the wall. Dino stays beside Lana, his jaw jutting and veins pulsing, his singed hair giving him a stunned appearance. All the while, the thing in the hallway slams against the door.

"This my ship now," the Dandy says.

He directs them away from the wall, to the center of the room to kneel and lower their faces. Lana notes that his shoes are purple and curled like an elf's. They could easily have a bell hanging from them. It is such an absurd detail that she laughs. She stifles it with both hands, but it comes out the sides.

"What is so funny, might I ask?"

The others study her with equal concern. She has lost her mind.

She shakes her head and bites her lip. If she speaks, she's going to laugh again.

Dandy stands directly in front of her in his little patent elf shoes.

Her shoulders convulse, but she holds the sound in her mouth.

She's going to die now at the hands of a man wearing elf shoes.

He grips her by the hair and jerks her face up to the ceiling. "Listen, bitch. I am going to cut your head off and feed your body to whatever that is out there."

She can tell he is not kidding. Reality hits like a slap in the face. She is manic, still in shock, probably on the verge of a genuine panic attack. Actually losing it.

Dino growls, "Leave her alone."

Dandy lets her go and faces Dino. "You know, the only reason I kept you alive was to see what the sphere would do. We know now. What reason do I have for keeping you around?"

No one speaks.

Lana's portable rings again. She wants only to see if it is Jack or Justin. She reaches slowly, trying to hide the movement.

The silver-haired man kicks her in the stomach.

Her whole body cramps and she cannot breathe.

Where are you, Jack?

*

His hands tremble and sweat. He's overheating in this claustrophobic cube. Bel's directions are simple enough. There are six wetware panels on rollers jutting out of place, gel-like circuitry that resemble lightning bolts visible in the clear casing. He slides the panels back into place, bracing his feet on the opposite wall for leverage. He turns the screws finger-tight. "Okay," he says. "You should be all patched up."

"Thank you, Jack. Preparing for reboot now."

"What reboot?"

"I must undergo a partial reboot for my AI system to activate, during which time non-vital systems will be temporarily shut down. Would you like me to rephrase this?"

"Which features?"

"Lighting, gravity, water heating, internal comms, door automation, surveillance systems, holo terminals, waste-disposal—"

"How long?"

"The reboot will last five to seven minutes. Two to three for diagnostics tests. One to two minutes startup time. Eight to twelve minutes total."

"Skip diagnostics."

"It is not recommended."

"I said skip it."

"Yes, Jack."

He tests that the panels are firmly in place, tugging on their ends. They don't even wiggle. "Bel, is there anything you haven't told me about the reboot process?"

"There are billions of things I have not told you about the reboot process. Would you like me to—"

"Never mind."

"With my AI features activated, I should be of more assistance."

"I sure as hell hope so. Tell me when you're ready."

"I am ready."

"Okay. What do I do?"

"To initiate restoration of artificial intelligence features, say *initiate*."

"Initiate."

The lights go out.

*

Darkness swallows the pod. Lana falls backward. The floor has vanished.

Maybe that kick to the stomach was worse than she thought.

"The lights!" someone shouts.

"What the—"

"Shoot them! Kill them!"

Somehow, her head bumps into the ceiling. Or maybe the floor. An arm brushes against her face. Then a foot. A hand grips her shoulder and lets go. Shuffling noises, shouts of, "Hey!" and, "Get off!" followed by the unmistakable sound of someone choking.

"How's that, fucker," Dino grunts.

Hunter says, "What's going on?"

"I've got the slimy prick."

"Dandy? Where you are!" An unfamiliar voice.

"I'm about to snap his neck. Let your weapon go."

Rapid breathing.

"Don't kill him," Hunter says.

Lana reaches out and pokes someone in the eye.

"Ow," Stetson says.

"Sorry." Her breath is back, though shallow and pained.

"Why'd the lights go out," Hunter says. "Stetson? Are you still here?"

"I don't know. It could be something."

"That's very specific."

They float in darkness.

"Listen," someone whispers. "The thing. It stopped."

Lana cocks an ear. No more clanging at the door. Where did it go?

A better question is why.

*

Jack's eyes adjust. It is not pitch-black. A pale green glow emanates from the cracks around the panels. He waggles his fingers in front of his face. Fat glowworms.

His work in this place is done. Justin is up on the third floor. He's not about to head that way blind, but if he crawls back out to the main hallway, he can wait near the exit for Bel to come back online.

He gets lost at the third turn. He holds fast to the dim tunnel, cursing himself. The ship seems to press in all around him. If he tries another way out, he could end up deeper in Bel's mainframe. He should have waited in the room. Why isn't there a damn map on the wall?

He vaults through the corridor.

Hasn't it been five minutes by now?

Halfway down the next passage, he senses something following him. A chill that goes beyond intuition. A charge in the air, and the faint scent of ozone. He pauses. Is he hearing things, too, or is there a slight shuffle and rustle, like scales on pavement? He drifts to the next intersection and waits, squinting back the way he came.

Tentacles wiggle around the far corner. They remind him of vines, the kind that wrap trees and sprout small pointed leaves, but they're slick and moist and move with intention. First there are just a few. Then a wave of them fills the tunnel. There is no central body that he can tell. No eyes.

It freezes. Tendrils slide along the walls. A couple probe the air.

It charges, the same sickly churning propulsion it used before.

He shoves back, spins and gropes the walls.

The lights come on and bathe him in a whiteness more blinding than the dark.

*

She thumps to the floor on top of Stetson. Before they can untangle, Dandy's men get back to their feet, making threats. Dino gets up too, one arm crooked around the Dandy's neck, revolver held to his temple. Dandy's eyes flutter. He hacks and coughs and slaps at Dino's meaty arm.

"Hand them rifles over or I waste this piece of shit. Five seconds."

The men share an uncertain glance.

"Four."

"Okay," says the one with the scar. "We do it." He shrugs the shoulder strap off and hands the weapon to Hunter. The other man is slower to respond, but eventually does the same. "Now you let him goes."

Dino smiles. He does not let go. He cranks his grip.

"Don't kill him," Lana says. "He might know something."

The whites of Dandy's eyes fill red.

"She's right," Stetson say.

With a sigh, Dino releases him.

Dandy stumbles forward and rasps, "Kill them."

His soldiers look away.

"I said kill—"

Dino grabs Dandy by the crown of his head and slams him into the side wall. "Shut the fuck *up* already." Dandy crumples, slumps sideways. Dino checks his vitals. "Alive," he says.

Alive.

She fumbles for her portable. There are three missed calls, all from Jack. She calls back. It goes to voice messaging. "No answer," she tells the faces around her. The shock of their predicament wearing off, she swallows the knot forming in her throat.

*

A female voice directs him down strobing passageways. "Right, left, straight ahead!" The voice has energy. Psychedelic lights flash and run in all directions. Shudders and thumps in the walls, like the mainframe is falling apart. "Turn right! Faster, faster!" It isn't until he is resting at another intersection that he realizes the voice is Belinda's. She sounds different. She tells him to wait, listen, and backtrack slowly. He lost sight of the creature as soon as the lights came on, but he heard it close behind. Somehow, it lost him.

She guides him to the main room with the tinfoil walls.

"Bel? What the hell happened back there?"

"I'm not sure. I woke up, and that thing was right on top of you. I sent localized power surges to the area to disorient it. I guess it worked." She sounds just like a person. Before he deactivated her AI all those years ago, she must have been like this. He doesn't remember, but he can't help feeling guilty, and grateful that she's back.

He pokes his head into the hallway. No creature.

She says, "I didn't have time to tell you, but you missed another call."

"Justin?"

"Lana."

"Patch me through."

She picks up after half a ring. "Jack! Are you alright!"

Unbelievable to hear her alive and well. He struggles to keep his own voice steady. "I'm fine, just—I'm on the second level. Where are you? Who's with you? Is everyone safe?"

"We're in the pod. Justin's missing."

"What about Dandy?"

"He's here. With two of his guys. He tried to kill us, Jack. We got their weapons."

"Good."

"Can you get here?"

"I'm on my way. Stand by the controls. You'll need to open the door from inside."

"Okay."

"You open them exactly when I say. We're in a bit of trouble here."

"I think I got that."

Belinda cuts in. "Jack, you should leave this area immediately."

Before he goes out, he closes the panel, but there's no lock.

"Lana?"

"Yes."

"I'm gonna hang up. I need to meet up with Justin. We'll meet you at the pod."

"Okay. We've got you on surveillance. Be safe."

He floats into the main hall, checking both directions. To his right, a dead end. To the left, a door that leads to the shaft landing. All white and still, deceptively safe.

He tries calling Justin back, but there's no response. *Great.*

"Bel, is the creature still in the mainframe?"

"One of them, yes."

"There's more than one?"

"I have surveillance on three, but there may be others where I don't have access."

"Where are they?"

"One is in the mainframe behind you. Another is in the first level hallway. Another is in the dining room on the third level."

"What are they doing?"

"I can't tell. They appear to be looking for something."

Hunting would probably be more accurate.

"Did the gravity in shaft three reset?"

"Yes."

"Amp it up again. 20 Gs. Do you have eyes on Justin?"

"I'm not sure."

"What do you mean?"

"The room to his quarters is open, and I see a partial human form inside, but I can't be certain that it's Justin."

They should have installed cameras in crew quarters. And in the lavatories. Anywhere the creature or creatures could be hiding. To hell with privacy.

"Okay. I'm going to get him. I need you to be my eyes and ears."

"Okay. I'll do my best."

He pulls himself along the handles and through the first set of landing doors and wonders what the hell he is doing. Justin is probably dead. Why else would he fail to answer his portable? Why else would his door be open? Jack is no savior. He should just get to the pod where Lana and the others are safely awaiting his arrival. Every man for himself. That's how it always was. You hoard for your own stash, not for your so-called friends. They'll toss you away when you're useless. Sick or unable to work, all you do is take up space. Sure, the doctors worry over you, sneak you extra rations, but then the guards come and they tell you food is already low and something must be done, and what happens then?

For God's sake, Jack. You aren't in the camp.

His breath is very loud in his head.

Something else is bothering him. "Hey Bel."

"Yes, Jack?"

"You said you would do your best. When I told you to be my eyes and ears. Why'd you say that?"

"I'm afraid I don't know much about the biology of these creatures. They don't conform to any known lifeform. I'm still analyzing their behavior, but I may be ineffectual at understanding when they've spotted you."

Careful to avoid the gravity shaft, he goes through the next set of doors, bracing for a wall of tentacles that isn't there. "How about this?" he says. "If one of those things starts moving very fucking fast in my direction, you let me know. Does that make sense to you?"

"Of course. I'm sorry if I've upset you."

"Let's just get through this."

"Alright. Currently, there are no creatures moving very fucking fast in your direction."

"I didn't know you had a sarcasm setting."

"I'm being quite sincere."

"You tell me if Justin wakes up. And keep trying his portable."

"Yes, Jack. And Jack?"

"Yeah."

"Good luck."

"Thanks," he says. "We're gonna need it."

CHAPTER 23

The Dandy and his men huddle against the inside wall, Dino across from them with a rifle in his arms and a *don't-even-try-it* look. Stetson pulls up surveillance. On the washed-out holo-display, Jack propels himself along the main corridor of the second level in Zero-G. He pauses often to cock his head and listen. Stetson asks Bel to put the creature onscreen. In the mainframe, it blocks the lens. Every now and then the darkness twitches and light filters between what looks like a number of eels. On the first floor, a small grayish wad or ball has tucked itself into a high corner near the forward grav-shaft where the soldier pulled his grenade. Strands of this creature dangle like the fronds of a nightmarish willow. The third one in the kitchen is much larger. Maybe seven feet tall standing upright. It's hard to get a sense of its shape. Far as Lana can tell, it has no central body. The tentacles or arms or whatever they are compress to form limbs, but as it moves they wind and unwind, in constant flux, with no distinct length or diameter. They slide over every surface. Floor, walls, stove, lights. It opens the cupboard, snaps the handles off the doors. Tosses pots and pans. Violence in these movements. Anything useless gets cast away.

"We should shoot them," Stetson says. "The turrets are functional."

Hunter clucks her tongue. "Not with Jack out there."

"All the more reason."

"We might just agitate them. They don't see him. For now, that's good enough."

Stetson grunts his disapproval.

Lana just wishes they could do *something*.

Stetson switches to a feed outside Justin's room. Through the doorway, the monitor shows a shoe at the end of a filled-out pair of jeans, lying twisted and still.

*

Jack comes up the middle shaft to the third level and steps back into gravity. His portable, which had drifted up near his head, falls against his chest. Justin's room is the last one on the right, the nearest to the panic pod. Jack heel-toes it, wishing he wore sneakers instead of clunky boots. No news from Bel so far.

He pauses at Justin's doorway, surveying the scene.

His nephew lies face-down in the middle of the room. Nothing else is amiss, but that's not saying much. There's really nothing to be amiss. Justin has been sleeping on his bare cot. He never even took his bedding out of storage. The only conspicuous object is the photograph lying by his head. With a start, Jack wonders if the kid killed himself.

He rushes in and turns him over. Immediate relief. A purple knot rises from Justin's temple, a spot of blood down his cheek. His chest moves up and down. He snores.

Jack sighs and sits back. He transmits to Lana, whispering, "Justin's fine. Looks like he knocked himself out."

She knows better than to respond. Any noise could stir the creatures.

He flips the photograph over. In it, a young Justin tips a birthday cake to the camera. Jack counts eight candles. Justin's missing both of his front teeth, grinning like he means it. His parents squat on either side, a little awkwardly, their hands on his shoulders. Jack's brother, Terry, has a twinkle in his eye. His sister-in-law has been caught mid-blink. A happy moment. Genuine. Jack feels a wave of sorrow rising. His brother's son. His own nephew. Look at all Jack has done for him.

Focus.

They need to get to the pod.

He tucks the photo into Justin's front pocket and grips his shirt and shakes him. "Wake up, kiddo."

Nothing. Not even a groan.

Jack raises a hand for a hard slap, but stops.

He slides his arms under Justin's torso and struggles to scoop him up. For a skinny kid, he weighs a hell of a lot. His head lolls back like a baby's, then he snorts and jerks upright and screams, pounding fists on Jack's back and head. "Got me!" he howls. "Help! Got me! *Heeelp!*"

Jack drops him hard and tries to shut him up. "It's me, Justin! Uncle Jack!" But he's beyond consolation, eyes wild, practically frothing at the mouth. He backs against his wardrobe still throwing his fists and doesn't stop until Jack jumps him and claps a hand over his mouth and tells him to shut the goddamn fucking hell up before he gets them killed.

"Jack," Belinda calls. "Get out of there. Right now."

*

Movement in Justin's room. Hard to tell what's going on. The cameras don't pick up sound. It looks like Justin is awake. That's a good thing. Maybe.

"Switch to the kitchen," Lana says.

Utensils lie scattered across the floor, and one of the stoves has been flipped. Wires stick up jagged from cracks in the tile. The metal legs have been snapped in half. The creature is nowhere in sight.

"What the hell," Stetson says.

"Hallway," Lana says.

"Oh no."

The dining room door is mangled, a hole torn through its center. Shards of jagged metal cling to the walls and ceiling. Stetson swivels the camera 180 degrees and there is the creature, bounding on thick legs, its movements fluid, each stride covering its full body length.

Hunter lifts her portable. "Belinda, hit that fucker."

"I am. Look."

Stetson changes to a camera down the hall. The thing charges ahead. The laser is invisible, but they can see its effect, or lack thereof. The creature unzips down the middle, but the two halves throw tentacles against the wall and ceiling, grip handles and swing forward to keep from falling. The halves reach for each other and seal together as if nothing happened, legs still moving below it. The turret, which can cut through bone like butter, is useless.

*

"Faster, goddammit!"

They near the doors to the forward grav-shaft, Justin unsteady, Jack shoving him in the back. The creature slams through doors behind them, one after another. Simple, thin, poorly made doors. Little more than partitions. They hardly slow the creature. It thumps and slithers after them.

Bel opens the landing doors. Jack and Justin leap across the shaft, buoyed by Zero-G. They flash through the next set. Before they're out, the creature crashes against the previous set, stressing the hinges.

The panic pod is fifteen paces away. Closed.

"Lana, the door!"

The panic pod opens and a figure steps out, backlit by white light.

Dino, a goddamn guardian angel. He comes nearer and Jack waves him back.

Bang.

The creature hits the final door. All that stands between them and it.

Bang.

He is just ten feet from the pod.

Justin makes it. Dino grips his arm and whips him inside.

Crunch.

The thing pours into the hall. C*la-bump, cla-bump, cla-bump*, it lopes like a horse on python legs.

Dino spots it. His eyes go huge.

Jack's body is electric, hairs on end, skin rippled with gooseflesh.

He is a field mouse with a hawk swooping in. It is no contest.

Dino grips his wrist and gives him a yank and shove. Jack trips across the threshold into the arms of friends.

Dino comes in after him. Hunter pulls the lever.

Too slow.

It happens in a fraction of a second. The creature punches a single ropy appendance through the shrinking gap between the doors, aiming for Dino's face. Dino reacts. With his right hand, he takes a mighty swing at the incoming tentacle, thrusting his arm through the doorway. Upon impact, the creature's limb blooms like a wireframe flower, wrapping Dino's forearm. The doors clamp shut, two sheets of reinforced alloy that crush Dino's arm just below the elbow. He falls back without so much as a grunt, the flesh severed cleanly, blood spurting across the walls and the ceiling and Jack. Dino falls against him. They lose their footing and go down. Lana lunges, producing a rubber tourniquet from a pocket like a magic trick, then jumps back, gaping at the end of Dino's stump.

Jack leaps to his feet.

Dandy and his men scatter.

A mass of brown maggots burrows into the folds of Dino's shattered limb. They eat fast and efficiently, doubling and tripling in length as the bone and flesh vanish.

Those aren't maggots.

"Hunter!" Lana screams. "Rifle!"

Dino stares at the stump in disbelief, holding it as far from the rest of his body as he can, as if he might just cast it away. He releases a sorrowful moan and kicks and slaps the floor. Hunter steps up with a rifle. Lana kneels on Dino's ankles to keep him still. Jack, realizing what is about to happen, drops onto Dino's good arm. Dino's muscles ripple and Jack wonders if it isn't already too late. The creature could be inside him, licking through his body, preparing to burst.

Hunter takes careful aim just below the ball of his shoulder and fires a steady beam, her teeth clamped tight. The flesh hisses and the bloody stump drops free, the wound flash-cauterized and black. Jack and Stetson and Justin drag Dino across the tile, away from the severed limb. Everyone gives it a wide berth. Because it is no longer a severed limb.

A slug-like mass about the size of a grapefruit sits on the floor, a miniature version of the thing in the hallway. A scrap of fabric lies next to it—what remains of Dino's shirt. A network of tentacles tests the air.

No one moves until it jumps at the nearest set of legs. Hunter's. She dodges. The glob slaps against the wall and stays there.

Hunter fiddles with her rifle settings, adjusting the laser, steps away and shoots the thing right in the center.

The cut heals instantly. No blood.

"No fucking way!" Justin screams.

"Cover it with some a thing!" screams the merc with the scar.

"With what!" Jack answers.

It leaps again.

They scatter.

It lands in the center of the room, quivers and sprouts centipede legs, and skitters lightning quick toward—

A helmet slams over it. Lana holds it firmly with both hands. Inside, the creature prods at the visor. For a long time, no one moves or says a word. They wait. For what, they aren't sure. For the helmet to explode, maybe, or the thing in the hallway to get the doors open, or Dino to erupt. Something else to go terribly wrong. But there is only the thing under the helmet, the lasting silence, and the understanding that they are trapped.

CHAPTER 24

Jack and Lana sit with Dino in the side room. They have lain out extra blankets for a bed, and Lana found a med kit in the main chamber, complete with antiseptics, bandages, and enough pain meds to knock him out. The cut is not in an ideal place, Lana says, right through the top of the humerus. He'll probably want a second surgery if they ever reach a hospital, and there they will take the arm cleanly off. He has lost a good amount of blood, but will survive if they stave off infection. He'd have transformed by now if any of the creature remained in his body. Probably.

"You can't blame yourself," she tells Jack.

Jack says nothing. He senses a presence in the doorway, turns to find the leader of the mercs, the guy with the scar. Gregorian. "This man save your lifes," the merc says. "Very brave."

Not long ago, this asshole was prepared to sacrifice Dino right alongside Jack and the rest of the crew for an expensive science experiment. Probably a lump sum. Now he wants to stand there and revere a fallen comrade. Jack never should have let them take the paintings in the first place. He should have defended his ship.

"Go to Hell," he says.

After a short silence, Gregorian says, "I was soldier too once."

"And I care?"

"This yours ship. No longer you are under occupations. I follow order of a captains."

"Do you speak fucking English or what?"

"I speak it, yes."

"Try harder."

Gregorian thinks a moment. "I am your crews now. The other, his names is Tarziesch. What you say we do, we will. We is, are, uh, under your commands. You tell us, we will."

"Fine. Whatever."

"Your crews are, uh, respect for you. This no is true for the man who hire me. He will to kill my men by these thing out there, these hydra. I am do this for money. I rather to be living. I rather to not be dead. I kill him if you are saying so."

"You're offering to kill the Dandy?"

"If you are saying so."

Jack understands that just fine. "I think I can handle it."

They leave Dino to get some rest and enter the main pod chamber. Justin guards Tarziesch and Dandy and sits on the helmet with the creature beneath. It is like a bug in an overturned jar. What did Gregorian call it a minute ago? Hydra. They need a better container, but there's nothing worth risking a failed transfer. There are some flimsy storage lockers, but they can't lift the helmet from the floor without unleashing the thing. The other option is to open the pod and toss it into the hall, except the one out there won't go five feet from the door. So under the helmet the hydra stays. They'll sit on it in shifts.

Hunter calls Jack to the monitor. Stetson paces behind her, whispering to himself and leaning over her shoulder to stare and curse.

"Will you cut that out?" Hunter snaps at him. "You're stressing me out."

"What is it?" Jack says.

She pulls up surveillance of the second level. Two hydras float like sentinels. They vaguely resemble sea urchins, spiky balls. They throw limbs along the wall to steer. "These came out of the mainframe," Hunter says. "Except there was only one at first."

"You saw it multiply?"

"Multiply, split, whatever."

"You think they're breeding?"

"I sure as hell hope not."

Jack leans back. This is not good news. "Belinda, are you listening?"

"I am."

"What are your thoughts about these things?"

"They are very foreign. It's difficult to formulate a theory."

"Does it seem like they're breeding to you?"

"I don't know that such a term is appropriate. The combined mass of the creatures to which Hunter is referring equals the mass of the singular creature when it was inside the mainframe."

"Meaning?"

"I believe the creatures Hunter is referring to are, in fact, a single creature. I do not believe any of them are distinct. I believe there is one creature that is capable of dividing itself. The divisions operate independently, so I cannot speak to their cognitive processes, if they have any. They may be conscious or they may not. And they only grow in size when they devour prey. In fact, the term *devour* does not seem appropriate to me. *Convert* seems a more fitting term."

"Anything we can exploit? Apparent weaknesses?"

"Not that I can tell, Jack. Energy-based weapons cause no physical damage. This does not seem possible, yet my observations are accurate. As I said, it is difficult to make definitive statements, but I have to voice my concern, Jack, that this entity is more resilient than any life form humanity has encountered."

Jack rubs his eyes. He could use a coffee. "How about the pod. Are we safe in here?"

"Safe is a relative term. Pod integrity is excellent. I see no way the entity can break through. I do not have surveillance cameras inside the pod, however, so I cannot comment on your current state. I understand you have a piece of the entity there with you. That is quite dangerous."

"Thanks. Let me know if anything changes."

"Okay, Jack."

He reaches into his jacket and grips the ivory handle of Dino's revolver. He decided to borrow it while Dino remains incapacitated. He slides the weapon from the holster and hefts its weight, studies it in his hand. Flecks of blood spot his fingers. He envisions Dino at a bar shooting liquor with his one remaining hand, people buying him sympathy drinks. Crippled for life. And for what? They have no business being in this predicament. Lana doesn't want him to blame himself. Fine. He can think of someone better.

Dandy stiffens when he sees Jack coming. He squirms back but is already pressed against the wall. Jack grips him by the hair, but the wig tears off. Dandy pats his natural hair back in place, strings of orange. "Hey," he whimpers. Jack twists the silk of his weird kimono dress in a fist and raises him up. He smacks him in the side of the head with the revolver. "Ach!" Dandy says. Jack slaps his other cheek and holds him against the wall by his throat, presses the barrel into his eye.

"I'm going to kill you," Jack says.

Dandy's face goes bright red.

Jack senses rather than sees his crew gathering behind him.

Dandy sneers, "You can't."

"I really can, though."

"Jack," Lana says, "he might know something."

"He doesn't."

Dandy masks his fear with a grin, grips the gun with both hands, pulls it harder into his own eye. "Do it. You'd be killing your family, too."

"You're full of shit."

"Those men who kicked your ass on Earth, they're still there, watching the clock. When it runs out, they'll do more than give your wife and kid a beating."

The curve of the trigger is so comfortable. So squeezable.

"Ex-wife," Jack says.

"Gee, sorry."

"What do you think is going to happen, Jim? You think we'll eject the pod, float a million clicks to the inner limits and hope someone finds us? We're trapped in a pod with no jump drive. Our mag shield will last another two weeks, tops. Then we'll fry. This is your fault. You killed yourself."

A frightened Adam's apple jerks under Jack's hand.

"You'd better find a way. Or your family—"

"What makes you think I care about them? You see this?" He leans back so Dandy can see the tattoo. "I've already been to Hell, Jim. I'm not afraid to go back."

Dandy searches the faces around him. Searching for what, exactly? Sympathy? Mercy? Forgiveness? Even Lana has gone silent. They must know that Jack is right. They won't survive.

Dandy coughs once, a dry hack. And again. His body trembles. Jack thinks he is crying, but no. He laughs. "Oh man," he wheezes. "Man oh man. Those turrets weren't on! I could have walked out the way I came in!" He gurgles and coughs. "You should have let me. If I die, then they die, and that's on you, Jackie."

Jack pulls the gun from his eye.

Dandy grins. "See?" he says. "You know I'm—"

Jack swings as hard as he can. Dandy's head snaps back, clangs against the wall. He drops hard. Jack works up a good lather and spits into his hair, kicks him in the ribs for good measure. Lana grabs Jack's shoulder. He shoves her. She falls, yelps. He could kick her too. He meant what he said about hell. What he didn't mention was that he brought it back with him.

Fuck you, Dandy.

Fuck you, Jack.

Killer. Coward.

He stalks down the hall, locks himself in the bathroom, jams the revolver to his chin. He sits like that a long time, tears running down his cheeks.

CHAPTER 25

Morale has flatlined. Stetson paces and bites his thumb, repeating that they need to get rid of the creature under the helmet. Hunter groans and sighs and asks him what he is going to do, flush it down the toilet? He waves his hands and says something about giving it a shot. Justin is set on executing Dandy and his men. He strokes the rifle that had been Dino's and before that Gregorian's, fiddles with the knobs, mutters how this is all their fault and they deserve it. They're going to die, anyway. Gregorian and Tarziesch plead that they are in the same situation and it's Dandy who got them into this. Lana wishes they would all just shut the hell up and let her think.

Dandy has an inch-long gash above his left eyebrow. She wipes away the blood and makeup with an antiseptic pad and pinches the wound and seals it with a dab of liquid stitching. His ribs feel fine, but there's no telling for sure until he wakes up. Not that she cares about his recovery. It's just that caring for a patient settles her nerves. Gives her purpose. She's not a violent person, but part of her wanted Jack to pull the trigger. Yet there are so many unknowns, so many things Jack should have been asking Dandy before he knocked him out.

Justin is still on the helmet. She crouches near the visor and peers inside. The creature has gone idle. It squats at the back of the helmet, looking like a clot of wet yarn.

Whack! It shoots a tentacle against the glass and retracts it, like a lizard tongue. She flinches.

"What are you doing?" Justin says.

"I wonder," she says. She duck walks backward, then very slowly slides one hand across the floor toward the visor. When her fingers are maybe six inches away, the creature smacks the glass again. "No eyes," she says. She drops to her hands and knees and swings around to the helmet's back side. "Gregorian, look through the visor and tell me what you see."

Gregorian positions to a better angle, keeping a generous distance. "It is just is sitting theres."

"Hang on." She repeats the same motion, inching her hand closer.

"It moves," Gregorian says.

"Where?"

Thunk. It whacks the back of the helmet.

"Can you stop doing that?" Justin says.

She leans back. "I'll be damned."

"What is this meaning?" Gregorian says.

Hunter and Stetson stand close by. Hunter says, "It can see through the back of the helmet."

"Maybe," Lana says.

"Am I safe here?" Justin says.

"You're fine."

"Why doesn't it attack Justin's ass?" Stetson says. "If it can see through the helmet, I mean. He's sitting right on it."

"It was," Lana says. "When I first trapped it. It kept hitting below my hands."

"Why'd it quit?"

"I don't know. Stop talking. I want to try something."

They go silent. She keeps her hand away this time, waits.

Gregorian whispers, "It putting up feelers."

She shushes him, lets the silence drag out. Then she snaps her fingers.

Thump.

"Oh shit," Stetson says.

"It strikes," Gregorian reports.

"It heard you," Hunter says.

"Yes."

"But you didn't make noise before. How'd it hear you then?"

"I really don't know."

"Extrasensory," Justin says. "Like, psychic."

She doubts it.

"Infrared vision," Stetson says. "Like a rattlesnake."

"That still takes eyes."

"Yeah? You take a course on alien physiology we don't know about?"

"Shut up, Stets," Hunter says.

"Don't tell me to shut up. I don't see how this is helping."

"Then I'll spell it the fuck out for you," Hunter snaps. "If we know how it sees, then we can hide from it, yeah? Then maybe we can get out of this tin can and onto the other ship."

"Other ship," Stetson says.

"Dandy's ship."

Gregorian says, "Not Dandy ship. My ship. Homunculus."

"If we get to the—The what?"

"Homunculus."

"If we get to the Homunculus," Hunter continues, "then we can fly the fuck away."

"Yeah, I got it," Stetson says.

"Great. Glad you're paying attention."

"Why do you have to push my buttons?"

"To make sure you're still functioning properly."

"Ha-ha," he says flatly.

Lana cuts in, "Is this really the conversation you want to be having right now?"

"Guys," Justin says.

Stetson jabs a finger at Hunter, "Seven years I've had to deal with this shit. You're a robot, you know that?"

"Cry me a river," Hunter says.

"Guys."

"You both need to cut it out," Lana says.

"I don't know if you know this," Stetson says, "but there's a monster outside the door! It maybe is just a little *fucking stressful*!"

"Guys!" Justin shouts.

They turn. "*What?*"

"Why don't we ask him?" He gestures at Dandy, who sits upright and runs fingers across the gash in his face, hissing air through his teeth. When he sees them staring, he drops the hand.

"Ask me what?"

CHAPTER 26

He cannot picture Kip's face. He knows it is an oval, that he has black hair, but the features are blank. He tries to focus on a memory. Something specific and vivid. Nothing comes to mind. He envisions moments that never occurred. A playground with a rubber floor, swinging the boy by the arms and laughing. That is what good fathers remember, right? Something from a commercial. Sitting with his boy on his knee while he imparts wisdom. How to deal with a bully or how to throw a ball. Instead, Jack slept with scrawny hookers in rented rooms while Ani raised his son alone.

Yet he recalls the bees at Ani's parents' place.

Her parents lived in a ten-bedroom farmhouse, and their backyard was fifteen acres of woods with a bubbling creek a few feet into the tree line. He'd been back from the war seven years but had been shipping for five, and still felt like a stranger, a visitor. He sat on the back porch watching Kip and wondering why he was here, buzzed on a flask he hid in his jacket. The others were inside the house, preparing salads or something. He liked the boy to have freedom, so he let him explore. He watched him wander into the trees to play in the creek. It was shallow that time of year. Every few minutes Jack would lean forward and shout, "How we doing, bud?" and the kid's squeaky voice would come back, "I found a fossil!" or "Crayfish!" or some such thing. Mostly Jack couldn't make out the words, but he heard it when Kip started screaming. A long wail, pained, confused, full of fear. Jack was in the woods in an instant, dashing between the trees. He found Kip running in circles slapping at himself and crying that he was being killed. Jack scooped him up and carried him back to the house. The bees had done a number. They clung to his knuckles, slipped down his shirt, tangled themselves in his hair. Welts covered his arms and legs. Ani and the in-laws crowded them, asking Jack what he had done. Jack ignored them, passed the boy off to Ani, slapped the stinging bastards from his own flesh, scooped the lighter fluid and matches from the grill, and bolted back to the woods. He found the nest in a rotten log, big as a basketball. A branch stuck out of its flaky side. Kip hadn't stepped or fallen on it. He'd found it and decided to mess with it. Still, he didn't deserve all that pain. Jack stood a good ten feet back and spurted the lighter fluid across the nest until it was soggy brown and the can sputtered. The bees swarmed. They crawled along his jacket and stung the sleeves, bit at his neck and hands. He ignored them and struck a match. The nest went up with a *whoosh*, erupted into tiny fireballs careening through the air. Water hissed from the log like small screams. He had heard that insects did not feel pain, but he hoped that was wrong. They needed to suffer for what they'd done. In short time, Ani's father appeared with a bucket of water, calling Jack a lunatic and saying he could have burned the forest down. They got the fire out and went back up to the house. Kip sat on his mother's lap with his shirt off, eyes swollen from crying, a pair of tweezers and a collection of stingers on the table beside them, white lotion dabbed on every welt. Jack said, "They're all dead," and grinned. The boy looked away and whimpered. Jack's heart sank. "What's the matter with you?" Ani scolded. "He's five years old for God's sake." *What's wrong with me?* Jack thought, indignant. He was only trying to help. Not his problem if nobody understood.

Thinking back on it now, Ani and her father were probably right. He was a lunatic, and his son saw it. Jack Kind, this man who called himself Dad even though he was never around, swaggering up the porch steps bleeding and smiling and smeared with soot. He'd become what he loathed, what he feared.

His own father was an engineer and an alcoholic. All summer long, he'd sit out in his toolshed where he stashed his liquor and get so drunk he'd sleep the night out there. Jack's brother said he was just avoiding their mother, that she had somehow worn him down. She was seeing other men, Terry would say. "Dad told me." She was the one who screamed and threw dishes, hit their father with closed fists, and he took it. For a long time, Jack believed Terry's view of things—their mother had lost her mind, hated their father, and tortured him until he could hardly stand to live in the same house. One night, when Jack was maybe ten years old, his father set up a second chair and invited him to sit. It was a cool night with a clear sky. His father swirled a glass and tipped it to his lips. Everything stank of wet cigars. They watched the sky for a long time before the old man patted Jack on the arm and said, "Never be like your mother, Jackie. She's weak. Have no patience for weak people." Jack wasn't sure what this meant. Eventually his father shooed him to bed. Through the wall, he heard his mother crying.

She left just before he turned seventeen. No note. Just gone. They all knew it was coming. Terry was right about her seeing another man. It had been going on for years. Maybe he finally convinced her to sneak away. At first, Jack was glad she'd left. He thought things would improve. The old man might come inside, spend time with his sons. By that point, Terry was always off at Greene's place ten miles down the road, taking cars apart and putting them back together. Jack occupied himself thinking about girls he didn't stand a chance with. It was a very lonely time, and the house was especially empty without his mother. In her absence, he saw what he couldn't before. She was the one who set and cleaned the table, cooked the meals and filled the serving bowls, paid for Jack and Terry's autocar tickets when they needed a ride. Without her, the house barely existed. She had not been the force driving them apart like Terry thought. And the old man still spent his evenings by the toolshed muttering angry mantras and kicking empties. He'd gotten worse.

About a year after she left, Jack confronted his father. Stormed out to the shed and stood with his hands on his hips, glaring. It was his mother's pose, and he spoke with his mother's accusatory words: "What would it take for you to be happy?" His father would not look at him. He burped loudly and pulled gulps straight from the bottle. He'd developed a massive gut and the lawn chair conformed perfectly to his body. This was his ruin. Unmown yard, garden bursting with weeds, the shed roof slumping in the center and covered in moss. There were no answers here. Whatever plagued his father, it was incurable, or at least the man would not seek its cure. He wanted to die sad and lonely. Considered it a badge of honor. So Jack did all he could do. When he turned eighteen, he enlisted.

The war had been going strong for nine months. It would take him across the solar system, far from that broken home. And they'd pay him. He would never be stationary like the old man. His mother had tried to wait things out, but realized in time that her own survival meant moving on. By that point, Jack and Terry were old enough to take care of themselves. She did what she had to. Jack understood. Respected it, even. He vowed that if things got bad in any one place, he'd take off too. He did not foresee being stuck in a POW camp for two years, a pretty big wrench in his plans. Yet it was the promise to keep moving that kept him alive. He saw what despair did to people. It got his father and it got men in the camps, guys who traded the morning work detail for a life-threatening beating, who remained in their bunks and smoked their last cigarettes and downed their last crumbs, the final burst of pleasure before their bodies began shutting down. Soon they would catch some disease or simply die in their sleep. He could not blame them. They had had enough. But he was not that way. He would outlast everyone. Stay alive till rescue came. He'd kill if he had to, and he did. Sitting now in the sinkless bathroom with the weird suction cup toilet under his ass, revolver plugged against his chin, he is not so sure he made the right decision. The ones who died had it easier. They didn't have blood on their hands. Didn't have to suffer through the nightmares. Didn't have to question. If he never returned to Ani, they never would have had Kip. He'd never have pushed her into the arms of another man the same way his father did to his mother. He'd never have seen his crew trapped in a panic pod with a monster ramming the door.

If he died all those years ago, how much misery would these people have been spared?

They aren't friends. They're coworkers. He is alone. Like always.

He's lost his chance at being a father. That's true. He'll never grow into that idol of paternal warmth he sometimes daydreams about. But there are people that matter more than him now. He can give his son a future and he can protect his crew. They have to get back to civilization with Dandy alive. Somehow.

He tucks the revolver away.

Coward.

He wipes the tears from his cheeks and opens the bathroom door.

Lana jumps back.

She stands with her fist raised, about to knock.

"Hey," he says.

"Are you okay?"

He shrugs. "Does it matter?"

She starts with some optimistic response, but stops herself, chooses a different course. She says, "You need to hear this."

CHAPTER 27

He can't think in the main chamber with Dandy nearby. Keeps getting distracted by thoughts of strangling him. So they sit in the side room with Dino again. Lana takes a moment to check his bandages, then sits on a storage chest across from Jack and tells him everything Dandy shared.

Eight months ago, a mining corporation found a reflective object drifting in the Kuiper belt. Some kind of sphere. About 300 feet in diameter, it was much too small and not nearly dense enough to have formed naturally. The team thought they'd discovered a relic from the war and reported to the Star Nation, per protocol, and have not been heard from since. Officially, their expedition vanished. Most likely, they were put in a military prison without so much as an official charge.

The object, codenamed Barbaricus—*the barber needs a haircut,* Jack thinks—was the first definitive proof of extraterrestrial intelligence. Turns out Dandy has been keeping tabs on the search for years, a self-proclaimed UFO enthusiast after he saw strange lights zipping around one of Jupiter's moons, and he'd been bribing sources in the government ever since. In a matter of days, he knew everything the Nation knew about the discovery in the Kuiper belt. The sphere was made of alloys that did not correspond to anything on the periodic table. Seismic tests showed it was hollow. Asteroids and comets had splattered across its surface, leaving traces of radioactive material, including a bit of zircon, which radiocarbon dating showed was at least four billion years old. If accurate, it meant the sphere was nearly as old as our solar system. Possibly older.

Surveys found an opening in its surface. A tunnel leading to a massive door with a manual locking mechanism. Inside, they found no alien crew. No bodies. No supercomputers. Not even any sign of a navigation system. The only contents were 360 objects about ten feet in diameter each, all spherical, like replicas of the ship—if it was a ship. They appeared to glow from within.

That was all Dandy's sources could get before they cut off communication.

Jack pieces the rest together himself.

His informants gone, Dandy decided to steal one of the spheres. First, he would have had to track the cargo to its new home, then study the security measures where it was held. He'd have contacts in place already. All he needed was a patsy and a way inside. A lot of people died for this. Innocents. People just doing their jobs. Lana confirms it. Gregorian and his mercenaries destroyed at least one research vessel, murdered the crew, stole access codes. At one point, they held an army general's daughter hostage and assassinated a senator. All in the span of a few months. Dandy threw his money here and there. It is how governments function. Cash in one hand, rifle in the other. Jack is just one more unwitting player in Jim Dandy's orchestra, and he had performed brilliantly. There will be no trace of Dandy's intervention. Records will show that Jack forged his entry to the facility and took the sphere by force. When all this is over, he'll have to answer for those supposed crimes. Yet one more reason to get Dandy back alive.

"Anything else?"

"That's the gist of it," Lana says.

None of the information proves particularly useful, and he says so.

"You don't think so?" Lana says.

"Maybe you know something I don't."

"Well, let's see." She ticks items off on her fingers. "For starters, I know that thing was in a container for several billion years, so it won't starve any time soon. I know that somebody put it into a container in the first place. So that tells me it must be vulnerable. Or at least controllable."

"For all we know, the hydra was made in that sphere. Maybe it was in cryosleep. Maybe the sphere was an egg."

"The kid reached inside and turned it off."

"So what does that mean?"

"The thing was inside a container. Someone contained it."

"Why? How?"

"I don't know, Jack. I'm just saying. Maybe it's not hopeless."

"Right. If only we had a microscope."

"That would help. I could examine it on a molecular level. I can't understand how it converts organisms without leaving waste. That's impossible."

Jack says, "I was joking."

"Well I'm not. And I'm not giving up because that thing is making scary noises. We're safe for now. We just need time."

"We don't have time."

"It takes eleven days to reach the nearest outpost. Dandy said he needs to be back in two weeks. That gives us three days."

"That includes today."

"It also assumes Dandy wasn't bluffing. Think about it."

"I can't take that risk. You know that."

"Yeah." She reaches across, places a hand on his knee.

He gives her hands a squeeze and looks into her eyes. There is sympathy in there, but also fear. They both know how unlikely it is that everyone will make it out of this. Perhaps it is her way of saying she understands his burden, but she doesn't. No one ever will.

CHAPTER 28

He paces the main room, studies the ceiling to avoid eye contact with the Dandy. He admires the lights set in transparent tile, walls that arc smoothly upward like an upside-down bathtub. He remembers the day he had the pod installed. Years ago now. They came in through the wall, tore a chunk out of Bel's side and rebuilt it around her. He hadn't expected that. Thought they'd haul it through the ship and set it against the wall, a childish concept in retrospect. He felt guilty for the modification at the time, worried he was causing unnecessary damage to his ship, as if he'd deemed her inadequate. And this late addition is the only reason they're alive. If they are going to make the long haul back, it won't be aboard Belinda. They'll leave her out here, alone, circling ever closer to the sun until she drops into the heat or a solar flare consumes her.

There are seven EVA suits in the panic pod, and nine survivors. If they are going to reach the Homunculus, at least two people will have to make the sprint. The Homunculus has only one airlock, which is currently engaged with Belinda, and it requires the fingerprint of an active crewmember to unlock while at port. So at least one of Dandy's men needs to come along. Gregorian volunteers. "It is my ships," he says. Jack will go with him. No arguments.

"Bullshit," Hunter says. "I'll go."

Justin throws his hand up. "Me too."

"Hunter, you're a pilot. We might need you to fly the Homunculus."

She says something but Jack cuts her off.

"That's the end of it. And Justin, I seem to recall finding you unconscious on your bedroom floor. You're staying here."

He flushes and lowers his face.

Once Jack and Gregorian disengage the Homunculus, the others can strap in and eject the pod. It has no docking capabilities, so the Homunculus will position nearby and the panic pod crew will perform a short spacewalk, making it to the new ship without having to deal with the hydra.

It's a nice plan. Would look very straightforward on paper. It's also naïve as hell to suppose Jack and Gregorian can just slip past the hydra. And if it sees through walls, that's pretty much the end of it. It is too fast to outrun in a straight shot. The best idea so far is to rush down the Zero-G shaft with the hydra in tow, get to the first floor, and have Bel reverse the shaft's gravity before the hydra clears it. That will leave only the hydra on the first floor to contend with. Hopefully it won't be waiting for them at the bottom of the shaft. If it is, Jack will distract it long enough for Gregorian to reach the airlock.

This part does not sit well with the crew. He asks them to submit alternatives, but they have none.

So that's it. The situation as it stands. No guarantees. No failsafes.

It's suicide and everyone knows it. Anyone stepping out these doors will be swallowed up in seconds, and where will that leave the survivors? In the same position, down two members. At least they won't have Jack to take orders from anymore. If by some miracle the sun's radiation wouldn't kill them, they could wait up to a year, rationing their food, hoping someone just happens to venture close enough to hear their signal. And they would die. One way or another.

Something nags at Jack. He keeps seeing Bel's mainframe in his mind. Those silver panels and humming corridors. The hydra wiggling like a giant slug. The memory makes his skin crawl. How close he came to being a meal. What saved him? If the hydra has extrasensory sight or whatever, how the hell did he make it out of there? Maybe it stopped chasing for the same reason it stopped banging on the panic pod door. It's not going to starve anytime soon, like Lana said, so it's simpler to wait things out. That doesn't seem right, though. Why chase him at all if it wasn't that interested? It wanted him and it could have had him. Should have. He knew it the moment it slid around the corner and sent those feelers up.

Feelers.

Feeling for what? Vibrations in the air? Like an eardrum.

But sound alone?

It sees through walls.

No. Not really.

He clicks his portable. "Belinda, can you hear me?"

"I can."

"When the hydra was chasing me in the mainframe, you said something about a power surge. Tell me again."

The others listen, wondering where he's going with this.

He faces the wall so their stares won't distract.

"When I came back online, I sent electrical pulses through my mainframe in an attempt to disorient the creature. It appeared to work."

"Why would electrical pulses disorient it?"

"There are a number of possibilities," Belinda says. "The strobing of lights would have confused its visual field, and the loud noise would do the same for its hearing."

Jack says, "It doesn't have eyes, Bel. Why else would electricity distract it?"

Belinda says, "Perhaps it can home in on bioelectric frequencies."

"Son of a bitch," Hunter says.

"That's not unheard of in nature," Lana says. "Bees can sense the electrical charge of flowers."

"Electric eels," Stetson says.

"Right."

Jack says, "Could we use power surges throughout the ship? Try the same thing?"

"Repeated surges can be dangerous to my components. I'm thinking of something else. Step over to the monitor. Tell me when you're there."

They crowd around. "We're here."

"Take a look at turret B1. I will calibrate it to roughly match the bioelectrical output of the average human body. It is not much. Keep in mind this is unlikely to succeed."

Hunter pulls up the display. They all hover a little closer. Something silky rubs against Jack's elbow through the shreds of his sleeve. Dandy. They come face to face. Dandy grins. The fucker thinks he still has the upper hand. Maybe he does. Jack resists the urge to drive a fist into that smile. He focuses on the screen, the red dot that represents the laser's target. Bel swivels the turret and the camera shifts left to reveal the coils of a hydra squeezed into a higher corner of the corridor, a brownish tangle of squid limbs. This is the smallest of them, the one on the first level. It just hangs there, motionless, maybe waiting for a victim to stroll into range.

Bel places the red dot on the wall next to the hydra.

The dot turns green, indicating that the laser is on.

Nothing happens.

Jack bites his cheek.

"Well there goes that plan," Justin groans.

"Wait," Lana says. "It's moving."

Jack squints, leans closer. Hard to tell. The picture is grainy and stutters often. The feed to the pod was done in a last minute rush at the suggestion of the installation team, and the turrets are antiques. He bought them at an auction years before, never expected them to work. And yet. The coils shift, tighten.

Bel widens the laser's diameter. The green dot grows.

The hydra throws a tentacle against the wall, directly over the laser. Bel swings it out of reach and the hydra pulls from the corner, extends stiff insectoid legs and crawls after it, whipping tentacles to try and snatch it.

The pod erupts with cheers. They are going to make it out of this. No one hears Belinda's hums of uncertainty as the hydra begins to slow, shoots more feelers into the air, points those long slender cilia at the source of the laser.

CHAPTER 29

Lana mops Dino's forehead. He's a little warm, but so is the room. Though the pod has ventilation, it's meant for around five people at the most. They've nearly doubled the capacity. The walls are slick with moisture. Now and then droplets of water fall and make the floor slippery. Their own sweat and breath surrounding them.

Dino wakes, disoriented. In the morning, they will need him lucid. If the term "morning" applies. Call it a window of seven hours instead, after which they will decide they've rested enough and put their plan into action. Everything is truly relative out here, far from the assuredness of solid ground. All that certainty is an illusion. The truer vantage—space—shows Earth as just one more scintillating pinprick in an overpopulated field of pinpricks. No cycle. No night or day. No atmosphere to nudge evolution along its path. There is only the calendar and the clock, governed by standard solar time, an invention she grew up with. Mankind attempting to impose order onto chaos. She remembers vividly the first time this realization came to her. She was young, but she had outgrown her phobia of looking into space, and she was walking through Observatory Park for some reason. She must have been around eight or nine. She can't recall now what she was doing there or why. Maybe a picnic with her mother and father. Maybe a playdate with friends. She ran along the stone path in front of the enormous window, the one looking out not at Saturn, but at the emptiness in the opposite direction. The starfield. She had seen it many times, but on this day, she stopped and stared. That old fear bubbled up inside of her, but she let it simmer below the surface, just enough to know that it would always be there, and she felt something that even now she has a hard time naming. It was more like a texture than an idea. It was as if she were suspended in the middle of a canyon, floating high above the ravine and its walls, and at any moment, if she broke her concentration, she would fall. This sensation evolved in time, became less terrifying, more conceptualized. She feels it now, the tenuousness of their position in the universe—in all of existence. Chaos is real. It's what Einstein left out of his theory. The way relativity itself is an invention because there is no one out there measuring things. That is what humankind does. Space has no need to justify itself. It just is. If we ever make it out of our little planetary system, maybe we will find that physics works differently elsewhere. Maybe there are no yardsticks other than what we bring along.

She explains things to Dino, and as she hears herself saying it, the whole plan seems very stupid. So the hydra can spot a circle of energy moving across the floor like a cat chasing a light. Does that mean the cat can't tell the difference between the light and a mouse? Can they say they truly understand this creature, or are they just floating above a cliff pretending they will never fall?

Logic only takes us so far. She knows this well after years of working on the human body, attempting to save lives, losing them for no apparent reason. She never met an experienced surgeon who claimed to have all the answers. Some bodies just quit. Others can be pushed well beyond their apparent limits and keep sucking air into their lungs and pumping blood through their veins. Sure, there are theories about this. White blood cell counts, immunodeficiencies dependent on age and lifestyles, etc., but death does not follow these rationalizations.

For a short period, she considered religion. At Starvation City, she made regular visits to the chapel. There was a nice chaplain there, an older woman who called herself Night Sister, a name Lana found pretentious until Night Sister told her it was her prostitution name. She kept it because she claimed she no longer knew the person her parents had named. Night Sister was the one who had gone through hardships. That other woman—that supposedly purer one—she had never existed at all. This was all shared under the presumption that Lana would open up about her own life, let her doubts spill to this gray-haired figure in a gray robe. She almost did. What would she have said? Something about being lost, feeling empty. But such emptiness is the state of the universe, so is it a negative thing to feel that way? That was borderline New Darwinism and she knew it. All their *space is cruel so we better be crueler* bullshit. Excuses to go around slaughtering innocent people. Yet that doesn't mean there isn't a kernel of truth in there. Whole civilizations murdered each other based on texts that preach peace and love and kindness. It doesn't mean peace and love and kindness are wrong. It just means the ideas had been perverted. If the New Darwinists got anything right, it's the inherent cruelty of the universe, but they were wrong about everything else. Where there is no air and no sea and no ground and no way for life to develop, life should be considered more precious, not less.

And yet, another possibility occurs to her. If in this cruel uncaring universe, something close to life were to form out here, something that could sustain itself over billions of years, something so strange that we might not recognize it as life at all when we encounter it, how brutal would that something—that non-lifeform—have to be in order to survive? What tactics would develop in its evolutionary line? And what would happen to any lifeforms that stood in its path?

She should sleep.

She helps Dino down a couple sleeping pills and enough pain meds to hold him over for the next few hours. He thanks her and squeezes her hand. She knows he hates being seen this way. He's supposed to be the invulnerable one. She tells him they will find him a shiny new arm when they make it back.

"Something with spikes," he says, and shuts his eyes.

Back in the main chamber, the flight chairs have been pulled up from the floor. Justin snores loudly and curls into a fetal position. Stetson sits on the helmet, but has managed to fall asleep with his chin on his fist. Dandy and his mercs lie next to each other at Stetson's feet. The room stinks of men. That musty fart smell and BO. It is a smell she will always associate with the shelters of Midland, their filthy walls and their hidden sicknesses and their cold rooms with bad lighting. Here in the pod, the lights have been turned pleasantly low. The only two figures still awake hover near the monitor at the front of the room.

Hunter and Jack watch the blobs on video. Jack turns when he hears her coming. "Hey." He wants to know how Dino's doing.

"He'll recover," she says.

He nods. "Good."

Jack does not look good. He has cut the torn sleeves from his jacket so she can see all the nicks and scrapes and burns along his forearms. In all this craziness, she forgot to clean his wounds. Dried blood and debris cling to him.

"A little salve will go a long way," she says.

He follows her gaze. "Oh. It's fine."

"Not really."

"I've dealt with worse. Trust me."

Hunter jabs at the display. "There's got to be a weakness." She says it more to herself than Jack or Lana. "I mean. No lifeform can just hang around forever without food and water."

"You'd be surprised," Lana says. "A lot of animals don't even have red blood cells. Sponges and crabs. Jellyfish. Worms."

"Bees," Jack says.

"Sure."

They get quiet. That they are even here right now is proof of their own lunacy. They could have done any number of things to avoid participating in Dandy's little game. They could have disappeared from Earth. Changed their names and their hair. All Lana had to do was stay put, and she couldn't even manage that. At the worst, they could have blasted the suspension cube off into space never to see it again.

And that is when it hits her.

The discovery in the Kuiper belt. The sphere. Three hundred and sixty smaller spheres inside.

She groans and rubs her tired eyes.

"What is it?" Jack says.

"We weren't supposed to find the ship," she says. "Nobody was."

Jack studies her face. "Lana," he says, "when's the last time you slept?"

"Hang on," Hunter says, "I want to hear this."

Lana says, "Think about it." And it all feels so simple. The way they are quarantined in their own ship. The same way the creature was quarantined in its pod. "This thing can't be killed, can't be destroyed."

"As far as we know."

"And it's extremely deadly. What do we do with our extremely deadly things, the things we can't just destroy? Our nuclear waste, our oceans of non-recyclables?"

"What are you getting at?"

"We bury it," Lana says.

Jack rubs his own eyes. "Okay."

"What if we had no ground to bury it in? Wouldn't we just blast it into nowhere? There are people doing it all the time. It's illegal, but they do it. That's why there's all that debris floating everywhere. Dandy even said the ship they found had no propulsion system."

Jack says, "I'm not sure I see—"

"Because it was never a ship. It's just a dumping ground."

Hunter nods along. "If it's four billion years old, our solar system didn't exist when they launched it. At least, not like it does now."

"Right. They sent it somewhere they thought no one would find it. A desert. Only it's not a desert anymore. And we did find it."

Jack says, "Even if that's true, why make it accessible? Why give it a door?"

She doesn't know the answer. All she has are guesses. "Maybe they were being optimistic. We always assume an alien race will be advanced far beyond ourselves. Maybe they assumed the same. That someone else would have a solution. A way to kill it."

Jack sighs and rubs the back of his neck. "What does any of this have to do with us?"

Lana stifles a laugh. "You never could read between the lines."

"Meaning what?"

"We don't have a way to kill it. You're right. And if we leave Bel out here, someone will find her the same way they found it in the Kuiper belt. They'll think they have a ship to salvage, and when they open the door..."

"Too bad for them."

"Think about the bigger picture." She sees in her mind the camps at Starvation City, the men and women and children struggling in their illnesses, their addictions, all scrambling over themselves, raising their hands to burning garbage. And in the sky, an explosion. A ship breaking apart, erupting with tentacles that slither where they land and clot what rivers are left, choke the oceans. Devour it all.

"You mean Earth," Hunter says. And from the look in her eye, Lana can see she is imagining some of the same things.

Jack sneers. "You said yourself we have no way to kill it."

"There's still somewhere no one could ever find it. Somewhere we'll never go."

"Where?"

"The sun," Lana says. "We shoot it into the sun."

"I'd have to program Bel manually," Hunter says. "From the bridge."

Jack raises a trembling finger. "No. Out of the question."

"Jack—"

"Gregorian and myself," Jack says. "That's it. I'll have my portable. You can walk me through it."

This makes sense to Lana. Frankly, she doesn't want anyone else to go out there.

Hunter shakes her head. "You'd be programming Belinda to destroy herself while her crew is onboard. Even if we set a timer and get to the Homunculus first, she'll fight you. You'd need to hardwire a workaround. I'm the only one who knows her navigation system well enough to do it."

Jack clicks his portable. "Belinda, is all of this true?"

"It is. I'm afraid I'm programmed to prioritize crew safety. Odds of survival are better out here with the creature than on the surface of the sun."

"There's got to be a simple override."

"No. I am the override," Bel says.

"Fuck that."

"I'm sorry, Jack."

"Alright, fine, so I'll hardwire the thing. The workaround. Whatever."

Hunter says, "You can't even read coordinates off a screen. I can do the hardwire in three minutes or less. You need me on this."

"I said no, damn it. You stay here. Everyone stays here!"

Justin snorts and rolls over. Stetson sits upright.

He wants to protect them. Lana understands that. But this is bigger than them, bigger than whatever guilt he's harboring. She touches his wrist. "Jack…"

He whips away his arm and storms off. She lets him go. There's no disappearing in here.

Hunter grips her elbow and tells her, "One way or another, I need to get to that bridge."

"I know. I'll talk to him."

"Yeah. Good luck."

CHAPTER 30

So he ends up back in the lavatory, hand propped against the door, preparing to push it closed. The moment lingers, as does his hand, as does the crack in the door. Why close it? What then? Sit here and fume about these choices which do not feel like choices? Like before. When he was crowded in a different cold room with a different type of threat outside the walls. When the officers—the people he fed for months with anything he could find—forced him into a decision he had no business making.

But is that true?

Was he really forced?

Couldn't he have sacrificed his own life, laid it down like so many others, just letting what remained of his strength dissolve away with the rest of him? Not with that promise to keep moving stuck like a bit of shrapnel in his brain. Nudging him steadily forward. It is still there now, though different because he is different. If he could go back, he wonders, would he make a different choice?

He does not close the door. Just stands, exhausted, the damaged skin along his hands and arms stiff and aching. His body in that drunken state of overtiredness, eyes remaining open by momentum only.

He has tried not to cause people harm. That should count for something.

He never wanted to be a father or a captain or a leader. He just liked the idea of a fast ship that could go anywhere and a home he could occasionally return to. If someone was waiting there for him, all the better. But things got complicated. Ani got pregnant and instead of feeling what he should have felt—some sort of joy—something in Jack receded. He clung to the comfort of the known unknowns, the dangers of space and the underworld he would come to navigate so well. And now look at him. Hunter is one of his oldest friends, like a sister to him, always over his shoulder with her no-bullshit attitude. In a sense, she's been co-captain all this time. He is supposed to ask her to come on a brisk walk beside a handful of unstoppable monsters.

If they get out of this, he'll go legitimate. That's what he told Lana. He hadn't known why at the time, but it must have been in his subconscious for a while. First thing he'll do is make sure all debts are paid. Then cut ties with the underworld. He'll return to Earth and drop in on Kip every once in a while. He won't try to make up for the past. He'll just be better. It's a promise he has made many times before, usually while slinking out of a hotel room still cloudy and reeking of booze, but this time is real. It has to be.

Nine years and he can barely picture his son's face. He doesn't know what hobbies the kid has, or interests, artistic leanings, talents, schoolboy crushes. Last time he saw him, Kip was into virtual reality entertainment. Quiet at first, he opened up when Jack asked him about his latest adventure. It was this bizarre-sounding puzzle game where all you did was stack oddly shaped blocks on top of each other in an attempt to reach a floating mountain. Kip had been at the first level for weeks, though he said he liked building the boxes in a lopsided way so he could climb up and ride the resulting avalanche. What a strange kid, Jack thought at the time. He's probably moved on by now. For all he knows, while Ani gets drunk each night, Kip is out there exploring the harder side of drugs at nine years old. It's not unheard of in shitty little towns like Nulleport. Maybe Jack helped transport the narcotics. Maybe Kip will become a dealer, or a smuggler like his dear old Pa.

He pictures an alternative future, grossly perfect: Jack clean-cut and embracing his smiling son, Lana next to him, a backdrop of rolling green hills and a soundtrack of chirping birds. They wear wedding bands and grin like dolls and wave at Ani on her porch, who waves back beside her perfect new husband. They all have very white teeth.

His laugh carries through the hall.

A coward sacrifices others before himself. He won't do it anymore.

A shadow slants down the corridor. He looks out.

Justin saunters into view and pushes on the door, startles when he spots Jack. He is mostly asleep, hair sticking up in chunks, puffy-eyed. "Whoa. You scared the shit outta me."

Jack clears his throat. "Sorry. Here, I'll get out of your way."

"I just gotta pee."

Jack slips past and into the hall. Justin's shoulders brush against his chest. Small, narrow bones. The kid seems far too young to be the same age as Jack when he joined the service. In fact, Justin is three years older. And still just a kid. How would he fare in the camps with his pale complexion and soft lips and girlish eyelashes, caked with filth, and those cheekbones showing through?

"You alright, Uncle Jack?"

"Yeah. No. Shit."

He stumbles back and bumps into the wall. He blinks, and Justin disappears. In his place stands one of the men Jack keeps submerged in the depths of his mind until they rip into his dreams. He knows this man, though he doesn't know his name. The way his lower lip and most of his chin are missing, chewed off by the latest bout of diseases sweeping through the huts. In the final moment of his life, this man saw Jack standing above him, one foot straddled on either side of his torso, pickaxe in his hands. The man was awake. What remained of his mouth twisted to form some unspoken question. His eyebrows creased, then raised, then a smile broke, as if the man above him had been revealed a friend. But Jack was no friend. He'd never seen the man before. His eyes were still open when Jack swung the axe.

"Uncle Jack?" His nephew is framed by the light of the doorway.

"I'm s—I'm sorry," Jack stutters.

"The hell are you sorry for?"

Jack shakes his head.

Justin helps him upright and studies his face a moment, then leans close, keeps his voice low. "You were right before, Uncle Jack. When I got separated, all I could think was to get to my room. I wanted to hide under the covers. Jesus fuck. When the gravity went out, I floated up, and I guess when it came on again I landed on my head. Knocked myself out cold. When you woke me up, I started screaming, 'cause I thought, like, I thought—" He looks away, shrugs. "I just mean thanks. I wish my dad could've seen us. He'd have shit himself."

Jack remembers the picture lying by Justin's head. In what he thought were his final moments, Justin had clung to that one happy memory.

"You miss them," Jack says. "Your mom and dad."

Justin shrugs. "Nah. They're dicks." He knocks on the doorframe. "This is home, Uncle Jack. This is family."

Jack isn't sure what to say. He wants to say the kid is naïve. Sentimental. Something.

"Uncle Jack?" Justin says.

"Yeah."

"I really gotta piss."

"Oh. Right."

Justin slips inside the bathroom, pauses, sticks his nose out. "Why do you think we stayed?" He shuts the door.

CHAPTER 31

Lana sits with her back against the wall farthest from the hall door. It hums lightly under her weight. Strange machinery inside works to keep them alive, filtering the atmosphere, recycling what they send down the drain. Hunter lies on the nearest seat, asleep or trying to sleep. Lana watches her. The slow intake of breath, release. They have never been close friends, but they have always been friendly. Some unnamed tension, a rivalry of sorts, wedged between them. It had something, maybe everything, to do with Jack. When Lana first came aboard she thought it was a sexual thing, like Hunter was jealous. If Hunter and Jack were in a room together, giving each other shit like they always were, and Lana walked in, they'd get quiet and blush. In time she realized it was not romantic rivalry. It was that Hunter didn't trust Lana around Jack. She must have seen it all coming. The way Lana fell for him, the way he started to fall for her, pushed her away till she couldn't stand it and left. Hunter was perceptive like that. Smarter than Lana, apparently, who had wanted to believe things would work out, that people change and real progress can be made. All that optimistic postwar sloganeering had gotten to her more than she realized.

Before Hunter dozed off, she'd taken one last look at Lana's face and must have seen the fear there, because she slapped her lightly on the cheek and said, "I promise I won't die," and winked. It was a joke the way she said it, and Lana laughed. She wasn't sure why she found it funny. How many billions have said it to their families and friends and lovers before sidling off to do battle with some faceless enemy, only to return in a coffin or not at all, their families and friends and lovers left to contend with the broken promise? It is exhausting to think about. You can't carry the burden of humankind's lunacy all of the time. Sometimes you have to see the lost souls in your mind and laugh and imagine they are laughing right back.

She's half asleep when Jack comes out of the hallway. He picks his way around the sleepers and sits beside her. She is supposed to tell him all the reasons Hunter has to go with him. *She promised me she wouldn't die,* she imagines herself saying. She says nothing. Jack has blood on his jeans. She forgot. She pulls the tube of salve from her pocket.

"What's that?"

"Hold out your arms."

She crouches in front of him and twists off the cap and squeezes a coil of balm into her hands. She rubs her hands together, then slides them along Jack's wrists to his biceps.

He hisses.

"Give me a break," she whispers.

His skin drinks up nearly half the tube, and it isn't until his arms are shiny and his head is back against the wall in a way that says he is feeling the tingle of relief that she lets herself feel the sensation of his skin against hers. She holds his wrists a moment. She drops against the wall, keeping her right hand on his. He squeezes.

He breaks the silence. "I'm sorry I pushed you before."

"Pushed me?"

"When I wanted to shoot the Dandy."

"Oh. I kind of forgot. I was pretty out of it."

"So was I."

"It's alright.

"No it's not."

She wants to tell him something nice, reassuring.

He says, "I can't get another person killed."

"Jack…"

"Let me finish." He sighs apologetically. "I just need to get this out."

"Okay."

"Hunter volunteered. She'll come with me and Gregorian. But I don't want her to. Remember that." He looks away.

Lana holds his hand tighter. "Okay," she says. She half expects him to pull away, retreat to his own place to sleep. The way he used to. Instead, he cups his hand around the side of her head, pulls her against his shoulder. She stiffens at first, allows herself to relax.

She pictures him in the clinic again, two black eyes, busted lips. He'd been so pathetic. Like a pet dog that bit her, ran away and got hit by a car, found the next morning whining on the front porch. So unlike the distant Jack she used to know. The one who didn't know how to ask forgiveness. And here, now, maybe it is because they might die in the next 12 hours, but she is comfortable against him in a way she never had been. Their time was always self-consciously fleeting, handled in haste and with a dash of shame, that much more thrilling for it. Like they were getting away with something. Wasn't that partially what drew her to him? Her immaturity driving the infatuation. Wanting someone for herself when he belonged to someone else. Girlish self-assurance. Greed. Yes. She hated that about herself and hated him for making her feel that way. That was why she left. Not just to escape Jack. He hadn't victimized her. She'd never admitted it before, but she did it to herself. She left because she needed to change.

And has she?

In this moment, pressed against him, she cannot believe this new feeling stems from that old immaturity. She does not want a momentary thrill. She wants this to go on. She wants them to be safe.

They fall asleep like this, together.

CHAPTER 32

Smell of coffee.

Steam under his nose.

Opens his eyes.

"Morning, hoss." Dino.

For just a second, he can believe they are in a hotel room or an alley after another drunken night, his personal security guard finding him with an offering of fast-food joe. The illusion dissolves. The room comes into focus. Dino's face remains along with the coffee. Dino holds out a worn tin cup, straining to keep it steady. Jack wraps his hands around it, savors the burn, sets it on his thighs.

The pod is alive with activity. While he slept, the others pulled pieces of the suits from storage and laid them on the floor. Gloves, helmets, torsos, pants, boots, air tanks, headsets, coolant liners, a box of adult diapers, and the bulky EM-packs. There are only four of these. Large white contraptions with fold-out arms. Between their nitrogen tanks and 55 microthruster ports, they weigh over a hundred pounds each. Lana sits on the helmet with the creature below, one of the EM-packs in front of her. Stetson points at various buttons and tells her what they do. There's an impatient edge to his voice. "Like I said, this here will push you forward. Here's your forward thrust for either side. That's how you rotate. The left arm handles pitch and yaw. Simple. Right?" She is lost in thought, runs her fingers gently over the buttons. Justin stands nearby scooping peaches from a can with his fingers. One slides free and plops onto the floor. He frowns at it, crouches down and picks it up and shovels it into his mouth, dust and all. Hunter sits at the monitor again, reading lines of code. Gregorian and Tarziesch appear to be in the midst of a prayer ritual, kneeling with their heads bowed to the deck. Jack can't decide if he should trust them. Who's to say Dandy won't make a deal with them once they reach the Homunculus? He probably has already. Their promises of loyalty to Jack could be a ruse to bring his guard down. If so, it has mostly worked.

Dino nods at the coffee cup. "Found a can in storage. Figured we could use it."

Jack blows on the rim and touches it to his lips. Burns his tongue. "Agreed."

"There's plenty of food. Canned or dehydrated. Take your pick."

Dandy stands directly across the room, leering at Jack.

"The hell is his problem?" Jack says.

"He's alive." There is a slight waver in his voice. He must be using a lot of energy just staying upright. He shudders and whistles.

"Jesus, Dino. You're missing an arm. Take a seat."

"Just wanted to test my legs. But, uh, I think you're right."

For once, it is Jack's turn to help his trembling friend. The big guy holds Jack's shoulder to support his weight. He grunts and hisses with every step. Punched the fucking hydra. It would be funny if the outcome weren't so awful. Dino drops into one of the flight seats. He winces and swallows a moan. Jack can do nothing more. They need Dino conscious and at least partially mobile for the spacewalk. Just in case. That means minimal pain meds. His eyes roll back. He says, "Shit, man. I'm gonna have to jerk off left-handed." A strained laugh comes out sounding like coughs.

Jack slaps Dino's knee. "Hang in there, alright?"

Dino nods.

Jack heads to the storeroom to find some food.

The others really raided the place. Cans with syrupy residue and a nest of foil wrappers cover the floor. He selects a can of pears and a packet of dehydrated pork and slides the military can opener from his pocket. He walks it around the tin, puckering the edges. He eats slowly, savoring this cheaply mass-produced shit. It could very well be his last meal. He's about to slide the opener back in his pocket, but stops himself. He opens his palm and studies it. A small wedge of metal, well-worn along the edges, scratched but still intact. It hardly weighs a thing. A gram maybe. He rarely had cans to open in the camp, but when he did, this little tool was a godsend. Twelve years later and he still keeps it in his pocket. Why? A compulsion. A habit formed by fear.

He tilts his hand. The opener falls to the floor, disappears among the garbage with a barely audible *clink*. A wave of anxiety passes over him. He shuts his eyes and wills himself not to go looking for it. *You'll starve*, a little voice says. Rationally, he knows he will not starve anymore than he will die of thirst. So he runs his hands along his belt and clicks the buckle free, releasing the weight of his old canteen. Water sloshes inside. He takes one last swig and sets it on the floor. Squat metal gourde. When he leaves, he closes the door behind him. There's something else he needs to let go of.

*

"Listen up," he calls.

They stop what they're doing and face him. He stands at the end of the hallway, feeling their eyes on him. He never wanted to be a leader. He has been thinking about Justin's words. *Why do you think we stayed?* He stands there not as their captain, but as their friend.

"You've probably all heard by now, but there's been a slight change of plans. Hunter will be coming with Gregorian and myself to the Homunculus. We'll stop at the bridge where she will program a new route for Bel. She'll put her on a timer, after which point Bel will make a grav jump into the heart of the sun. That means we need to be off this ship and to a safe distance before the timer runs out. Six hours is the maximum allotment. That should give us plenty of time." He looks back at Hunter, finds her nodding. They're waiting for more. A speech. A rally. He's never been good at this. So he will tell them something else. A story about survival. He clears his throat.

Standing in front of his friends, Jack Kind finds himself slipping into a memory. A young man again, he shivers in a different room where other men await an order he cannot possibly give. They are his superiors, but they've passed this responsibility to him. *Lead us through the gates of Hell.* After this, he will never think of himself as a good man. Just a survivor.

Lana cocks her head: *Are you okay?*
He licks his lips. "I've never told this to anyone."

CHAPTER 33

The officers stood near their bunks with their heads hanging. There was no way to digest the guards' pronouncement without assessing their own humanity. Who among them could be capable of doing what they've been told to do? Jack, still reorienting himself after the morning beating, missed the order. He asked Capt. Wojak to explain it. And even then Jack thought he heard wrong, asked him to repeat it. Wojak shook his head and said, "That's all there is, Chef."

Jack laid in his bunk and rubbed the knots on his skull. This was a joke, a taunt. Soon the guards would come back and—

And what? Jack thought. Have a good laugh at everyone's expense?

Even if it was a joke, it was deadly serious. All things are in war, just as they are hilarious and inconsequential. A group of young men "just fooling around" meant murdering a group of civilians, dragging them naked through soiled corridors and stacking them in an airlock and blasting them into space. Jack had heard of occurrences like this throughout the solar system, and they were not relegated to any one side. A man he considered a close friend in the camp, a Pvt. Gerome, had turned to him at one point and confessed that during the guerilla raids on McLaughlin Station, his squad stumbled upon a room full of elderly women and young girls and took turns with each before lighting a smoke grenade and sealing them inside. The funny part, Pvt. Gerome said, was that he'd forgotten about it until this very moment. Jack said nothing. Gerome was a harmless looking kid with a big nose and an underbite, great at scrounging from the guards. They never spoke of it again, just continued to barter until the camp was liberated. He probably went home to his family.

That was blood on someone else's hands. This was different.

"I won't do it," someone said.

"I'd rather die."

"Suit yourself."

"Fuck you."

"I'm serious. It's an option."

"And I'm serious. Fuck you."

"There's gotta be a way around it."

"I don't understand. Why make us choose?"

"We can ration better."

"There's nothing to ration. That's the point."

"I won't do it."

"Me either."

"Why make us choose?"

"To torture us."

"They think they're being fair."

"Fuck that."

"I won't do it."

"Someone has to."

What they were talking about was this: Food was so scarce prisoners were dropping dead on work detail. Some were too starved to rise out of bed or wield a hammer. This was not a form of punishment. The guards were short on food, too, though they weren't yet starving. The outpost relied on supply drops, and those drops had ended months ago. The guards wouldn't say why, but the homemade portables in the camp said the war was picking up in the region, meaning FROST's supplies were dwindling along with their abilities to transport them. Yet the prisoners were constructing what was supposed to become a major colony for FROST once the fighting settled down. The work could not stop. And if the food supply could not be increased, then the number of mouths had to be reduced. The guards' solution was to make the officers choose who would be executed. And execute them. One hundred and fifty men. That was the requirement. They had 120 hours, or five standard solar days. If they failed to meet these requirements, the guards would return and kill indiscriminately, starting with the officers.

The officers decided Jack should choose. He knew the camp better than any of them. He had friends everywhere. Guys who had become trading partners, guys he gave bland cookies to in return for favors, guys who trusted him, guys like the doctor and the doctor's assistant, who could tell Jack in confidence exactly which men were too sick to recover. These would be the first to go. The remainder would be thieves and hoarders, and there were plenty of them to choose from. Like the group of fifteen men who'd set up a gambling racket. They played for food and water and they never lost. Desperate delirious men continued to play.

At first, Jack protested. The officers circled his bunk and told him it was this or it was all of them. He could not argue.

The most difficult aspect was finding men to help with the executions. Four officers volunteered, Wojak and Keshawn among them. None really knew what they were getting into. The rest they bribed with promises of extra food, which would come from the officer's very quarters, since they very rarely went on work detail and could make due with less. Fifteen men in total would kill ten times that many.

They could not tell the rest of the camp what was happening. It would start a riot, which was maybe the guards' true intention. In secret, they went after the thieves first, many of them loners.

Wojak showed the assassins how to kill a man with a knotted sheet or piece of rope, twisting it around the neck, turning your back to your victim's, bending forward, pulling the rope over your shoulder. Of course they had considered more humane means, but the doctors could not spare morphine or syringes, and other poisons would have been more painful than hanging. The gamblers put up the biggest fight. Keshawn lost three fingers and suffered a severe gash on the head when one of the guys pulled out a saber he meant to keep as a souvenir. They went after the hospital the next day. When the doctor realized what was happening, he tried to stop them, but he was overpowered, held down in the distance where he could not hear the slaughter. They killed 130 sick men. After the gamblers and the thieves, it was easy and shameful and Jack would forever be haunted by the sound of his axe crushing the skulls of the sick, and although in the coming days the officers would try to explain to the rest of the camp the rationale for these actions, Jack could not blame the prisoners who abducted Wojak on his way back from the latrine one day and beat his head in, nor could he blame Keshawn when he killed himself, nor the men who came for Jack and held him down and tattooed him as a killer and a coward and a traitor and wished him a long life remembering what he had done to his brothers.

And now 13 years later, as Jack says these words for the first time, he relives the details he thought for so long would destroy him. But they do not destroy him. He wonders instead at the way nobody in the camps ever mentioned to him that their stomachs were noticeably fuller, the color in their cheeks noticeably pinker, or that his process of selection included the maximum number of inevitable casualties—sick men who would have died regardless and were in fact taking more than their allotment as treatment for incurable diseases—or how they discovered below the concrete pad of the gamblers' hut a massive store of canned goods and bottled water which those men had been gorging themselves on while so many others clutched their ballooning stomachs and died. These things were not mentioned because it was easier to believe that Jack had made the wrong decision, was a killer and a coward and a traitor, that certain lines cannot be crossed, even according to men who in the eyes of society had already crossed so many. What could Jack say to this? Today, what can he say to it? They were right, and they are right, and although the camp was liberated, he will never be free, and this is what his friends should know on this ship before they open the panic pod doors, if he should never see them again. And they should also know that suiting up before the doors are opened will prove much easier than waiting until things are in motion, because once Jack and Gregorian and Hunter reach the Homunculus, the pod will need to be ejected, and it's hard to put a space suit on in Zero-G, so better get to it.

CHAPTER 34

The hydras have not moved from their original positions. Hunter gives them names for reference. The small one on the first level will be known as Thumper. On the second level, slightly larger, they have Squiddy, and outside the panic pod doors, Big Bear. The ship has six internal defense turrets: one in the forward airlock, one in the cargo hold, two on level two and two on level three, above the forward and rear Zero-G shafts. Hunter and Gregorian will take the laser rifles, programmed to the same intensity as the turrets, a frequency so low it would cause a mild sunburn at worst. They will sprint to the bridge. Hunter will program Bel while Gregorian slips through the emergency hatch down to the airlock and unlocks the Homunculus. When Bel is good to go, Hunter and Jack will follow.

Meanwhile, the survivors in the pod will standby to eject. Lana has still not fully processed the fact that she will be performing a spacewalk in a matter of minutes. She tries to think only about the plan and how to work the EM-pack, seeing in her mind the field of stars and such vast blackness all around and hearing over and over Jack's confession about the camp until she wants to scream.

There are things people should never experience. The human race was scandalized by The Great Solar War, but the individual stories are what break the heart. He could have told her this in their time together, she thinks, but knows it is not true nor fair. But she has a clearer portrait of Jack than before. All his running around, incapable of an emotional connection, the drinking, what he said before about nightmares. Like so many others, he was a textbook case of PTSD, untreated and left fending for himself.

She used to have nightmares, too. Patients who wouldn't stop bleeding. The lights going out, operating in the dark, feeling their wounds with her hands, pressing into their guts, being swallowed by them.

She could have helped Jack through it.

Couldn't she?

They could have helped each other if they'd only been honest. That's how real relationships are supposed to work. Even now, he avoids looking at her as he talks with Gregorian and Tarziesch yet again about the layout of their ship. A layer of oil sheens his face, strands of hair pasted to his forehead. He must be exhausted.

"Hey." A hand grabs her wrist.

She jumps.

Stetson pulls away, stabs a finger at the nearest EM-pack. "Just follow my lead and you'll be fine. Right?"

"Yeah. Right."

His smile is all sympathy. "You're not gonna talk to him?"

She's never really spoken to Stets about her relationship with Jack. Or really anything of consequence. Like Hunter, Stets always maintained a comfortable distance. Friendly but not too friendly. She always respected him, though, and his opinion. "It can wait," she says.

"Can it?"

CHAPTER 35

Jack has not been so focused in years. No fear about whether or not he has made the right decisions, if he is a fuckup or unredeemable. No guilt. There is a problem to be solved and a solution to implement, and all that needs to happen next is for things to go smoothly.

Except.

There is something. A needle of anxiety in his mind, like he's holding back tears though he isn't. Whatever it is, there's no time to deal with it now.

The turrets are functioning. The rifles have been calibrated. Belinda is prepared to open and close the correct doors, lead the hydras to the ship's stern. The panic pod diagnostics check out. His shoes are tied and his heart pumps blood and he is ready, but when he looks in Lana's direction he feels a pang in his chest. They are all reassessing him now. That's unavoidable. You learn secrets about a close friend and your mind backtracks to process the pieces of a puzzle you thought you'd already solved. Otherwise, you ignore it, in which case you aren't actually friends.

He leans over the holo-screen to get another look at those unnerving tentacles. Lana comes up behind him. They need to talk, she says. She leads him to the hallway and into the side room, and they shove through the wrappers and cans. Jack kicks his canteen out of the way. Lana's body language says she is upset. How much more pain is he going to cause this woman?

She closes the door behind them.

"What is it?" he says.

She shrugs. "Tell me you aren't trying to martyr yourself."

Jack sinks. "What?"

"Just tell me."

"Martyr myself?"

"Nobody here wants you to die for them."

"Why would—"

"Just shut up and listen." She steps toward him. Then again. And again. Until they are face to face and Jack's breathing slows, and he can almost feel what the monsters must feel when following their prey—an electric warmth around her body, some kind of glow. It has always been there. Even in that clinic seeing her for the first time in years, still half-drunk and barely able to hold his head up. He'd been trying to ignore it. But now she's got that gleam. She was always the dominant one, pulling him into her room and fiddling with his belt, the pursuer.

She lays a hand across his neck. "This is bullshit," she says.

He flinches. "What?"

"This." Her hand bears down on the flesh of his neck. "This thing, this tattoo. It's bullshit. You did what nobody else could. They were the cowards, not you." Tears in her eyes. Hand trembling. "They had no right."

He doesn't know that he agrees. Probably he doesn't. But he is stunned. He's not sure what he expected—disappointment maybe, or anger directed at him, or feelings of disgust and shame at having slept with a man who helped murder 150 people. She has no right to feel bad for him, or worse, forgive him. He has to look away or he is going to lose it.

She grabs his chin, turns him back to her.

The needle in his mind slides into his throat. He tries to swallow it, but it's stuck.

"I'm not asking you to deal with this right now. Just tell me you want to live."

He stammers something about whatever happens is going to happen—

She pulls his lips to hers and everything he was going to say melts away and seems very stupid. They pull apart, and he leans back and looks into her face, soft features, dark eyes, knee-trembling beauty. "I want to live," he says. And means it.

CHAPTER 36

Double-check everything. Portable is working. Hunter's tool belt with screwdrivers, wire-cutters. Everyone wearing the torsos and lower halves of their suits. Holding off on the gloves and helmets to preserve maneuverability and oxygen. Hunter jumping up and down and shaking out her limbs, stretching her neck. Stetson at the control panel, spacing out, that blank stare as he fights his mounting agitation. Justin beside him with a similar expression, chewing the inside of his cheek. Dino in one of the chairs, teeth gritted and eyes clenched in pain. Gregorian kneeling and praying with Tarziesch—Tarziesch who disapproves of the bulky old-style space suits, wishes he'd worn his own. Lana on the helmet with the creature, studying the floor. And lastly, the Dandy, gripping Jack's arm and pulling him aside and saying, "I have one final order, Jackie."

The makeup has faded, wiped away by attempts to clear his sweat. The spacesuit makes him look like a mascot of some doomed sports team. Tiny head poking out of a marshmallow body. Pale complexion, smattering of acne scars, the shadow of a kid who never grew up. Is this what child kings looked like, acted like, felt like, with nobody questioning their authority as they fed their subjects to lions? These patterns of history play out on the Dandy's face. "I'm not leaving here empty-handed," he says. His little hands grip the inside of Jack's elbow.

"Get the fuck away from me."

Dandy does not seem to hear this. "I want you to go to the cargo bay and retrieve those gems. The ones from the sphere."

"You've lost your damn mind."

"Just hear me out."

"I am. I did. This is me hearing you out." Jack taps his ear. "Now stop touching me."

Dandy licks his lips and blinks. His face goes red. How long since someone talked to him this way? "Alien technology, Jack. Think how much it'd be worth. We'll be rich. Both of us."

Jack laughs. "You think I'd cut a deal with you? The only deal I'll offer is to let you live. That's it."

Dandy grins. "Alright, Jackie. Maybe when we get back, I'll order your family—"

In a single motion, Jack peels away and swings Dandy against a wall, pressing a forearm into his throat. "You threaten me one more time I might just pop your ugly head off." Jack shoves him and he falls to the floor coughing, the weight of his suit pinning him there.

Everyone watches them.

Jack trembles with anger.

No more delays.

Memory of Lana's lips on his. Ghost sensation. Calming.

He has their attention. He says, "Time to go."

CHAPTER 37

From her purchase on the helmet, Lana can't see the display. The others crowd the console and hold their breath as Belinda sets her lasers to work. This moment has snuck up quick. She still half-imagines an alternative will come along and save them. Maybe the hydras will bite through the airlock and blast themselves into space. It doesn't seem fair that this is the best option. The only option. She has always imagined she could sneak her way out of any disaster. Probably everyone feels that way.

She shifts inside her suit, her back sore from the weight. The things are bulky and outdated. Just bending her elbows is a struggle. Jack probably got them at a discount. Or for free. An old friend once warned her not to board a ship without a suit set to her own specs and accessible at all times. "It's like taking a gun into battle. You don't take one that's untested." Not that her friend, who'd been a plastic surgeon at home during the war, knew anything about battle. At the time, she'd come up with what she thought was a clever reply: *If I cared about safety, I'd go to Earth.* Funny that she followed through so many years later. So why did she leave?

"They're taking the bait," Stetson says, his voice wavering.

"Look at them," says Justin. "Fuckers are fast."

Jack, Hunter, and Gregorian move toward the door.

Belinda buzzes in: "Your path is clear."

The door's handle is a red lever resembling a breaker switch set into the wall. Jack steps up beside it. He calls for Justin to stand by and prepare to close it. His shoulders slump and he turns to face Lana. She tries to force a smile, but nothing comes. He nods, straightens his shoulders and puffs out his chest and reaches for the lever.

The door pops open with a clang.

The floor outside has been scratched to its underlying frame. Plastic chips and particleboard lie scattered like confetti. Like a dog had been scratching to get in. Even from where she sits she can hear the creature somewhere down the hall—*thud, bang, thud*—slamming against every surface, trying to catch an uncatchable beam of energy.

This is not going to work. She is certain of it. But Jack and Hunter and Gregorian have stepped outside, and Justin cranks the lever again, and the door seals shut.

*

They speedwalk down the corridor. A sprint would be too noisy. All Jack sees: the narrow tunnel of his ship's upper hallway. Feeling more and more like a cave with no exit.

Something snorts grunting breaths directly behind him, possibly above. All around.

The hydra. It has found them. No warning from Bel.

He holds his panic in long enough to realize the breathing is his own. Hunter and Gregorian keep pace directly behind him. And far behind them, a series of broken down doors.

The corridor dips and the ceiling opens into the observation area, shielded now by a black carapace. He visualizes the starfield surrounding them, the universe holding them in its strange expansive web. How many stars and planets are younger than the creature hunting them now? What else is out there, beyond the veil of our limited reach?

He holds tight to his portable, resisting the urge to call Bel and ask if everything is still going well. Has it heard them, is it chasing yet, how screwed are they on a scale of one to ten? A gentle breeze trickles overhead. Bel circulating filtered air. It shocks him for some reason, this mundane detail, how he has felt that same rush of air a thousand times in this same corridor, and never once considered how precious that air really is, how much he enjoys breathing.

Bel opens the bridge doors.

Soft blue light bathes the room. They hurry down the steps to the navigation table. The sun hovers above its surface, a white ornament, flickering. Hunter unzips her tool pouch and slides on her knees to a panel at the table's side. She pops the panel and plucks out a handful of wires. "Here we go," she sighs.

"Mr. Jack," Gregorian whispers. He raises his arms, lost.

Jack leads him to the emergency hatchway, twists the handle and lifts the lid.

The ladder rungs disappear into darkness.

"God dammit," Hunter hisses. She kisses a couple of fingers.

"What?"

"Shocked me," she says.

"Be careful."

Gregorian backs into the duct. Jack tells him to be careful, and quiet. Gregorian flashes a thumbs up, then ducks below.

"How we doing, Bel?" Jack says.

"The creatures are occupied. Big Bear has gotten into food storage."

"Is that a problem?"

"For now, no. But Big Bear is becoming very big."

*

Stetson notices it first. He's watching Jack and the others on the monitor when he swivels to report that everything's alright and shoots to his feet and shouts, "Why the hell is that still here?"

He points at Lana. *Don't I belong here?*

"I don't think we want that floating around in microgravity."

He's not pointing at her, but at the helmet underneath her.

With everything else going on, she didn't think about it. Nobody did, apparently.

"We can open the door," Justin says. "Have Bel distract it."

"I'll do it," says a voice from the interior hallway. The Dandy has removed most of his suit. He wears only the torso. "Tarzan, help me outta this."

Tarziesch fidgets uncertainly. He looks from face to face.

"Do what I say!"

Tarziesch jumps and obeys, lifts up the heavy torso so Dandy slinks out of the bottom. When he's free, he snaps his fingers at Lana. "Up."

"Excuse me?"

"I'm going out there. Might as well take that thing."

Justin has been sitting next to Dino. Now he balls his fists and stands. "Like hell."

"What's the big deal? Those things are idiots. Jackie Boy is safe, isn't he? Have your robot girlfriend distract the things and I'll meet them at the airlock, yes?"

"Go sit down," Lana says.

Dino groans. "Just kill him already."

"I don't think Jackie Boy would like that."

Justin crosses the room.

Dandy backs up to the manual override. Justin reaches out and grabs his shoulder. Tarziesch looks on, his loyalty flicking from one figure to the next. Lana frozen helplessly on the helmet just a few feet from them.

"You're not going anywhere," Justin says.

"Watch me." Dandy throws the first punch.

*

"The bottom of these shaft are stuck," Gregorian reports. "It will not opening. I think it is seize, like old screws."

"Kick it to shit if you have to," Jack says.

It has been less than a minute. Still feels like they're taking too long.

He pulls up surveillance on three separate holo-screens to show each of the hydras. The nearest camera to food storage is in the dining area. From the camera's angle, he sees what appears to be an enormous slug hanging out of the open storeroom doors. It seems to pulsate every few seconds. With each shudder it looks...bigger. There's over five tons of food in there.

There's something else. Something much, much worse. On the other two screens, Bel makes her lasers dance, but Thumper and Squiddy sit perfectly still.

Bel seems to know what he's looking at. "We don't have much time."

"Hunter, how long?"

"Two minutes."

"We may not have that."

"Perfect. Any bad news?"

In the shaft, a rhythmic beat as Gregorian kicks at the bottom hatch.

Belinda says, "Jack, there seems to be a disturbance in the panic pod."

"What do you mean, a disturbance?"

*

It was a sucker punch that caught Justin in the chin. His head snaps to the side and when he rights himself, he throws his body at Dandy. They hit the wall. Lana screams for them to stop before they're all killed. Stetson watches from the other side of the chamber, ashen, and Dino claws at the seatback and grimaces. Justin and Dandy trade headlocks, pound each other in the ribs and crotches. Dandy lashes out with long nails, tears flesh from Justin's cheeks. Tarziesch injects himself between them, catching stray blows. They roll against the door. Tarziesch wipes blood from his nose. He looks up, furious, and charges, gets an arm around Dandy's neck and cranks him away from Justin. Dandy leans back and kicks his legs in the air, throwing Tarziesch off-balance. Dandy manages to strike the sidewall. They lose their balance, fall over Lana.

She braces herself, knocked from her perch.

Her skull raps hard on the tile and everything stutters.

When she glances toward the door again, she sees the helmet rolling free.

*

Thumper is on the move. Two feelers prod the air atop what could tentatively be thought of as its head. It walks on six spindly legs. Sometimes more. It is in no rush, just feeling the air, looking, listening, paying no attention to the light circling and bobbing around it.

Jack: "Gregorian, you need to hurry."

Gregorian: "Almost there. Almost now."

He makes a hell of a lot of noise. It's a matter of time before Thumper comes close enough to hear. And Jack can't get anyone from the pod on his portable. He has a clear view of the doors but they are just doors. No sign of what's going on inside.

"I'm going back," he says, leaping out of his chair.

Hunter: "You're not leaving. Thirty seconds."

"It won't matter if they're dead."

"Well they'll *be* dead if we don't get to the ship."

He pauses, curses and kicks the nearest object, his broken mug from earlier. It shoots across the floor and cracks on the far wall.

"There!" Hunter says. She pulls up a keyboard. Her fingers flash over the letters. The sun rotates, and the arrow representing Belinda points at its heart. "Coordinates are set, motherfucker."

There is no time to celebrate.

"Gregorian needs to stop making that noise immediately," Belinda says.

"Gregorian, did you hear that?"

"I have almost there," he says. More thuds, sharper, echoing up the shaft.

On screen, Thumper runs for the prep chamber doors. Thirty feet down the hallway and closing.

*

Tarziesch lies across her stomach, pinning her. He pats the floor and fights the weight of his suit to right himself. He paws at the wall for a handhold, but there isn't one. Finally, he stands.

Lana's head throbs and when she tries to sit up white spots pop in front of her.

Tarziesch sways like he might tip over.

Dandy gets up, too, and reaches for the door handle. Justin has somehow fallen toward the pod's hallway. He doesn't try to stop Dandy, attention focused instead on Tarziesch's leg.

Lana sees it, too. Wants to scream. No point.

Tarziesch looks down, goes pale. Like some insectoid starburst, the hydra clings to his right shin, long dark limbs circling his thigh and ankle. The limbs squeeze and dimple his spacesuit.

He hollers in Venusian and kicks his leg like he might fling it off.

Dandy takes this opportunity to open the door. In a flash, he slips outside. Gone.

The hydra stiffens, needle-sharp tips pushing down.

Justin shouts: "Take off the suit!"

No time.

The legs puncture the suit and all at once the hydra slithers inside.

Tarziesch goes quiet.

Lana claws at the ground, army crawling away. Too heavy to stand.

Tarziesch lurches. "Ach!" he says, tongue lolling. "Oooohm."

He throws his head back and tentacles spray from between his lips, a blast of gore and slime. They lick at the ceiling. The skin over his neck pulses. Tears form in jagged red lines.

Justin, still near the hallway, lowers his shoulders, steps forward. Lana sees what he's going to do, knows that it is the only way anyone will survive. Still, she tells him to stop.

He charges.

Justin connects with Tarziesch at waist height. Tarziesch's head erupts in pinkish clots and a bundle of waving appendages. Justin heaves against this hideous mass, the hydra already wrapping him. He lifts with everything he has, barrels out of the room with a monster on his shoulder. They crash just outside the door.

Stetson does not move from the command console. Lana screams for him to get the door but he's gone catatonic. Dino clutches at his empty sleeve, reliving the loss of his arm, perhaps.

From the hallway, sounds of ripping fabric and Justin's high-pitched screams.

She shoves against the floor—hardest pushup she's ever done—and throws her feet beneath her. Every muscle strains as she totters upright. She spins.

The handle is just a body-length away. Just two or three strides.

Corner of her eye: tentacles slither along the floor. Inches from the doorway.

She leaps.

Falls.

The floor slick with blood and mucus.

She throws her arms out—for the handle, for anything.

Her fingers grip it, cold metal. The weight of her fall pulls it down.

Before the door closes, she catches sight of them. What used to be Justin and Tarziesch. Their suits shredded, wet with blood and slime. Two hydras knotting together, leaping for her.

The door shuts them out.

She drops, rests her forehead on the cold linoleum, not quite sure if she is alive or dead.

*

Jack watches the horror playing out on the monitor. Dandy running out, his nephew and Tarziesch disintegrated. *Converted.* His nephew is gone. Son of his brother and brother's wife. If Jack makes it out of here, he will tell them directly. He'll look into his brother's face and say, "I am responsible." If he hadn't put him down earlier—

What had he said? *I seem to recall finding you unconscious...*

He gave a young man something to prove, a cause for taking unnecessary risks.

Gregorian: "I am through." And the banging sounds from the emergency hatch are gone.

It is all too late. Thumper is just feet from the chamber door. Bel amps up her lasers, no longer a decoy, slicing Thumper with mathematical precision. As quick as Thumper loses limbs, they reabsorb, so it seems to convulse down the corridor.

Bel displays a view of the prep chamber. A rectangular shadow hangs from the ceiling, swings slightly. The busted hatch. Gregorian slinks out of the opening, lands hard, body folding into his knees, then upright, dashing for the airlock. And in his haste he does not see the bench in the center of the room. He trips and tumbles headfirst into the storage lockers, lies prone facedown.

Jack slams his fist on the controls.

Hunter clamps her hands to either side of her head.

Thumper reaches the room. The thin door explodes into splinters.

Gregorian scrambles upright, careens toward the airlock.

Thumper comes apart, solid form diffusing into a gossamer net that coats the air and every surface it contacts, flowing through the room looking almost harmless, almost beautiful.

Gregorian reaches Bel's airlock door. He spins to see his approaching end, and loses his footing and falls backward into the chamber. The hydra's sinew coats the camera lens in darkness.

Jack and Hunter hold on, breathless.

A moment later, Gregorian's transmission: "This is Kilo Gregorian onboard the Homunculus, awaiting orders of Captain Jack Kind."

Jack and Hunter silently throw their fists in the air.

Hunter whispers, "Jesus fuck, Greggy. Walk much?"

"Not sure I am understand."

Jack says, "Nice work, Gregorian. You had me worried for a second."

"Oh him of the little faiths. Can you make it to airlock?"

Onscreen, Thumper condenses, pulling from the camera. It rubs against the airlock door, seeking a weak spot. Something to pry.

Jack says, "I'll have to get back to you."

"Copy. I will be prepping systems for disengage. Await your command."

Jack considers telling Gregorian that his friend Tarziesch is gone. That Dandy and Jack may not be joining them on the Homunculus, after all. He says, "See you soon."

CHAPTER 38

"We lost Justin and Tarziesch. Dandy escaped."

"I saw." Jack whispers back. "Are you alright?"

Lana's alive, but *alright* doesn't really factor in. "What do we do?" she says.

He doesn't want to say. She'll think he's playing the martyr.

He doesn't have a choice. He has to get Dandy. His nephew is dead. Ani and Kip are still in danger. Hunter is out here with him, vulnerable. The only way forward is to save the one man who put them here, a man who won't answer Jack's calls, and now sits cross-legged in the cargo bay with a screwdriver, prying at the gems imbedded in shattered bits of an alien sphere. He still thinks the hydras can be controlled. It's pure luck they haven't spotted him already.

Jack tells Lana to standby. They'll be out of this soon.

He explains to Hunter what is about to happen.

She screws up her face. "Are you kidding me?"

"Tell me something better."

"I can't. But you can't—"

"I can and I will. I'm the captain here."

She holds her hands up in defeat.

He studies the screen one last time, making certain that Thumper is still at the airlock door, no surprises in the corners ready to ambush him once he's down there. Belinda assures him that what he sees is accurate. For now, Thumper is thoroughly occupied.

"You're up to speed on this, right Bel?"

"I am."

"Are there alternatives I've overlooked?"

"Given your physical constraints, your plan is solid in theory."

"In theory."

"I'm a computer, Jack, not a fortune teller."

"But you've computed the odds."

"At this moment, I don't believe sharing statistics would prove useful."

"Probably right. Just watch my back."

"I have been."

To Hunter, he says, "Don't move till Thumper takes the bait."

She nods, studies him a moment. She wants to hug him or something. But that would signify goodbye. "Don't be an idiot," she says.

"Too late."

He straddles the hatch. Thirty feet below, the prep chamber glows, a bright square. Thinking of his previous encounter, he pauses to pull off his boots. Then he starts down, slow as a sloth, his breath already making the walls sweat, his feet silent on the rungs.

CHAPTER 39

They wait to eject the pod. Stetson's fingers poise above the touchpad. The scent of blood and something fouler linger in the air. Don't look at the slickness on the floor, and don't step in it. Just like those packed rooms with their beds, soldiers bandaged and moaning, the Alliance unwilling to spare tissue regenerators on such low priorities as suffering men. Lana's hands shaking, gloves wet. It was a different time but it keeps come back, all that suffering and loss. All you can do is apply more bandages.

"The hell is he doing?" Stetson says.

On the holo-screen, Thumper continues to slap at the airlock. Jack has yet to drop out of the hatch. Lana's not surprised this was the best plan he could come up with. Consciously or not, the moment the hydra arrived, he recognized his chance to sacrifice himself. That's why he confessed about the camps and why he wouldn't look at her after. He can go to the grave feeling lighter now, having said his peace. Nothing to do anymore but watch for the cloaked angel with the skeletal face. Because the future is harder to see when it is open.

A scraping sound from above disrupts her thoughts. Metal grinding metal.

Stetson doesn't notice, absorbed in the screen.

The sound again, louder, joined this time by a chorus of raining pebbles.

Not pebbles. Claws.

So she won't have to see Jack's death onscreen. She'll beat him to the other side.

"Stets. It's in the ceiling."

He hears it too. Tilts his head back. "How?"

He switches cameras. This one shows a familiar view of the closed pod, the white doors with their divots and scratches, the floor battered to chips. There is a new piece of destruction now.

Twisted fixtures hang from the ceiling. Nanotubing and ceramic shielding and fiber optics dangle from a jagged hole.

The hydra found a way to skirt the doors.

"Will it hold?" Lana says.

"It should. It's designed to."

"Not good enough. We need to eject."

Stetson isn't so sure. They should be safe, he says. The hydra couldn't get through the doors, so why would it get through the hull? Plus, the pod is like a reinforced train car on a magnetic track, its doors butting against the hallway. This track runs through an airlock and into a long chute where the pod's rear thrusters will activate to launch her. Does Lana really think the creature can 1) hold to the pod during launch, and 2) survive in outer space, without an atmosphere, and this close to the sun?

He isn't thinking rationally. "Even if the hull holds, the longer we sit here, the longer it has to get a better grip. And we still need to do a spacewalk."

"Shit," he concedes. "We should confirm with Jack."

"You call him now, you'll get him killed."

"Right. Dammit."

"Do it, Stets." She drops into the flight chair beside Dino, pulls the safety belt over her shoulders. A few helmets and gloves still lie on the floor, but the heavier equipment—EM-packs and air tanks—have already been secured.

Stetson doesn't act until another screech erupts overhead.

"Good God!" He clicks himself into the pilot chair. "Belinda, have you been listening?"

"I have. You'll need to activate the launch sequence manually. Jack has trained you on this, I hope?"

"Yes. Basically."

"You sound uncertain."

"I'm just a little shaken up, Bel!"

"Understood. Good luck out there. It's been lovely working with you."

"Yeah. Sure."

Screeeeee, goes the ceiling.

Stetson fiddles with the controls. Lana leans back and shuts her eyes. *Just go already.*

He calls Hunter first. "We're ejecting. No time to explain."

"Copy. Bel said the hydra got into the ceiling."

"Well I'm glad she told *you*."

"Second in command, Stets. I'm sorry. I thought you knew or I'd have—"

"Gotta go, Janessa."

"You'll do great. I'm not patronizing."

"Patronize this," he says, and smacks the controls.

The pod lunges sideways. A dizzying sensation as it spins to face the chute.

CHAPTER 40

He feels his way, one rung to the next. The hydra slams again and again against the airlock and the sound echoes up the shaft twisted and amplified. The air tastes musty and thick. As he nears the lower hatch, he hears, in addition to the banging, that stomach-churning sound of the creature's body rubbing against itself, slick and wet. It will waste no time turning on him. He'll be helpless but for his feet and Bel's reaction time. No way to kill it. No way to stop it. It has shown its intelligence, but is it conscious? Does it feel any which way about him, about them, these little moving wads of meat? Does it feel pleasure when it wraps its body around its prey, a rush of elation? He thinks of the bees that stung Kip. How they erupted out of that rotten log. Insects are not conscious, are they, and yet they can show panic. Has the hydra ever faced an enemy it could not run down? How many worlds has it destroyed? Does it remember the things and people it has absorbed? Are they in some way still alive inside of it? Does it sleep, and if so, does it shoot up in the middle of the night seeing their faces?

His feet find the final rung. He clings, shaking and cold. The hydra's efforts reverberate through the ladder and his bones. It is just a mechanism, a force of destruction, a black hole with a will, and Jack teeters just outside the event horizon. There is nothing to do now but drop inside.

So that is what he does.

CHAPTER 41

The pod shunts down the track, a bumpy few feet that jostle them side to side. She checks Dino's safety belt and holds hers at the shoulders. Dino drips with perspiration. Every time the pod shakes, it jostles his stump. "You're alright," she tells him.

"Yeah," he grunts. "No sweat."

She grips his glove, but it's empty.

The hydra's efforts have increased to a steady scream. The hull should hold. It has to. It's required to withstand millions of degrees of heat and forces that could liquefy bone. The hydra is powerful, but it can't be that powerful. Can it?

Stetson watches a wireframe illustration of their coming journey down the track, narrating with a flat voice, his attempt to keep the terror at bay. It's not working. "The airlock's coming up. The track is actually very short. See, the, uh—This airlock was added when they installed the pod. Behind us, the track will be pressurized with the rest of the ship. It's actually kind of a wasteful, uh—Waste of good oxygen, honestly, if you ask me. If I designed it, I'd have, uh, I'd have added a secondary door in the hallway here, see? That's what I would have done."

"You doing alright up there, Stets?"

"Makes no sense to have an airlock way down this way. Double-doors would solve that."

The pod takes a sudden leap forward.

Something in the ceiling goes *crunch*.

"See! Then we wouldn't have to deal with all this *fucking noise!*" He throws his head back and screams. "I fucking hate you, you piece of shit!"

The mind controls the body. Once it goes, the body shuts down or does something irrational, like the worst kind of drunk. Either he'll hyperventilate and pass out or go manic. Confined areas and the constant stress of space will do that to anyone, no matter how long they've been out here. One of her more memorable patients during the war was a lieutenant who lost it during a raid and opened an airlock, blew his whole squad out. He was the only survivor until he stole a syringe of regenerative tissue and shot it directly into his heart.

"Hey Stets. How many walks will this be for you?"

He makes a strange sound. Whining and whimpering.

"I need you here, Stets. You're gonna have to guide me. I'm relying on you, okay?"

"*Hoooo*," he breathes. "That's a good one. I'm alright. I'm okay. *Hooo*. We're inside the airlock now. Ten seconds. Put your head back. There's no grav drive. Just good old-fashioned thrust."

She presses into the seat, takes whiteknuckle hold of the armrests.

They jerk ahead, more bouncing.

Clang, clang, goes the hydra.

"We're clear of the airlock. Preparing for launch. Let's hope this knocks our stowaway off, hey? Three. Two. Blastoff." He jabs at the control pad and that is the last thing Lana sees before the force sucks her into her seat and socks her in the gut. The oxygen in her brain slides to the back of her skull and the pod shrinks to a pinpoint of light somewhere far ahead.

CHAPTER 42

Death collapses time to nothing, stretches it to the infinite. The moment is there and not there. Seems to flicker between these two states. Later, if you survive, it will feel as though it never happened, and you'll repeat the story to yourself, trying to make it real, to build it into your ongoing timeline. That time death reached for you and barely missed. A piece of you will wonder if it didn't. If all of this is just a ghost's dream. In fact, it is, but you have always been the ghost. Somewhere far ahead, or far behind, death has already found you. In this moment, Jack looks upon death—not for the first time—and he sees that it has a thousand shifting arms in tangles, yarn that meshes and ties and slides through itself smooth as glass. Gashes appear across its surface like so many mouths. It comes for him, tentacles growing and gliding.

He dashes for the hallway. Moves on instinct, bolting toward the forward gravity shaft. Hears the hydra *thump thump thumping* after him.

Into the hall.

Grav shaft straight ahead.

Creature just behind.

He hurls himself into the air, finds the handholds at the lip of the shaft and flips his body up and into the tunnel. Head still poking out, he has an upside down view of the hydra. It has taken the form of some kind of giant millipede with legs sprouting in every direction. They shuttle it forward, propelling off the walls, ceiling, floor. As it nears, the front end splits apart. He doesn't wait to see what shape it takes next. He pushes off the sidewall, rising feet-first, slaps the ladder to spin his body upright in the shaft. He glances down and sees the hydra not twenty feet below, tentacles boiling. He kicks off the ladder at the second story landing, glides into the corridor.

Belinda knows what to do.

She cranks the shaft's gravity in reverse, forcing the creature to the third level. It whips past quick as a hypertram, a pale tangle. An appendage lashes out and misses his foot by inches, leaves a dent in the wall.

Bel reactivates the gravity on level two. He isn't expecting it and drops to his knees before stumbling back to his feet, keeps on running toward the rear of the ship as fast as he can, his right knee aching. Bel says something he can't quite make out over the sound of his footsteps and gasps. *Let it be something good.* Maybe Hunter made it to the airlock. Or Lana and the others have ejected safely. Or his path is clear.

She relays the message through her onboard speakers. "Squiddy is straight ahead."

This is not good news.

"Faster," Bel says. "You can make it."

He takes her word, sprints full-speed. She opens each door, white flashes.

"Up the mid-shaft, down the stern," she instructs.

The landing doors part. Jack's heart stutters but his feet behave.

Squiddy burbles out of the doorway across the shaft. The ladder is all that separates them.

He jumps, hits the ladder at an angle. One hand slips between the rungs. His face slams into metal. He scrambles to correct his grip.

Squiddy unfolds, each tentacle doubling or tripling in length. They reach.

He ducks and leapfrogs from the ladder to the wall, pushes off and up, and glides toward level three.

A tentacle smacks the wall between his legs.

Squiddy follows him up the shaft.

Jack tastes blood in his throat, ignores it.

He reaches the third floor landing.

The rear doors are already broken. He leaps from shaft to hallway, into gravity again. Lands on his feet. Thumper crashes out of the fore corridor just as Squiddy erupts from the top of the shaft. The two hydras intertwine, twin strands of bile. The floor shudders, and the combined hydras suck down the hole as Bel cranks the gravity. "Faster," she commands.

Across the final landing, dark shapes clog the far corridor, a wall of tentacles careening out of the kitchen. Big Bear. This enormous growth larger than any animal, its anatomy shifting in disharmony, as if a hundred life forms have been mashed together and it can't decide on one—here a loop of tentacles and there what appears to be the snout of a dog and here bug-like mandibles and there an arm that could be human except for the extra fingers.

Is it imitating these shapes, or were they absorbed in its past?

Belinda shouts, "Jump!"

He dives into the shaft headfirst.

The bloated hydra throws itself after.

He falls five times faster than Earth gravity. The ladder is a silver blur. A glimpse of tentacles at the second level. The combined Thumper-Squiddy hydra, lashing out too slow. He drops into the cargo bay, through the mangled remains of the grav shaft. The cage has fallen away, shattered during his first chase with the hydra. As he nears the floor, Bel cranks the G forces in reverse. He jerks upward.

The hydra bubbles out of the shaft after him. The very end mushrooms, holding fast to the surface around the opening like a blooming grappling hook. Slowly, steadily, it swells into the chamber.

Bel's voice squawks from his portable: "Talk to me, Jack. Say anything. There's not much time." The force of the fall and the rebound did a number on him. He can't quite place where he is or why he is bathed in a field of light. A demon oozes out of a metal hole nearby. He recognizes Jim Dandy below, hands on his hips, gaping. A jolt of hatred courses through him. He remembers everything. He floats in the air near one of the ceiling lights. Bel must have targeted him for selective Zero-G.

Dandy waves. "The hell you doing up there, Jackie?"

CHAPTER 43

Someone left the storage room door open. Garbage clutters the panic pod's cabin. Foil wrappers, crumbs, the flattened carcass of a cockroach. A minor annoyance in what is shaping up to be a successful trip. Two pieces of great news: First, Hunter made it safely aboard the Homunculus. Both it and the pod are maneuvering into Bel's shadow for the spacewalk. Second, there's no sign of the hydra since blastoff. It must have dislodged. It's probably still in the ejection chute or maybe fried in the sun's heat, not so invincible afterall.

Free of Belinda, the ride is much smoother now, though Stetson is an engineer first and a pilot second. His handling of the pod's navigation system is fitful at best. Each time he touches the controls, the pod jounces as if kicked, and Stetson curses the design.

Dino has passed out. He may have snuck some painkillers before takeoff. More likely, the loss of his arm has lowered his blood pressure, and microgravity proved too much. At least they got his suit on before he went limp.

Lana takes the copilot seat. The pod has no window or external cameras, so the wireframe model of their surroundings on the holoscreen is the best picture they'll get. The pod maps its environment by bouncing photons off nearby objects, except this close to the sun it can't compensate for the background radiation. It looks as if they're flying through a network of octagons. That's what you get when you're inside the sun's corona, Stetson says. Outside of Bel's shadow, they can't get a frequency clear enough to hail the Homunculus either, so they communicate by transmitting lines of text several hundred times a second until the onboard computers receive enough to unscramble. It's time consuming, but better than a collision.

Homunculus: *g0t y%u in 1iNe of sight. Cont1Nue stra1gh+ 5000 feet.*

Lana counts seconds in her head, not sure what number she should anticipate. If they're moving a hundred feet per second that would give them, what, five minutes? A little more, a little less? What does 5,000 feet even look like, say, on a road? She's too shaken to do the math. Something about not seeing what's out there is getting to her. And not knowing how Jack is fairing. He could be dead.

She reaches 145 seconds before another message beeps through.

Homunculus: *cro$sin# shadoVV meridi&n now. rot@te 180 degrees port. Ple@se respond.*

Stetson and Lana share a glance. He brushes away a stray bit of cracker that floats from above and types back:

Panic: *We read you, Homunculus. What's the problem?*

He says to Lana, "Maybe positioning for the spacewalk."
Lana doesn't think so. It's not smart to read tone into half scrambled text, but there's urgency there. *Please respond.* Hunter and Gregorian are worried. Something's wrong.

Homunculus: *Humor mE.*

Stetson spins the pod with a series of shudders. "At least the text is clearing up," he says.

Panic: *That better, Homunculus? Requesting reason for spin.*

A long stretch with no reply.
"Come on, kids," Stetson grumbles.

Homunculus: *Will need to keep |/essels separated current distance. Will be a lon%er walk but proceed as plan?ed.*

Panic: *Why separated?*

90 seconds pass. No response.

Panic: *Hunter? Need reply. What is the problem?*

When the reply comes, Lana's breath hitches in her throat.

Homunculus: *Bogey on y0ur hull.*

CHAPTER 44

Jack wastes no time once his feet are on the floor. The hydra forms stalactites, rigid spikes struggling out of the shaft, fighting the upward pull. Dandy looks on, dumbfounded, screwdriver limp in one hand, staring as Jack runs toward him waving and shouting, "Run, you asshole!" Dandy doesn't run. The stalactites slide out of the grav shaft's influence and leap toward the floor. Globules vault at Jack as soon as they land. Bel does her best to alter their aim, switching the gravity on and off when they jump. Jack dodges. One zips by his left ear. Another careens for his chest, split in half at the last moment by Bel's overhead turret. Both halves whip by his shoulders.

Dandy finally gets a handle on the situation. "Holy shit!"

"Airlock!"

He looks around, uncertain.

Jack points behind him. "The ramp!"

Dandy steps, pauses, stoops to take something from the floor. His cape. The corners have been tied into a makeshift sack or bag. It sags with weight. Something shiny inside.

The jewels.

With death literally raining down around them, Dandy prioritizes his wallet. Jack reaches him, grips the shoulder of his shirt and drags him ahead. Dandy tries to wrench free. Jack holds tighter.

Bel opens the door to the inner chamber, a doorway angling out of the floor. It will be the final room they ever see, no doubt. Last stop in a lifetime of bad decisions. Dandy trips on his own feet just short of the doorway, goes down. Jack seizes a fistful of hair. Dandy yowls. Jack looks behind. Enough of the stalactites have fallen for the hydra to take one of its more animal forms. Twin arms burst from its back on either side of its body. They stretch into flat fans, expand horizontally, so thin they're nearly translucent. Then those enormous protuberances, seven feet long each, *flap*. Of all the horrors he has witnessed, Jack has never moaned with fear, but he does now. This compulsory noise builds in his throat and just comes out, startling him. The hydra has grown *wings*.

And with a flash of her laser, Bel slices them off.

Jack laughs, then chokes on it. The hydra grips the grated floor and hauls ass toward him. Bel dices it up to slow it down. More gobs drop around it, diving and burrowing into its mass.

Jack drags Dandy through the passageway. The door claps shut behind them and the hydra clangs against it. Dandy stops to catch his breath, hands on his knees.

"That door won't hold!" Jack shouts, grabbing again for Dandy's shirt.

"I thought you could control it!"

"What the fuck does it look like!"

As the upper door gives, they charge into the main airlock with the two shovers. Bel shuts them inside. The hydra hits the door, which trembles, but holds.

Jack slumps against the cold surface. The hydra's efforts reverberate through him. Five tons of goddamn food. Why did he ever need that much?

Dandy paces in circles. He carries his sack of alien jewels across his shoulder like a gaunt Santa Claus. He's been talking to himself. Something about how this is all Jack's fault. If he'd done like he was supposed to and let Dandy leave before they turned on the sphere, none of this would be happening. Jack is too exhausted to respond.

Dandy reaches some climax in his rant, storms into Jack's face, points a finger. "You better get me out of this," he says. "Or I'm going to make sure your family—"

Jack head-butts him. Dandy snorts and drops onto his back, unconscious. The gems spill from his cape, shiny blue rocks. Jack steps around him, kicks Dandy in the gut. "I warned you."

CHAPTER 45

Stetson helps her with the helmet and gloves. She does the same for him. With the suits fully pressurized, it's like being inside of a raft underwater, the material stiff with air. She fights for even the slightest movements. There's hardly enough room to secure their EM-packs, but they manage. Fully suited, Stetson types his final commands into the console. The pod's remaining air goes sucking into the ventilation, taking much of the garbage with it. Lana's suit bulges, even stiffer than before.

They strap Dino—still unconscious—to Stetson's chest, facing forward, and Stetson gives her a thumbs up.

They take positions at the door, Lana in the lead. At least the comms should work better in Bel's shadow. As long as they stick near each other, they'll be able to talk.

"When you're ready," Stetson says, "pull that lever. Get clear as fast as you can. We'll be right behind you."

Last time she pulled this lever, it was to seal the hydra out. It feels insane that her hand is about to reach for it again, this time to open it. The hydra is out there, on their hull, waiting for them. They tried telling Hunter to shoot it with the Homunculus's cannon, but the solar wind crippled the targeting system, so they'd have to aim manually. As in, by looking out of the window. It's a risky shot even with the computer. Flat-out homicidal otherwise.

She peers around Dino into Stetson's visor. He sweats heavily, struggling to maneuver with Dino and his EM-pack. Lana says, "If I lose control of this thing, promise you'll come and get me. Don't let me drift alone out there."

He actually laughs. Static shrieks in her ears. "You'll do fine."

"I hate space, Stetson."

"Everything's in space. That's like saying you hate oxygen."

"Just promise me."

"If you start to drift, you won't get far. You pass out of Bel's shadow, you're toast."

"Is that supposed to make me feel better?"

"Does it?"

She turns to face the door.

"I promise," Stetson says.

She pulls the lever.

CHAPTER 46

Dandy salvaged fifteen blue opals. Less than Jack expected. They're big as chicken eggs, maybe a pound each. They are merely minerals. Pretty colors. The same as we use to decorate our monuments and furniture. This is what Dandy risked his life for. Jack leaves them.

He releases a single shover from its tie-down straps, hops into the machine and drives it so the forks press against the outer door. According to Gregorian, the Homunculus's airlock opening is contractible to fit different ports, with a maximum height of seven feet and a width of ten, and it is roughly twelve deep. There should be plenty of room for the shover to squeeze inside.

There are no EVA suits down here. Terrible contingent planning in retrospect, but the cargo ramp was never meant to open into the void. It's meant to form an umbilicus, docking to another ship's airlock, and that is also why the shover's controls are unenclosed, for working in a breathable atmosphere. So Jack digs through the storage lockers searching for anything useful. He doesn't find much. Mostly hardware he forgot to put back in suspension storage. A soldering iron that's bent into an almost unrecognizable shape, squashed dust masks, shredded duct tape, an exploded bottle of dried superglue, gloves that have been so forcefully compacted into balls that they tear when he attempts to flatten them out. He also discovers a tarp, a couple of tie-down straps, razor blades inside a broken case, and a remarkable amount of dust. Minus the lattermost, he sets these items aside.

Hunter should hail him soon. He asks Bel for updates.

"They are preparing for crew transfer. Judging by the data, there have been one or two serious complications."

"Don't tell me. Not yet." He can't handle more bad news.

"Okay."

The hydra keeps on giving the airlock door a workout, much stronger now with its improved size. Until the Homunculus gets into position, he and Dandy are stuck. Sitting ducks. He busies himself by slicing the tarp into strips. Dandy coughs and rolls over, awake. He touches his nose and hisses through his teeth. Jack glances at him, then back to his work.

"The hell are you doing?" Dandy says.

Jack ignores him.

Dandy stands, moans, and notices the prearranged shover and Jack's handiwork with the tarp.

"Wait just a fucking second here. You're not planning what I think you're planning."

Jack says nothing.

"Without suits?"

"Do you have a better idea, Jim?"

"Don't call me that, you son of a bitch."

Jack shrugs.

"Oh God," Dandy moans. He leans against the wall. "This is it."

Jack lets him have this moment of crisis. It's not supposed to be pleasant to witness, unless you're a sadist, but in this particular case, Jack anticipates the show. Dandy rocks back and forth and mutters how unfair it all is (true), that he deserves better (false), that he will be remembered (in infamy, no doubt), and that everyone responsible will pay (probable, since Dandy is mostly at fault). He runs through the stages of grief in fast-forward, circling back to anger, which he directs squarely at the one man trying to save him. "You were so easy to play, Jackie. Do you know that? How predictable you are? You're just a good dog, that's all."

"Keep talking, hero."

"I'm serious. You're just a sad little man. Though I will say I was surprised when I saw you holding that old rifle. I should've let Greggy take your head off. But I wanted you to see the sphere. I wanted whatever was inside to kill you slow and painful."

"Charming."

"You keep on thinking you're untouchable, Jackie. Pretend these words don't matter. Deep down, you know. I played you from start to finish. It's what I do best. And you can look at me and think I'm this despicable man who lies and kills to stay at the top, and that may be true, but at least I'm honest about it. When I took power, the people knew what they were getting. They were sick of corporate cronies providing the illusion of freedom. Every choice preselected. I gave them the truth the old fashioned way. By standing up and declaring that I am the meanest motherfucker they'd ever lay eyes on. And if you don't submit, I will rip your head off without laying a finger on you. That's power. That's what the people wanted. And I brought it to them."

Jack sets down the razor. The menace this man is capable of. It cuts through him, makes his palms sweat. Suddenly the revolver inside his jacket feels very heavy.

"Then there's you," Dandy spits. "You disgust me. All your self-loathing. Grow a pair and be proud of what you did in that camp. Once upon a time you had what it took to survive. Now look at you. All I had to do was say the word *family* and you curl into a useless ball. A whimpering dog who forgot how to bite."

Jack's spine goes stiff. Did Dandy just admit it? Could he be so stupid?

Dandy throws his head against the hull and screams at the inner airlock. "Cut it out or kill us already!"

Amazingly, the hydra goes quiet. As if even it obeys this psychopath.

As for Jack, he has removed the revolver from its holster. Now he stands.

"It was a bluff," he says. His voice unsteady, betraying his emotions. "The whole time."

"Oh, fuck off! Of course it was a bluff! Like my associates don't have better things to do than stalk two of your idiot relatives!" He spots the handgun, rolls his eyes. "Oh, what, you're gonna shoot me now? Like you even have the—"

The revolver bucks.

CHAPTER 47

She stands in the open doorway, looking out. The Homunculus blinks in the distance, a barely discernible network of lights against the stars. Everything is huge and tiny out here, no sense of scale to gauge with. She wastes no time easing herself forward with a nudge at the right control stick.

Something grabs her foot.

She falls. The stars rush upward.

She misjudged. Falling into the sun.

"You're alright," Stetson says. "Your boot hit the doorway. Calm down and correct it."

Not falling. Rotating.

She taps the controls on the left arm of her pack. Gas sprays frontward from shoulder-height. She finds herself facing the pod. A stark white rectangular vehicle with the edges molded soft. Too bulky to be aerodynamic. Stetson hovers upside down in the doorway.

No, she corrects herself. She is upside down. She must have done half a summersault on her way out.

Stetson comes forward, but appears stuck. He jostles from side to side. "We're caught," he says. He fights for control, his pack spraying out behind him.

She spots the culprit. The glove of Dino's empty arm has somehow wedged between the handle and the wall. If Stetson doesn't stop fighting it, he could tear the suit and kill Dino. "It's the release," she says.

He continues shaking from side to side.

"Stetson, you've gotta—" The rest of the words won't come.

A large *thing* shambles across the hull. Multiple legs creeping in unison. Twelve or more feet across. It comes right at her.

She jets backwards.

Stetson spots the glove. He yanks it free and gives her a thumbs up.

He must see the look on her face, or perhaps the reflection in her visor, because he freezes and his mouth drops open, and then he blasts forward as fast as he can.

He's too late.

The hydra has perched above the door. As he zips through the opening, it whips a tentacle down and wraps the base of his EM-pack. He screams and opens his rear jets wide, but the hydra tethers him to the pod and he swings wildly to the left and smashes against the side of the vehicle. Nitrogen crystals dance. The hydra twists Stetson and Dino to the other side where they crash again into the hull. Dino's left leg folds the wrong way beneath him. Stetson shoots them forward with a hard burst, and before the hydra wrenches them back again, Lana acts.

She propels herself forward into Dino, gripping the safety harness over his chest. The hydra shakes back and forth like a shark tearing at its prey. The harness has a central push release. With all the movement, she can't seem to hit it. They swivel right. Dino opens his eyes.

"*Help me!*" she says.

But his left arm dangles, useless and broken.

They skitter, the force of Stetson's pack fighting the hydra's impossible strength.

She loops her wrist under the safety strap and holds tight to Dino's body, punching repeatedly at his chest. The button is stuck.

When she looks up, Stetson's facemask has filled with eels. They press against his visor until the helmet pops off with an explosion of gore. The blood freezes, small shards of colored glass.

She pounds the harness release dead center. Dino slides free.

Stetson's EM-pack explodes. What remains of his body goes shooting straight up, taking the hydra with it long enough for Lana to get a better grip on Dino and spray them backward. Stetson's suit tears open and he is gone, just gone, his body replaced with folds of the hydra. It coils, preparing to strike. Lana's off-center grip spins her and Dino in circles. She adjusts, releases him. He careens away from the pod. She holds back, steadies herself.

The hydra lashes at her.

She rams Dino full speed, aiming for his center of mass. Her momentum holds them together. The hydra doesn't touch her, its base still stuck to the pod like a leech.

CHAPTER 48

Dandy lowers his hands, looks down at himself, and sees that he is unharmed. Confusion changes to relief, then to outrage. "The fuck are you playing at!" The bullets left dents in the metal around his head. It could have killed them both—firing eight bullets in an enclosed space like that—but it didn't.

The barrel smokes. Jack pulls his collar down and rolls the metal along his neck, across the tattoo. At first he feels nothing. Just smells burning hair and hears a hiss. Then the stinging sets in and he fights the instinct to pull the gun away.

Dandy scowls with disgust.

Jack is nothing like this man across from him, this killer coward. He did terrible things in the past. That is true. These things will haunt him until his death, but he is not now who he was then, and it is only right that he remain haunted. If his conscious were clear, then he would be like the Dandy.

At last he pulls the barrel away. A bit of darkened flesh hangs off the end. He flings it into Dandy's lap.

Dandy leaps up and swats at himself like he's on fire.

"You're on your own," Jack says. He slides the handgun into its holster and returns to the plastic sheeting. There are no more strips to cut, so he wraps them around his arms, legs, and torso. He uses the tie-down straps to cover the remaining gaps. It's no spacesuit, but to slightly diminish the exposure could mean the difference between life and death. In Bel's shadow, with no air to transfer the sun's radiation, the temperature dips near 3 or 4 Kelvin, very close to absolute zero. Outside of that shadow, forget it.

Dandy, sniffing back blood, steps forward and into Jack's face. Still pretending he has the upper hand. "What does that mean, exactly, I'm on my own?"

"Let's hear your interpretation."

"I don't know how to operate these!" He kicks at the shovers.

"Then I guess you're in trouble, Jim."

"That's very fucking clever. You look like an idiot in that getup."

"And you look like a dead man."

"We're both dead men."

"That's probably true." But he hopes not.

CHAPTER 49

The Homunculus's airlock is at the very tip of her bow, sandwiched between the plasma cannon and the viewing window of the bridge. Lana floats inside. Like being swallowed by a metal giant. She releases Dino and slips out of her EM-pack. Air rushes through the ceiling and gravity tugs at her legs. She ends up on her knees. A light flashes and a pair of boots step into view. She cannot lift her head. She is not quite sure where she is anymore, or what happened to Dino, but she knows she has to help him. They have to get to the Homunculus. Where is Hunter?

Something knocks against her helmet. She turns away.

Her helmet twists up and off.

The air tastes like burnt metal.

Something warm touches her face.

"It's okay," a voice says.

She looks up. The hydra is there, dressed in a space suit. It forces tentacles into her eyes.

She gasps awake.

Hunter leans over her, face full of concern. "It's okay," she repeats.

Something heavy holds Lana's back to the floor, keeps her paralyzed.

Still inside the airlock. Pinned by the weight of her spacesuit.

"You blacked out," Hunter says.

Gregorian lifts Dino by the legs and starts to drag him into the ship.

"His leg!" Lana shouts. "It's broken!"

Gregorian makes a face and tenderly lowers Dino's feet.

"Stetson's dead," she says.

"I saw," Hunter says.

"Jack?"

"Let's get you inside and out of this suit, okay?"

"Hunter, where's Jack?"

"He's still on Belinda. We'll get him, but first I need you up."

Lana wants to scream, to punch something, but it's like someone has turned her upside down, shaken her empty, and she is so cold. She just wants to go to sleep. It will all be over soon, one way or another.

"Lana. I don't know what to do. If Dino's hurt, you have to help him."

Dino. It's possible he's already dead.

Hunter helps her out of the suit and fetches a bottle of water, which she sucks down immediately. Gregorian rolls Dino onto a gurney and pulls him into the main chamber beside a red medic's bag already open on the floor. The suit is too thick to cut, so they pull it off piece by piece. She diagnoses the femoral shaft fracture right away. The bone has torn through the coolant undersuit at the thigh. It stabs outward pinkish yellow. Blood loss appears negligible. His arm is in slightly better condition in that it is not an open fracture. She injects him with tranqs to keep him sleeping, then feels along the arm to judge the break. Gregorian produces a small ultrasound machine with a holoscreen on the back. She's surprised by this before remembering that they are on a combat ship. They expect grievous injuries here.

It's a two-part fracture along the shaft of the humerus. Fairly clean. Gregorian helps her set it, holding Dino's shoulder while she pushes the bone into place. She looks it over with the ultrasound, satisfied with the result.

The leg will require surgery. And even with the right tools, she's not a surgeon and they don't have time to deal with it. The best she can do for now is clean the wound, apply a splint, and get him into a grav tank where there will be no risk of infection or further tissue damage. It'll heal in the fluid, so if they ever make it out of here, their first stop had better be to a medical center.

Gregorian leads her to the tanks. There are no stalls like on Belinda, just six tanks arranged like a star, the heads touching in the center. At least they're low to the deck. She measures Dino as fast as she can and programs the tank without checking the hardware. Gregorian helps her lift. Together they slide Dino from the gurney into the liquid, nearly spilling him onto the floor once or twice. When it's all said and done, she finds herself drenched with sweat, even with her coolant undersuit on. They've lost another hour.

She calls Hunter. "Dino's in the tank. We did everything we could."

"Copy that. Get to the bridge. We're in position."

"In position for what?"

"To catch your boyfriend."

CHAPTER 50

"Hey Jack? It's Lana. Are you okay?"

He has strapped himself into the shover's seat, hands on the controls, imagining what it will feel like to have the air involuntarily expelled from his body. When exposed to the vacuum, any open orifice is subject to that squeeze. He'll be sure to clench.

"Yeah," he says. "Doing fine. A bit warm, but I bet I'll cool down in a minute here." There's a 20 second delay between messages sent and received through his portable. Bel relays everything through her comms, and there's a lot of interference to wash out. He just wishes he had something better to say, something more worthwhile. But then there are so many things. Too much. Things that can't really be formed into words.

For now, the sound of Lana's voice will have to do.

From what he understands, the crew made it safely aboard the Homunculus. Now they await his return, after which point they'll slip into their grav tanks and head for the nearest known system, which is a few million miles inside Mercury's orbit. More likely, he'll pass out as soon as the airlock opens, lose control of the shover, and smash his skull against the side of the cargo ramp. The average person can remain conscious for 90 seconds in the vacuum, depending on the conditions. Then there's the enormous dose of radiation he's about to receive. With any luck, he'll be inside the airlock within fifteen seconds. They've aligned the ships just so. When he blasts out, he'll reverse the shover at full speed. The concept is a bit like paddling backward in shitty canoe while bobbing down a very fast river.

"We're all set," Lana says. "Pulling away from Bel in five seconds. Four. Three…"

If the Homunculus were to remain still while Jack and his shover entered the airlock, he would smash inside so hard they'd never find his teeth. So the Homunculus will pull away—with the airlock still aligned—and slowly accelerate close to his speed. By the time he reaches the airlock he should drift inside at a nice walking pace. As if that very fast river ends in a very fast waterfall with a net at the bottom. The net needs to move with the falls so he doesn't get diced up when he hits it, like a gravball player swinging his glove down to lessen the impact of a falling ball. It's a maneuver that would not be possible without Homunculus's onboard computer.

"...one," Lana says. "You can do this, Jack."

"Thanks. I'll be there soon."

"Fuck this!" Dandy has tied himself in tangles with the remaining straps. They hang loosely off, barely covering the joints of his arms and legs. "I need more!"

Jack does his best to ignore him. There is a much more pressing issue he has been thinking about. The airlock itself is pretty small. The volume of air would likely fail to fill the entire cargo camp, which allows for the possibility that the air will simply rush past him, leaving him and Dandy sitting here in their shovers, suffocating. The only way to guarantee enough air and enough force to eject them is to access the rest of Bel's air. And that means opening the interior airlock.

"Hey Bel."

"Yes, Jack."

"You have to open the inner door."

"I know, Jack. I will."

"Thanks."

"No problem. You and your crew are my top priority. I'm sorry to see you go like this."

"Me too, Bel." Of course, it's just a thing she says. She is not conscious. At least no one has proven it. Then again, you can't even prove another human is conscious, so who knows? He'll just have to take her word. And with that in mind, he says, "I'll miss you, Bel."

"I appreciate that, Jack."

"You both make me puke," Dandy growls.

"Hey Bel."

"Yes."

"When I deactivated you before. Did you leave phantom programs behind? To mess with me?"

A few seconds pass. How long is that for a super computer? Several hours? Days?

"Of course not," she says. "What do you take me for, Jack?"

He smiles.

A loud bang startles him. Dandy kicking the storage lockers. "There's nothing here!"

"Ten seconds," Bel says.

He turns the ignition. The shover hums, the dashboard lights up. Plenty of thrust left in her. "Jim, you might want to get in your seat."

"Nine."

"Fuck you, you motherfucker!"

"Eight."

Jack shuts his eyes. Feels his breath. He may not have many left.

"Seven."

"You're not leaving me!" Dandy screams.

"Six."

An arm lashes out, smacks Jack in the mouth.

"Five."

The hydra rattles against the door.

Dandy pulls at Jack's neck. "Give me those straps! I need them!"

"Four."

Jack's wrappings are too stiff for him to fight back. He's like a mummy.

Dandy tugs, brandishes the screwdriver.

"Three."

"Let me in!" Dandy rams the pointed metal between the straps, stabbing Jack in the ribs. Hot pain shoots through his body. He howls. Dandy throws his body into the shover, over the controls. Jack grips him by the lapels and pushes him onto the hood, between the forks.

"Two."

Dandy stabs at Jack's arms, but the blows can't pierce the reinforced straps. Jack holds him at a distance.

Dandy's free hand flexes, searching for a handhold, anything.
Jack blows all the breath out of his lungs.

"One."

The airlock flashes open. Air slams them from behind. They rocket forward. Dandy blows off the hood and twists up and away, pinballs against the ceiling. The force folds him in half. Jack and the shover spin past him, out of control, whipping down the cargo tunnel. His body tingles. Too much movement. Rows of ceiling lights flick past his head. A dark shape behind, long tails waving, a wall of snakes. He spins, vapor spirals, vibrations in his back, a tornado's mouth, everything dark, white all around, and silence, silence that hurts, silence that burns. Tumbling blackness and dark, dark everything, everything silent and dark.

CHAPTER 51

He lies in a hospital bed in an unfamiliar room. The walls flex and bulge, but it's just in his head.

"Keep still," Lana says. "You've had a hell of a trip." She stands at the end of a dim corridor with a forced smile, holding a plastic drinking bulb. "This will help." She comes to his side, presses him back into the foam headrest, tips the straw to his lips.

He gulps cold water down a raw and swollen throat. "Thank you."

"How ya feeling?"

"Like a horse that should be put down. Are we on the other side?"

She rolls the empty bulb between her hands. "Other side of what?"

"Of the jump. What system are we at?"

She looks down. "We're still here. We haven't jumped. We can't."

"Why? What do you mean?"

She inhales long and deep. "Jack, Dandy is dead."

He almost laughs. He tells her about the bluff. "Ani and Kip are safe."

She wipes a swollen tear from one eye.

"Why haven't we jumped, Lana?" His palms feel hot and swollen.

Another tear runs to the corner of her mouth.

"Hey." He reaches for her.

She takes his hand.

"What happened?"

"It's Stetson. Jack, he's dead. The hydra…"

Suddenly Jack feels very heavy. Swollen. His ribs ache, a throbbing in rhythm with his pulse. "Dino?"

"Asleep. He's in bad shape. But he'll make it."

More senseless tragedies. He can't dwell on it. Not now. "Why haven't we jumped?"

Her breath rattles. She doesn't want to put it into words. It can only be one thing.

He says, "The hydra."

"It followed you. It almost got into our airlock. If Hunter didn't close the door when she did—" She swallows, looks down and then back up, her complexion turned steely. Playing strong. They're all at their wits' end. This fucking thing has killed two of their crew, almost all of Dandy's. And it won't let up. It never will. "It's on the hull, Jack."

"How long?"

"What?"

"Before Bel dives. How long do we have?"

"A little over three hours."

"Damn it." He sits up. Pain shoots through his side. "*Damn it.*"

"You're in no condition."

"Help me. Please."

Despite herself, she lends a pair of steadying hands. His feet are bare. They swing out from under a blanket and over the end of the bed. Both sets of toes are black except for the big ones. He grits his teeth to fight the building scream. It's like standing on daggers.

"You weren't wearing boots," Lana says. What she doesn't say is if they don't get him into a grav tank before long, he might lose them.

"Help me to the bridge. I need to talk to Hunter."

CHAPTER 52

"The bad news is our sensors are shot. The really bad news is that without the sensors, we can't aim, so the plasma cannon's useless." Hunter sits in the pilot's chair, straddling the back, chin resting on her arms.

The bridge is smaller than Bel's. Military grade. Jack takes up the gunner's seat. He wouldn't know where to begin with the controls. "We've got to have options," he says. "Think."

Hunter says, "I'm sorry, Jack, but it would take at least six hours to replace and calibrate the necessary parts. We just don't have the time. And this close to the sun, even in Bel's shadow, the hardware can't handle the exposure. The software either. It's not happening."

"I'm not talking about hardware and software and timelines. Could we shake it off? Roll so hard we dislodge it?" He winces nearly every other word, ribs throbbing with pain, jolting his lungs. Lana said nothing is broken, but his muscles and tendons took a beating, and the vacuum sucked out an uncertain amount of blood through the hole Dandy put in his side. It's nothing a few days in a grav tank couldn't heal, but in the meantime he'll have to deal with the shooting pains and the liquid stitches tearing every time he moves.

Lana lingers by the door, arms crossed. "It held to the pod when we ejected. I don't think we can shake it off."

Hunter adds, "And we'd have no way to tell if it worked unless someone goes out there."

Gregorian looks up. He hasn't said much. Probably just trying to keep up with the language. He locks eyes with Jack. "Hunter idea is best. Someones go out there."

Hunter balks. "That's not what I said."

"It is only option. Someone give lines of sight. Manually."

"How?"

"Comms. Outside persons call out trajectory. Like, uh, ancient artery."

"Artillery."

"Yes."

"Will comms be functional?"

"Almost definitely."

"Hunter? You know the technology. Does this sound doable?"

She rubs the back of her neck. "It'll be dicey. Worst case scenario, we only get a few minutes of functional comms."

"Okay, then. Unless there's a better approach."

"I will do this," Gregorian says. "It is my ships."

Jack says, "You're the only one who's ever worked a plasma cannon. You stay here. And before anyone else says a word, I'm still captain of my crew, and I am going out there. That's final. Hunter, Lana, is that understood?"

Lana throws her head back and stares at the ceiling.

Hunter makes a face.

"Well?"

Lana says, "Jack, you can barely stand."

"Exactly. I'm better off in zero G." It's meant to be a joke, but no one laughs.

"You've lost a lot of blood."

"We're not safe. If we do nothing—"

"I should go," Lana says.

"You're not practiced out there."

"I saved Dino, didn't I?"

"You did. But I'm the one who got us into this. Dandy chose me. Not you, not Hunter. If it weren't for me, none of you would be here."

She glares, then storms into the next room where she slides down the ladder into the main chamber.

Jack sighs. He knows how she feels, but she doesn't understand. "Gregorian."

"Yes."

"Tell me everything there is to know about the plasma cannon."

CHAPTER 53

Encased in clear gel, Dino's leg looks unreal. Rubbery, almost. The bone protrudes through a flap of flesh that could be pale lips. It will heal that way, and whenever they arrive at the nearest medical center, the flesh will have to be cut again, the bones rebroken and properly set.

But that is assuming they make it out of this. And it seems with each assumption like that, something goes terribly wrong. What's that old saying? Expect the best, but prepare for the worst. Maybe it's best not to prepare at all. To just sit and wait to be acted upon.

Killing time, she checks the grav tanks. They're newer than Bel's, the hardware sleeker, polished, all smooth edges. She can't find the slightest indication of neglect. No corrosion. No useless wires hanging from disabled ports. One of Gregorian's guys must have spent a lot of time down here, caring for these. The way Stetson used to care for his electronics. She keeps seeing his helmet popping off. First, a slithering wetness over the headset. Then silence.

And that thing wagging at her, reaching for her.

She leaves the room.

The ship is small, a conservative setup. Cubbies cover every free surface, filled with who-knows-what. She cannot find a kitchen. Just a single storage unit brimming with dehydrated food. The cramped corridors feel more like the passages on a submarine than an aircraft. Most of the ship consists of a single corridor, the bridge positioned above it. The setup reminds her of early spacecraft designs. Those antiques she's only read about. Like the ISS before they let it burn up. So delicate and piecemeal, a series of crates wired together. The first generation of ships was like that, for the same reasons the first sailboats wouldn't have had reinforced hulls or torpedoes ready to launch. There was nothing to fight at first but the elements.

She could blame humankind for this predicament. The whole race clamoring over itself for the best place among the stars. All that early passion for exploration steadily polluted with greed until finally the powers-that-be or had-been forced a new conflict. One much worse than any before. She could entertain the idea that those early explorers—the idealists, the scientists, the astronauts, the ones who were not searching for power or wealth, but for knowledge—would have thought twice about their efforts if they saw what lay ahead. If they could have read the fate lines on mankind's bloody hands. But she knows better. Because those people, the righteous ones, they know that if you are trapped in a cave, sometimes you have to go deeper into the darkness to find the true source of light.

The suits on the Homunculus are a formfitting mesh far more resilient than the bulky elephant suits on Bel. She finds them in a drawer just next to the airlock, folded up like any other piece of wardrobe. Even the helmets are small and aerodynamic, transparent all around and auto-tinting in UV. She struggles with the breathing pack, nearly suffocates herself putting the helmet on first. She hooks up the hoses and tries again. It must weight 60 pounds. The EM-pack she finds weighs about the same as the other, but there are no control arms, just a wire that adheres to her suit, running from her back to her wrists, ending in controllers that dangle there for ease of access.

Top-heavy, she wobbles to the airlock door.

CHAPTER 54

An alarm shrieks and a red light bathes the bridge.

What now? Jack wonders.

A smooth male voice declares something in Venusian. It sounds serious.

Gregorian says something back and the alarm cuts out.

Jack says, "What the hell's going on?"

Gregorian types at his monitor. "Lana," he says. He pulls up an angled view from above. She faces the wall, jabbing at a control panel. Beside her rests an assortment of twisted metal, specks of debris that could be ice particles. It dawns on Jack that he is looking at the inside of the airlock. The wreckage must be the shover he rode in on. Lana wasn't kidding about how lucky he was. But now is not the time to reflect on it. Lana means to get out.

He lunges to his feet. Pain sends him sprawling onto the floor.

Hunter helps him back. "I don't think you're going anywhere, bud," she says.

When he catches his breath, he tells Gregorian to open the inner airlock.

Gregorian's hands hover over the controls. "Negative. Lana have activate outer door. It cannot override."

"What are you talking about? I said open it."

"You are not understand. If outer door is being tamper with, inner door lock. Security protocol. Lana must disengage outer door first."

Onscreen, Lana continues to type at the panel.

"Can she get out?" Jack says.

"Not without passcode. No."

Hunter whistles. "So we can't open the inner door, and she can't open the outer."

"Okay. But I still need to go out there."

"I don't see her letting that happen, hoss."

Lana turns to face the camera. Her voice buzzes through the onboard comms. "Are you watching, Jack?"

"Yes. I'm watching."

"Open the door." Her expression is grim, distorted by the curved glass of her faceplate. "It's the only way."

"That's not going to happen. Come on back inside."

She shakes her head and points at the outer door.

"Lana, I'm still in charge here."

"Listen to me. You're seriously hurt. You've lost a lot of blood. You could pass out the second you hit Zero-G. It's not safe for you."

"It's not safe for anyone. You know that."

"You're being reckless."

"Am I the one in the airlock trying to get myself killed?"

"It's where you want to be, isn't it?"

"Come back inside."

She prods at the control panel, which sets off the alarm again. Gregorian shuts it down.

"Lana, please. We're wasting time."

The comms click, but all that comes through is a crackle of static. Like ocean surf. Her breath. She says, "You're not the one making this call, alright? Whatever happens to me, I chose it. That's how this is going to work."

"I give the orders and you obey them. That's how it is."

"This isn't your burden, okay? It's mine."

"That's bullshit."

"I know what you're afraid of. I'm afraid too."

"Just come back inside. We'll talk about it."

"Gregorian, Hunter, are you listening? You know I'm right. It can't be Jack on this. You'll walk me through what I have to do. I've already programmed the grav tanks. If I don't make it, you just get in and close the lid."

Jack punches his thighs. "Damn it, Lana. You're not doing this."

"It's alright."

"No it's *not!*" His voice strains. "I won't have you getting killed. I won't have it!"

"Listen to yourself. It's not your decision anymore, Jack."

"No one else is dying on my watch!"

"Gregorian, open the door."

Jack snaps, "Gregorian, don't you fucking move."

Hunter touches Jack's shoulder, gently. "She's got a point."

"Fuck you!" He throws her hand off.

Gregorian leans over the controls, thinking.

Lana says, "Like you said, we're wasting time. Gregorian. It's your ship."

Gregorian turns to Jack, and Jack knows he has made his choice. "I am sorry."

"Just wait," Jack begs. "Lana, you made me promise that I wasn't trying to get myself killed. Can you make that same promise now?"

She laughs. "Sometimes you are so stupid."

"Don't evade the question."

"You're not dead, are you?"

"What does that mean?"

"Gregorian. The door."

Gregorian types.

Condensation brushes across the airlock floor. Debris stirs. As the gravity lifts, the metal shards hover like snowflakes.

Jack mutters, "She didn't promise."

Hunter rolls her eyes. "She said you're not dead."

"I don't understand."

"It means she doesn't want to die. It means she wants to be where you are."

CHAPTER 55

Her first time on a rollercoaster, she cried the whole way up the first hill. She gripped her mother's hand and begged for them to stop, but her mother assured her she would enjoy it once it got going. It was one of the smaller coasters on Mars, at Olympus Thrills, and this particular coaster was built on the edge of Olympus Mons where a vertical drop had been cut through the escarpment. Miles of sheer rock face, perpetually shadowed. An abyss. When the ride got going, and her stomach lifted into her throat, air whipping so fast she couldn't catch her breath to scream, she knew she could never trust her mother again. She spent the rest of the day in a hotel room, watching holo shows below the air conditioner while her parents sulked. When she was a teenager, she had the opportunity to go back there and conquer her fear. A couple lousy friends goaded her into it, but when she strapped in and the car started forward, her screams and cries were so severe the operator stopped the ride to let her off.

"You still read me?" she says

"Clear as crystal."

They have pulled close to Belinda, with a clear view of her dark underbelly, the cargo ramp still extended, looking like some kind of drill. The directional part of her mind that evolved over millennia on a planet where up and down were certainties interprets the view as dangerous. She feels she is floating above that darkened vessel, and the moment she steps out of the airlock, she will fall toward it. In a way, it's true, except that everything around them is falling in synchrony toward the sun, including the planets, falling sideways so fast they constantly miss. This knowledge does little to move her out of the doorway, but she is not going anywhere otherwise. She tries to take a step and is surprised to find that her feet will not lift. Somehow, they have fused to the floor.

"I'm stuck," she says.

Slight undulations in the Homunculus's position have caused bits of the shattered shover to float around her. They find their way out of the chamber and shimmer in the external lights.

"Your boots are magnetic," Jack says. "Lift harder."

She tries again. It feels as though she is pulling herself from quicksand, but with some effort, one sole at a time, disconnects from the floor. "This won't work. I'm too slow."

"There's a panel on your left wrist. Like a plastic bracelet. Open it. You'll see the controls."

When she flips the device, a red message flashes warning that she is being poisoned with radiation. She relays this to Jack, who says there is nothing they can do. Solar wind. This far into the corona, they've been bombarded with charged particles since they arrived. The ships' magnetic fields have shielded them for the most part, but a lot of energy sneaks through. It's nothing a few days in a geno-module couldn't reverse. Still, best not to be out there too long.

She swipes away the message and finds the boot controls, turns them off. With a tap of her toes, she drifts outside. She tests the EM-pack with a tentative spurt and finds the controls significantly less responsive than before. This is a plus. It means she won't go spiraling with a simple tap.

Clear of the airlock, she moves out farther from the bow and spins to face the ship. The airlock has sealed. It has gone from a door to a wall. A sense of despair, desperation. Her heart races. She wonders if she will ever share the company of another human being again. It doesn't matter now. There's no screaming her way off of this ride.

"You still hear me?"

It's Hunter who responds. "Copy. We're all ears. Tell us what you see."

"Nothing yet. I'm heading to the gun emplacement."

The ship is just like a giant V, with the bow at the point, and the plasma cannon on the bow's underside. She dips toward it. Black metal rushes up. The cannon's singular barrel measures twenty feet long and half that in diameter. A long black tube with a round ball joint at its base. She gets out in front of it. Even while it points down and away, the sight gives her chills. She doesn't know much about the make and model of this ship, but she knows that vessels with full swivel plasma guns on their bottoms were designed specifically for bombing terrestrial targets. And this machine is certainly old enough to have been in use during the heaviest fighting. How many outposts did it destroy? How many civilians ran from its shadow, vaporized before they found shelter? She can practically hear the ghosts crying out.

"I'm here," she says.

"Copy."

"Do me a favor and turn the cannon 180 degrees."

"Copy."

The ball joint spins and the cannon faces the ship's belly.

"Hunter, is it possible that we can hit our own hull?"

"It's entirely possible. That's why it's so import— keep — tact."

"Say again, Hunter. You broke up."

"I said, it's why we need to keep in contact."

"Right. No pressure."

"None whatsoever."

"Alright. I've got no vantage here. I'm going underneath."

"Be careful." Jack's voice.

She keeps a healthy distance, flips so her feet point to the hull. Simpler to keep her bearings that way. Far above—or below—she spots what appears to be a distant satellite blinking through the darkness. Hope of rescue rises within her, but sinks just as abruptly. That series of lights is just the panic pod, still drifting nearby like a monument to their failures.

She thrusts onward, scanning the hull for movement. She could be flying over farmland at night, the landscape just one big shadow. Two black dunes distinguishable only by the blinking lights at their bases mark the ship's landing gear. Worst case scenario, the hydra is up on the ship's back where there's no way to hit it with the cannon.

It is nearby. She feels it.

The ship's sole gravity drive rests between the twin ends of the V. Three stories tall, its outward design is deceptively simple, a piece of conical silver that in another time could have been mistaken for an enormous warhead. There are no markings at all. And on either side of this seamless fixture, dotted along the back of the ship's wings, is a series of powerful thrusters lined up in sequence. The farther from the grav drive, the smaller they are. These are the reason Bel could not outmaneuver the Homunculus. Tapered cylinders with holes pocked all around their surfaces, they resemble carefully carved pumice stone. Each of those holes is a secondary port that helps the ship steer.

And maybe it is just her imagination, but squinting at that polka-dot pattern of metal and shadow, she could swear she sees something in there, something long and thin, winding through the hollows like a worm through the flesh of an apple.

"I think I found it," she says.

CHAPTER 56

To calibrate the cannon, they fire into the void. Enormous orbs of supercharged gas, bright as the sun itself. Lana calls out degrees, hanging back to check line of sight. The projectiles move slightly faster than the speed of sound and would blind her without her visor, so she focuses on their reflections in the hull to save her eyesight. By increments, they lower the barrel until the shots skim less than ten feet above the ship's surface, low enough to hit the hydra if it's as big as Jack says it is. The tricky part will be getting it into the open.

To protect against heat and radiation, modern spaceships generate powerful magnetic fields (magshields) which deflect most of the cosmic energy that can damage onboard equipment or irradiate the crew. They'd have died much farther out if it weren't for this technology. In their current position, they are protected by the combined strength of their own shield and Belinda's. The safest way to draw the hydra out of the propulsion jets, Lana theorizes, is to bombard it with radiation. If it is as sensitive to electrical impulses as it seems, then the sun's energy should overwhelm it, possibly even render it blind. To accomplish this, they'll deactivate their own magnetic shielding and drift to the edge of Belinda's, just far enough out for sunlight to hit their stern. When the creature comes out, they'll hit it with the cannon, and that should dislodge it from the hull, permanently.

*

On the bridge, Jack bites his cheek and watches Hunter at the controls. They've already lost 45 minutes since Lana left the airlock. That leaves about an hour and a half before Bel's grav drive kicks on and sends her and anything in the area straight into the sun. And there's a good chance reaching the edge of Bel's magshield will cause serious damage to their propulsion systems. This pressure has no visible effect on Hunter. She backs them steadily into danger.

Through the observation window above them, Belinda floats, adrift beneath a white halo, still protecting them from a distance.

*

Lana plants herself beside the cannon. The ship thrums through her boots. There is no telling where the end of the magshield lies. All she sees is the ship releasing pressurized gas from the same ports where the hydra hides. Most of the vapor is invisible, but she startles when sudden green flares ignite around her. She suspects an explosion or hull breach, but no. The green phosphorescence swirls in arching patterns, blinking in and out, shimmering electric dust. She feels silly when she realizes what it is. The ships have created their own cloud of debris, including oxygen and nitrogen and water vapor, some from the vents and some from when Jack left Belinda. As their magnetic fields fight against the sun's, this cloud of gas and ice interacts with the solar wind exactly like it does in the atmospheres of planets. Lana is inside an aurora. It's stunning, and she could almost forget the danger she is in. She reaches out to swipe at the sparks, but they vanish as they appear. A photon here, a photon there. Twinkling.

A broken voice crackles in her headset. "Crossing mer— ... — erily."

"Say again, Homunculus."

"—ossing meridian momen—y."

"Copy. Hunter, there's a lot of static."

"We're —ing interference, too."

"Keep in contact."

"Roger th—."

Their passage through the horizon is obvious when it happens. And it nearly kills her.

The Homunculus takes a hit of intense sunlight. The propulsion jets burn white hot. Though black, the surface is mildly reflective. It scatters the energy that lands upon it. Lana sees a white flash in her left eye, then nothing. An alarm bleats inside her suit. On reflex, she jets backwards. Her boots come free of the hull and she drifts back by the ship's bow.

She's been hit, she realizes.

Hit by what?

The left side of her faceplate has been blacked out. Maybe burned. She reaches up to touch it, can't feel anything through her gloves. Her face feels hot and stiff from her forehead to her left nostril. She blinks, waves her hands in front of herself, turns her head frantically side to side, but the blackness remains to her left.

Oh no.

It's not the faceplate. A sunbeam has ruined her left eye.

This must be how all those wounded soldiers felt during battle, before they were carried out and brought to her crying. When something hit them and they tried to stand but found their legs useless or their guts hanging out or their lower jaws missing. It must have dawned on them slowly, just like this. The battle would go on, not pausing to regard their injuries. How hard must they have fought not to panic, like she fights now, wondering why Jack and the others are not responding to her calls.

*

Alarms blare and warning lights pulse. The calm male voice Jack now recognizes as the Homunculus's AI unleashes a string of syllables he cannot make sense of. Gregorian attempts to translate, fumbles for the words.

Jack barks: "Make this thing speak English!"

Gregorian changes the babble to Jack's native tongue. The list of damages just keeps on growing: "Rupture in exhaust ports 11, 18, 22, 29, 30, thrusters unresponsive, grav drive offline, coolant leak in main thruster 2, atmosphere regulators offline, magshield controls offline…"

"Turn that shit off!"

The AI goes silent.

"Get us into shade. Now."

"I'm trying!" Hunter says. "She's not responding!"

"Run diagnostics. Reboot if we have to."

"Rebooting now."

The lights go dim and red. With the gravity offline, Jack floats up from his chair. The ship jolts forward and his seatback hits him from behind, sending him spinning toward the ceiling. "Christ!" He clamors back into place. A moment later the lights and gravity come back on. He settles into his seat. "Report."

She reads from her screen. "Minor damage. Systems functional. She's putting out some fires, but we're alright. Jesus fuck, that was not okay."

"Call Lana."

Hunter tries. There's no response.

CHAPTER 57

When she's certain their shielding is back up and they are safe from the light, she lands on the hull and walks carefully back to the cannon. She is so lost in anxiety, half-blind, worrying why the others haven't responded, that the sight of the hydra running toward her hardly registers. It tumbles like a ball of yarn, tall and wide as a house.

She leaps, blasting her thrusters. She falls through blackness, away from the ship. Fifty feet. A hundred. One-fifty. With her back turned, there's no way to tell if it has leapt after her. No way to hear it coming. Just that tingle on her scalp that lets her know it is inches behind, reaching. When that sensation fades, she brakes and turns.

Before her in the emptiness of space, the hydra sways, a long strand of seaweed. It snaps at her like a snake with its tail nailed down.

"—ou read?" Hunter's voice.

"Hunter, are you there?"

"Thank the fucking stars. Comms are back up."

"I've got the hydra. Fire. Fire now."

A blue ball flashes too far to port, a miss she anticipated.

She calls out the adjustment.

The second shot is a miss, too, but not as wide.

She adjusts by two degrees.

All the while, the hydra waggles and snaps.

The third shot splashes a white flare at the base of the hydra's trunk.

The stalk rotates away from her, the snake's tail tugged sideways. Free from the hull, both ends travel toward their center. It bulges into an oval like a water droplet in Zero-G, ridges rippling along its surface, so many tongues flicking at nothing.

"Direct hit!"

Their celebration on the bridge hisses through as static.

One good blast from the cannon should send the hydra soaring off. Yet something is wrong. The hairs on her neck stand at attention. She feels watched. Targeted. From behind.

With a twist of her controls, she turns in time to see an enormous pale insect falling out of the darkness, crooked limbs reaching to embrace her.

The hydra from the panic pod.

She spins, shuttles out of its path.

Too slow.

An appendage hits her from the side but can't get a grip. It's a glancing blow that throws her into a violent spiral. Vapor whirls and the alarm in her helmet returns. The EM-pack won't respond. She spins right to left, the Homunculus flashing past again and again and again, smaller now, farther. Either her thrusters or her air tank has ruptured.

Corner of her eye: the pod hydra splashes into the first. Its momentum sends both creatures rolling back to the Homunculus.

Lana tumbles, fighting her controls, nearing the edge of the magshield and oblivion.

CHAPTER 58

"What the hell was that?"

They all felt it. A sudden vibration in the hull, a collision.

"Lana?" Jack tries her on comms.

A wash of static in response.

Hunter pulls her hands from her screen as if burned. "We lost her."

"What do you mean *lost her*? Where'd she go?"

Hear now the *ratta-tat-tat* of the hydra scrambling over the hull.

"I don't know. The signal's gone."

This cannot be happening.

"Find it!"

"Too much interference. It's like she vanished."

"She didn't vanish!" He limps out of his chair. Every muscle protesting. He never should have let her leave.

"Jack!" Hunter calls.

"I'm going out there!"

*

The spinning does not stop. If it were her air tank, she'd have suffocated by now. The rupture punched through the left side of her EM-pack at a forward angle, very near her torso. No air comes out. The pack is empty. The controls dead. She feels nauseous. Going to pass out. Everything turning turning turning.

Get a grip.

Dancers slow their spins by holding out their arms. She tries it.

It slows her enough to get her bearings. The Homunculus shrinks away from her, a black triangle with a few flashing lights. It's too far to see specific features or movement, like whether or not the hydra has managed to get back onto the hull, or what kind of damage it is trying to do now. She's probably too distant for them to see her. But maybe if they look out the viewing window at the right moment, they will witness her passing into the solar wind. Is there enough oxygen in her suit to light a flame, or will her skin just blacken and dry like charred meat?

She puts these thoughts away, disgusted with her mind. There has to be hope. This suit has a beacon that activates with the alarm. She checks her wrist panel, and the blinking red letters confirm this. They should be able to pinpoint the signal and come get her.

Too close to the sun.

Her comms are too weak to reach them from out here. Why would the beacon be any different?

She wants to scream and never stop.

Concentrate.

Spinning, spinning.

The panic pod. A blinking light. Impossibly, it is almost level with her center of mass, as if they are both on a plane. With each rotation, it looms larger. Her depth perception is pretty much gone, but she's close enough now that she can distinguish the open door and the steady light inside. It must be around 1500 feet away, roughly ten degrees left of her trajectory. If she had any fuel left, it would be so easy. Maybe if she vents her oxygen. The suit comes equipped with an emergency air line that fits over her mouth and nose, a last resort in the case of a breach. She could sever the main line and direct it like a hose.

She reaches for the latches over her neck, finds the release, and starts to tug.

She stops herself.

She's not thinking straight. Pulling her helmet off would be suicide. Nevermind the pod. Even with an oxygen line she'd be unconscious in seconds. Then what, even if she could reach the pod? Pray the controls are intact? And how exactly would she steer with no pilot training?

Although...

The pod has spare EM-packs. And a comms system powerful enough to reach the Homunculus. Those are better odds of surviving than spinning helplessly into the big nothing.

Now, to find a way over there.

She searches her mind. She doesn't know much about physics beyond her school lessons more than ten years ago. Even then, her focus was biology. She dated a theoretical physicist once, briefly. He had long greasy hair and untrimmed fingernails. He'd been pleasant enough, but a bit too ungrounded for her taste. Their first night out together, he kept saying he didn't want to talk about his research, then went on to talk about his research. Something about grav drives and how they alter spacetime. Their lingering trails not strong enough to measure with current technologies, but in a few hundred years the combined forces could alter the orbits of small bodies, with potentially serious consequences.

If these are her final minutes of life, why is she thinking about Dan the theoretical physicist? There's plenty else to reflect upon. But there is something about this memory. Something important. That stinted awkward conversation over wine. She politely nodded, lonely and desperate for human contact, heady and bored and guilty and sad, faking interest in the differences between grav tech and traditional acceleration. How grav drives open a hole in the space around them—like a zipper, Dan had said, oblivious to the sexual connotations—whereas physical acceleration comes from expelling mass at great speeds. Equal and opposite reactions. Good old Newton. You throw out energy in one direction, the energy throws you in the other.

Of course.

There is only one item she can think to use. And its mass is great enough that it might actually work. It just has to be perfect.

*

Gregorian stalks beside him while Hunter hounds him on comms, both stressing all the reasons Jack absolutely cannot go outside. He knows them already, but he also knows that even if Lana is alive, she's no use with her portable down, which means *someone* has to go the hell outside with her, don't they? Neither Gregorian nor Hunter have rebuttals to this.

Gregorian helps him suit up in the main chamber. They're just about to secure his helmet when another shudder racks the ship, accompanied by a drawn-out metallic howl. The lights flicker and the gravity comes and goes in pulses. They hold to the walls.

"Hunter, please tell me that's you."

"Jack. Get back up here."

"I told you I'm going—"

Something gives. The floor falls away and Jack bounces off the ceiling. The ship sways, groans. He collides with the floor, the wall. The gravity throws him down again. The Homunculus's voice booms throughout the ship: "Catastrophic failure in weapons system. Damage to ceramic shielding. Hull integrity questionable. Repeat."

"Holy shit," Hunter announces.

"Talk to me!"

"Jack, we just lost the plasma cannon."

*

Lana misses the immediate flash, but knows something is wrong on her next rotation. The Homunculus now faces her at an angle, and a bright white field of debris expands outward. She can't dwell on what this signifies. The panic pod is coming up fast, and if she doesn't act soon, she'll be too close to change her path.

Sliding out of the pack proves trickier than she anticipated. With the straps unclipped, her angular momentum tugs the EM-pack away, shifting her center of mass and altering their spin. Like when two kids face each other holding hands, whipping around in circles. Not only must she throw the pack off at just the right angle, but must compensate for the spin, timing her separation so she doesn't kick off facing the sun or the nothingness.

She manages to shift her mass. While maintaining a grip on the pack's harness straps, she tucks her feet against its inner side. It is as if one of the the spinning children lifts their feet and presses them to the other child's chest. With every rotation, the pod passes straight overhead.

She watches and waits, tucks into a ball, legs braced, ready to kick off. She tests herself by counting and guessing where the pod will appear, repeating this until she's confident she could make the leap with her eyes closed. Yet with each rotation, how many feet does she travel? And each foot lost widens the angle between herself and the pod, which decreases the chance of this working.

No more delays. *This rotation.*

When the pod nears its zenith, she kicks with all her might, releasing her grip and stretching out straight, arms extended, toes pointed. The EM-pack spins erratically away. She turns about half as fast now, eye on the pod each time it rotates into view, drawing nearer.

*

Thrusters are down, Hunter says. They are paralyzed.

Both airlock doors have a round viewing porthole. Jack peers through, rendered mute by the sight. The hydra must have ripped the cannon from its place. And it exploded, releasing a cloud of plasma, charged particles that could vaporize steel. A glowing murk flashing with lightning strikes that savage the Homunculus. As if flying this close to the sun wasn't bad enough, their own weapon unleashed a radiation storm, the kind designed to destroy ships just like theirs. So far they are holding strong. The initial eruption dispersed most of the plasma's energy away from the hull. But this shit hanging around could still eat through their thrusters, paralyzing them.

He tries not to think of Lana.

He can't go out there now.

Ratta-tatta-tatta goes the hydra, somewhere nearby.

"It is alive," Gregorian says. "How?"

Jack punches the door.

Something flashes by the porthole. A shadowed amalgamation, unspecified shapes.

"I am think I saw something."

Jack raises one hand, indicating silence.

The hydra comes back, slower this time, settles over the airlock, blocking most of the view. It is seriously very fucking large. Bolts of lightning snap across its manifold arches, having no effect at all. It presses against the exterior door, blotting out all light. And then the *ratta-tatta-tatta* starts again, and everything begins to shake.

Jack backs away. "I think we might be in trouble."

Gregorian just nods.

*

Slow motion. Two objects nearing each other. One, a woman in a tight blue suit, turning in circles, reaching out her hands, kicking her legs as if she is underwater. The other object an abandoned escape pod decorated with scratches and dents, surface damage left there by a monster. The hydra must have kept on punishing the pod after Dino and Lana left. Maybe searching for food. Maybe testing the strength of its hull. Maybe just smashing out of anger. A sea of garbage hangs around this useless lifeboat. Scraps of fabric might be bits of Stetson's suit. And tiny red specks of frozen blood. She tries not to notice these things.

Inches. If she misses the pod, it will be by inches.

Fifteen feet and closing. Absurdly, she must have kicked off the EM-pack too hard, overcompensated for the angle. She will overshoot her mark, skim right past the open door and around the curved edge of its stern. Inches.

Still she reaches and kicks at empty space, refusing to believe that she brought her worst fear upon herself. She has a contingency plan. She will find a way to plug the hole that vents her air and she will breathe exhaust until she dies sleepy and warm.

As it all comes true, as she misses the surface by little more than six inches, fingers flexing, every molecule in her body trying and failing to stretch, the pod lights blinking innocently, she comes around the rear of the pod, rotating fully one more time, now facing the rear thruster ports she could not see from her previous angle jutting out of the pod's back by a good eight inches. She stretches one last time. Those beautiful cone thrusters, like bullhorns. Her right hand clamps an inner lip. She hangs on. Even when her body whiplashes. When the muscles, tendons, bones, everything that makes up her right arm screams in protest, she hangs on. Her momentum slams her against the hull, beside yet another thruster port. She wedges a foot against one to keep from bouncing off. She hangs on.

CHAPTER 59

"Here's our culprit," Hunter says, pointing at a string of floating numbers. "Diagnostics found it almost immediately."

Jack does his best to hold it together, but grits his teeth to keep from shouting. Every moment they stand here in front of this abstract display of data, the hydra is that much closer to ripping the airlock door off its hinges. "We don't have time for guessing games. Tell me what and where it is."

"It's a short. Somewhere in the ignition system. Jack, it could take hours to find. Maybe days. I need to go through the schematics one section at a time. There are thousands of them."

Gregorian clears his throat. "Are you forgetting me? I know these error codes."

"Be my guest," Hunter says with a dismissive wave.

He puts his face to the floating screen, eyes practically crossed. "I know where. See these letter, upper case, lower case? This indicate quadrant. This is inside ship. I can fix."

"How long?" Jack says.

He raises his arms uncertainly. "Twenty minutes."

"You've got five."

He raises his eyebrows, then nods and bolts out of the room.

Jack calls: "You need help?"

"You slow me down!" he shouts.

Jack sinks into the copilot's chair, slaps his face with both hands. Until they get out of the plasma field, there is absolutely nothing they can do, and they can't get out of the plasma until the thrusters are back up. Hunter pulls up the view inside the airlock. The porthole is a circle of squirming shapes, as if a pile of intestines has been smashed against it. Even the camera vibrates. Hunter points to a fluctuating number in the top right corner, indicating the pressure. The numbers rise and fall: .998, 1.003, .998, 1.005, .993. The changes are to a few thousandths of an atmosphere, and although there hasn't been a breach, they prove that the hydra is able to flex the material of the door, sucking it out and pushing it in, expanding and contracting the chamber itself.

Jack could use a drink. Something tall and very strong.

"We're not getting out of this, are we?" Hunter says.

What can he say? Justin is dead. Stetson is dead. Lana...

He can't bring himself to think it.

Something *blips* on the holoscreen, and a new window pops up.

Jack ignores it. Probably some new error code. Hunter leans forward. "I don't believe it."

"What now?"

"Look!" She smacks him in the ear, flails her hands at the window.

He hardly believes it himself. But there it is, unmistakable.

Panic: *Lana here. Do y0u Read?*

"How?" Hunter says.

He grins. *Thank the stars.* "Answer her."

Homunculus: *We read you. Assumed the worst.*
Panic: *You don't 10ok so good your$elf.*

Jack wipes his eyes. He knew she was okay. She had to be.

Hunter punches his shoulder. "I knew she had a sense of humor."

"Get her up to speed."

Homunculus: *Homunculus's thrusters are down. Gregorian working on repairs. Will come to you when done.*
Panic: *Field of plAsma? What happened?*
Homunculus: *Hydra.*
Panic: *No+ much time before jump. 45 mins by my count.*
Homunculus: *You count correct. There is another major problem. Hydra has secured itself over airlock. No way in or out.*

This message sits for a long time. Jack imagines her in that derelict pod, alone and anchorless, reeling from this news.

Finally, a reply:

Panic: *Need to get hydra off.*

Hunter clucks her tongue. "No shit."

Homunculus: *Ideas?*
Panic: *Yes. You will need to suit up.*

CHAPTER 60

Lana perches along the pod's exterior. Secured into a freshly charged EM-pack, she holds to the door and watches the Homunculus change course. The thrusters release controlled bursts, and when the bursts hit the glowing plasma, they set it spiraling. Lightning dances, but the ship slides steadily away, turning as they swing into position. It looks effortless, spanning that distance with such precision, and she is struck with awe that they have come this far, not just in spite of the creature, but of space itself.

The Homunculus settles several hundred feet from the panic pod's stern, the bow pointed at Belinda.

Lana tests the comms: "Do you read me?"

A scratchy voice replies, half-broken: "Inter—ence. Re—eat."

"This is Lana to Homunculus. Do you read."

"-ead you. C— ... mission?"

It's no use.

She pulls back into the pod and types at the main console.

Panic: *Still too much interference. Will try again when closer.*
Homunculus: *Agr3ed. Hydra is almost through. Hurry.*

With that, she exits the pod for the final time, through the doors and across the emptiness toward the Homunculus's very tip. The hydra burrows into the airlock, an infected yellow growth. She hangs at a generous distance, too far for her comms to work, apparently. They must have been slightly damaged when the sun hit her facemask. Yet the only way this will work is if she has contact with the others. Cautiously, she glides up and over the top of the ship, hoping the hydra won't spot her. Finally, she gets a response.

"Read you loud and clear," Jack says. "Where are you?"

She never thought she'd be so desperate to hear a human voice. She could cry. "I'm up near your back. Are you prepped?"

"We are. Are you sure this is a good idea?"

"No. You just let me know when that bastard's down the chimney."

"Down the chimney? Not sure I follow."

"Like the Big Bad Wolf. Three Little Pigs?"

"Never read it."

"I don't know about you sometimes, Jack. It ends with a big wolf stew."

"I'll get the water going."

*

The moment comes without warning, as these things tend to do. One second Jack is sitting there jabbering like an idiot, watching the pressure readout fluctuate as before, and the next, something *pops* and the hydra floods the airlock, a rush of tentacles, and the pressure shoots up to ten atmospheres, then twenty and climbing.

"It's in the chimney!" he screams. "Repeat! Lana, go now! Now!"

"Going."

He double checks the connections in his suit. Gloves, boots, torso, neck. He tugs at the belt holding him to his chair. He feels a little silly until he spots Hunter and Gregorian doing the same. "Gregorian, will we be able to get the inner airlock open with the outer door gone?"

"Yes."

"But the security protocol—"

Gregorian shakes his head. "No such thing."

"No such thing? But you said—"

"I lie earlier. Because Lana was right."

Hunter laughs.

"You little shit."

"Sorry, Captain Kind."

"Fuck it. We're still alive. Are we one hundred percent sure these seats are secure?"

Gregorian gives a thumps up.

Hunter points one gloved finger at the holo screen. "Tell your girlfriend she needs to hurry the hell up." The screen has gone black, the hydra pressed against the camera lens. Or maybe the lens has snapped. The only sign that the chamber is still intact is the wildly fluctuating pressure.

"Lana, do you read me?"

"I re—" A flat line of static.

"Lana? Come in."

"Get— ... pos—"

"Goddamn it!" He unclamps his belt.

Hunter screams over comms: "Where are you going! Jack!"

"Airlock!" He skitters out of the room and starts down the ladder to the main chamber.

"Are you crazy! Get back here!"

The ladder vibrates as if a jackhammer rattles its base. "We need eyes on the hydra. If we can't reach Lana, we won't know when to pop the seal!"

Hunter curses, but concedes. "Find something to hang onto."

"I plan on it."

He enters the chamber. An ongoing earthquake, handles of the storage compartments rattling. Inside the airlock, the hydra licks at the porthole. He's still uncertain how he's supposed to know when the time is right. He really did not think this through.

CHAPTER 61

There are less than three minutes before Belinda's jump.

Lana arcs out and away from the Homunculus to keep the hydra from sensing her. She repositions straight out from the airlock, several thousand feet. The hydra is a mess of fibers. Even this far back, she can distinguish the confused nature of its shape, all those limbs like ropey muscle. She throttles forward, very aware that she will need to reverse as soon as it spots her. It'll be a while. But the thing has proven intelligent with the way it leapt from the pod. She half wonders if it doesn't know what they're up to. If this is some incomprehensible ploy to get them right where it wants them. One way or another, they will find out.

She closes the distance foot by foot, hailing Jack every few seconds. At last, she gets a response.

"I thought I lost you! Christ!"

"I had to swing out, but I'm closing in."

She can only guess at her distance. Somewhere around a thousand feet by now, the height of a hundred story tower. Like she is falling down, down, soon to splat along the pavement.

Nine hundred fifty.

The hydra has taken a strange pinkish hue. Like it's excited. Eager for its coming meal. Maybe, for once, it can sense the ticking clock. It roughly resembles a dome now, the outer limbs suctioned to the hull. The center of the dome buried in the airlock.

Six hundred fifty feet and closing.

Any time now.

Five hundred feet.

Four fifty.

It shows no sign.

Three hundred feet.

Time running out, she cranks the throttle.

Two hundred.

One hundred.

The edges of the dome slide toward the center. A suction cup inverting, the edges flaring suddenly up and in.

It launches at her. All at once. A tendril pounces from its center.

It was a trick. It waited for her to be within reach.

She dashes right.

The bulbous end shoots by, missing her by an arm's length. The limb snaps taut and bends toward her. She blasts out of reach and circles up and away, suddenly dizzy again. This time, she's sure to face the hydra while backing up. And just like before, it follows, thinning out, stretching.

"It took the bait! Pop that door in thirty seconds!"

CHAPTER 62

"One minute until the jump!" Hunter calls. "Holy shit. I've got eyes on the hydra!"

Jack lingers helpless in the main chamber. There is nothing but the ladder to hold onto, but he doesn't trust it. Coming down here was foolish. Now it's all about timing.

He starts up the ladder, but he stops, seeing something from the corner of his eye.

A shape inside the airlock.

A figure pushed against the glass.

A form made of that alien tendon material, but not alien in shape.

A human form.

His heart hammers in his chest.

There, on the other side of the circular porthole of the inner airlock door, stands Justin Kind. Jack's nephew. Flayed raw but staring, accusatory. Blaming him. Jack knows that he should climb the ladder back to the bridge. He sees his hands on the rungs, holding tight. He sees the open hatch above. And when he looks back to the door, like figures coalescing out of flame, others have joined his nephew. They crowd behind him, gliding close. He recognizes the young boy who opened the sphere. And Tarziesch. And another of Dandy's men. And coming up through the others, one of his oldest friends. Stetson. Empty eyes blinking in confusion. Jack wants to go to them. To take them out of that airlock and get them to the grav tanks where they can rest until they make it out of this. They pound against the window.

"Jack!" Hunter howls.

He hears her in the distance, tinny, crackling. Not quite real.

They need him to help. He should help them.

"If it breaks through the inner door we cannot repressurize!"

Dead.

They are all dead.

He tears his vision away. They are lies. Imprints. Tricks.

He pulls up the ladder to the second level, feeling the glare of the ghosts.

He rushes to his seat, stunned when he looks up. Beyond the observation window, a great stalk extends from the ship into the darkness, a nightmare umbilicus. He dives into his seat and claps the buckle together, amazed his shaking hands can accomplish such a feat. "Now!"

And with a press of her finger, Hunter blasts the ghosts from the airlock.

The umbilicus shoots away.

CHAPTER 63

It almost happens as she imagined it. The airlock opens and the force thrusts the hydra out and away. It whips toward her, flailing. She pulls out of its way and watches it strike again and again, too far, and its limbs take the unmistakable shape of human hands. The palms must be ten feet wide, fingers as tall as her. They grab at nothing, muscle without flesh. This terrible mass pinwheels up toward Belinda where the sun's rays still splash out behind her like a perpetual sunrise. Seconds left before Belinda's grav jump.

Lana rockets down toward the airlock at full throttle.

She nears the doorway.

"Start thrusters!" she calls.

But time is up.

Behind her, Belinda's drive revs to life. She feels it even this far away. It reels her in like a tractor beam. The Homunculus begins to recede. She falls up with the hydra. Toward Belinda. Toward the sun.

The Homunculus lunges at her. Fast.

The bow rises slightly as it comes. She spots her friends on the bridge, lit up inside the viewing window. Hunter actually takes one hand from the controls to wave.

The ship rams at her. Blackness engulfs her. She falls through the open airlock, into gravity, into light. She slides along the main chamber floor, hits the ladder and holds on.

Impossibly, Hunter scooped her out of space.

CHAPTER 64

"Give her everything!"

"This *is* everything!"

They turn from Belinda, from the hydra, from the sun. Hunter grunts into the controls. Belinda fights them every inch, her grav field closing in. If they don't reach its edge before she jumps, it won't matter how great a pilot Hunter is. Space will warp around them, sucking them through a tunnel into the heart of their nearest star.

"Booster!" Gregorian howls.

Hunter looks at him. "What?"

"Booster!"

Jack groans.

Of course.

It's a military vessel. Capable of more than your average thrust. Hunter shakes her head. "How!"

Gregorian, finally taking his role as copilot, flips a small switch on the main panel.

The stars melt across the observation window. The force pins Jack into his seat. This is the end. He knows it like he has never known anything before. Belinda has jumped, and they are being pulled backward into the sun's hellish interior. His thoughts in this moment are of Lana, who must be getting crushed against the main chamber's wall, and of Kip, who will grow up without his father—not much of a loss for the boy, all things considered—and of his lost friends. Not only the ones he lost to the hydra, but those he lost to the war, to the camp, at their own hands or someone else's. And he thinks of the men he killed. Their sense of calm when all the life leaked out of them. How peaceful they seemed. That is how he feels now, and he knows they are not angry, but glad that he will be among them soon.

CHAPTER 65

Lana hobbles to the crew quarters, following the sound of echoing voices. She wears a brace on her right ankle, but tries not to put too much weight on it. She broke it when Gregorian activated the boost thrusters, throwing her against the wall. It could have been much worse, but she'd been wearing one of the Homunculus's advanced spacesuits. The fabric, when acted upon by sudden force, goes rigid as metal. Suits like that are well worth the price, she keeps reminding Jack. If Dino had been wearing one, he might not have broken so many bones. As she moves toward the voices down the corridor, she slows her pace and tries not to make a sound.

Hunter and Gregorian have been at each other's throats since the close call with Bel's grav jump. It's been two weeks and they're all a bit stir-crazy on this tiny vessel, but there's more to it than that. Though they're all hurting from the loss of their friends, Hunter has taken Stetson's death especially hard. She won't talk about it, but it's there. The other day, Lana overheard her through the lavatory door having a one-sided conversation with no one. "You stupid bastard," she had said. "Caught your sleeve on the damn doorway?" Lana had shared the particulars of Stetson's death with Jack, who must have passed the info to Hunter. She had it wrong—it was Dino's sleeve that caught in the doorway—but this was not the time to correct her.

"Jack might've forgotten who you work for, Greg," Hunter says now, "but I haven't."

"You forget same man responsible for your friend death also get my crew kill. I am no loyalty to Jim Dandy or his peoples."

"Without men like you, there would never have been a Jim Dandy."

"There is no point in this arguing."

"When we get to where we're going, just stay far away from me, alright?"

There's a long pause. Finally, Gregorian says, "I am sorry for your friends. They die noble."

"Don't preach at me, Greg. I know all about noble death."

"Then you are knowing this is more than most peoples can say at the ends of their life."

"Sure. I also know that if you don't stop talking, I'm going to put my foot up your—"

Lana clears his throat and enters the room and immediately wishes she hadn't. The crew quarters are cramped. It's a reduced gravity room with two triple-decker bunk beds. Hunter and Gregorian share one of the bottom bunks, and both are completely naked. Hunter sits at the edge, her elbows on her knees. When Lana comes in, she crosses her arms over her breasts, more a gesture of annoyance than modesty. Gregorian lies in the bunk with his hands under his head. He makes no move to cover himself, just raises onto an elbow and looks at Lana. Most of his torso is covered in burn scars similar to hers. This jars her more than anything. Reminds her of the wet salve on the left side of her face and that until she hires a plastic surgeon, she'll be subject to the stares of strangers. At least Hunter and Gregorian don't look at her funny. Not even now.

"Can we help you?" Hunter says.

"Um." Lana backs out and calls from the hall, "The tanks are ready when you are."

On her way to the grav tanks, she doubles over with laughter.

*

Jack watches on the bridge's monitor as Lana helps Gregorian and Hunter into their tanks. She takes their weight and leads them to their pods and provides steadying hands as they settle into the fluid. Sleep seems like a good idea.

Jack rubs his toes. They've lost some feeling, but managed to stay attached. Gregorian found an ointment designed for severe frostbite in their medical supplies. The stuff burned like hell at first, but did its job. Another week and he'll be able to wear shoes again. He's grateful for this and for other small mercies.

It's in his nature to feel guilty. He knows that now. But he's fighting it like a cold. What happened to Justin and Stetson is not his fault, he tells himself. It is becoming a mantra. Lana says they wouldn't blame him, and that seems important.

He is still processing the fact that they survived. He'd been certain in those final moments before Bel's jump that they had failed. That he had failed them. It is like a deep bruise somewhere on his body, but he can't place it. Sometimes he forgets it's there, but something will remind him and he will feel it pulsing, and he'll shut his eyes and repeat his mantra. He told Lana about this. She says he's learning to let go. He isn't sure of what, but she is probably right.

He meets her down there right after she finishes with Hunter.

She rests on the edge of Hunter's tank. When she hears him coming, she pivots to face him, squinting slightly.

"How's it going?" he says.

"They're all set. Down for a long nap."

"I think they've earned it."

"Me too."

"It's just us now," Jack says.

"Yes."

She has regained partial vision in her left eye. Enough to register light and murky shapes when they're close. When they get to civilization, she'll buy an implant that should bring her sight back to 20/20. The scarring can be dealt with in a number of ways, but there will always be remnants of the damage. The eye itself has gone a cloudy white. The skin from the corner of her lips to her hairline appears smooth as wax. He can tell by the way she holds herself that she thinks she's ugly now, but she's wrong. She is still Lana, and that's all that matters.

"The other tanks?" Jack says.

"They seem fine, but I want to comb through them one more time."

She's been borderline paranoid about the grav tanks, but with good reason. They escaped Bel's jump by the skin of their ass. People have reported odd things occurring in close proximity to grav fields like that. Objects going missing. Screws unwinding themselves. Wires crossing or corroding in no time at all. And the occasional hallucination.

No one else saw the shapes the hydra made, but they were real. Clear as anything. The first night afterward, Lana assured him that it absorbed its victims' physical forms, nothing else. They'd seen it take other odd shapes. The way it chased them down the hall on all fours. Just imitations, she said. She was trying to comfort him, but there's no real proof either way. He isn't sure if he believes in souls, but that doesn't assuage the fear. After what they've been through, anything seems possible.

"Let's wait on the tank inspection," Jack says.

The Homunculus is too damaged to make a grav jump. The hull sustained serious damage from the cannon, and they are one airlock door away from depressurization. The stress from a jump could rip the hull wide open. Grav tanks are versatile, but they won't work at absolute zero. It's not a risk worth taking. At their maximum speed, it will take a little over 14 months to reach the nearest outpost, which means it will be close to 16 months before Jack sees Kip again. Not that it'll matter to the boy. If he's anything like his father, he'll weather whatever this life throws at him. But if Jack can manage it, he'd like to be there to help out when he can. If he can.

So Jack and Lana have two options. They can go down for a year long nap like the others and let the ship wake them when they reach the target outpost, or they can spend those months together, uninterrupted. It would be time enough to catch up on important things. And there's plenty to share. Not to mention all they should prepare for ahead. Technically, they did steal a piece of alien technology, along with the alien inside. Then there's whatever else Dandy framed them for. Any records he forged will be airtight.

Yet as dangerous as these things may be, Jack is not afraid of the future.

"I think we should stay up for a while," Jack says.

"You do?"

"Yeah. I think I'd like that."

Lana stands and cocks one hip. "Gee," she says. "However will we pass the time?"

They go to each other. She wraps her arms around his waist. He holds her to his chest. He missed her terribly. He can admit that now. Funny how we bury so much inside, attempting to spare ourselves pain. It always erupts.

THE END

ACKNOWLEDGEMENTS

Thank you to Severed Press for bringing my debut novel to the world, and for involving me in the cover design and editing process. This is the book I wanted to write and the book I wanted to share.

Many thanks to the array of teachers who have challenged and sculpted my writing over the years. At SUNY Oswego, Leigh Wilson, Brad Korbesmeyer, Donna Steiner, Robert O'Connor, and Chris Motto all offered much needed early guidance. These days, I'm honored to call them colleagues. At MNSU Mankato, the entire Creative Writing Department helped me develop the skills and discipline needed to complete novel-length projects. I'm especially grateful to Diana Joseph, Geoff Herbach, and Roger Sheffer for their tastes and talent.

Much gratitude to my friends who provided feedback on early drafts: Ben Wheeler-Floyd, Ashley McNamara Fritz, and Sam Hastings. You guys rock. I hope you're up for reading many more drafts in the future!

The following people influenced the direction and completion of this project from a distance: Hugh Howey, thank you for your relentlessly sunny disposition, your generous advice to strangers, and your reader-first attitude. I read *Wool* during a creative slump. It knocked something loose and made writing (and reading) fun again. I can't tell you how grateful I am for that. Jeremy Robert Johnson, thank you for your killer prose and your words of encouragement. Michael J. Seidlinger, King of Social Media, I don't know how you do everything you do, but it's inspiring as hell. Joshua Cohen, thanks for your willingness to chat, for offering advice where you could, and just being genuinely brilliant. The members of Rammstein, thank you for providing an unofficial soundtrack to this novel. All those who run, work for, publish with, or buy books from indie presses, thank you for being ravenous. You are the future of publishing.

And finally, endless love and gratitude to the person who keeps me from coming apart at the seams, the only one I can talk to about works-in-progress, my best friend, my hero, my wife, Carey Feagan-Allocco. Thank you, thank you, thank you.

ABOUT THE AUTHOR

Benjamin Allocco lives in Syracuse, New York, where he's writing his second novel. You can keep up with his writing at www.benjaminallocco.com.

SEVEREDPRESS

facebook.com/severedpress

twitter.com/severedpress

CHECK OUT OTHER GREAT SCIENCE FICTION BOOKS

IN PERPETUITY
by Jake Bible

For two thousand years, Earth and her many colonies across the galaxy have fought against the Estelian menace. Having faced overwhelming losses, the CSC has instituted the largest military draft ever, conscripting millions into the battle against the aliens. Major Bartram North has been tasked with the unenviable task of coordinating the military education of hundreds of thousands of recruits and turning them into troops ready to fight and die for the cause.

As Major North struggles to maintain a training pace that the CSC insists upon, he realizes something isn't right on the Perpetuity. But before he can investigate, the station dissolves into madness brought on by the physical booster known as pharma. Unfortunately for Major North, that is not the only nightmare he faces- an armada of Estelian warships is on the edge of the solar system and headed right for Earth!

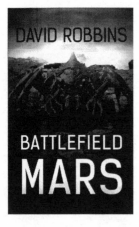

BATTLEFIELD MARS
by David Robbins

Several centuries into the future, Earth has established three colonies on Mars. No indigenous life has been discovered, and humankind looks forward to making the Red Planet their own.

Then 'something' emerges out of a long-extinct volcano and doesn't like what the humans are doing.

Captain Archard Rahn, United Nations Interplanetary Corps, tries to stem the rising tide of slaughter. But the Martians are more than they seem, and it isn't long before Mars erupts in all-out war.

SEVEREDPRESS

 facebook.com/severedpress
 twitter.com/severedpress

CHECK OUT OTHER GREAT
SCIENCE FICTION BOOKS

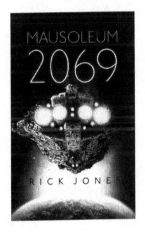

MAUSOLEUM 2069
by Rick Jones

Political dignitaries including the President of the Federation gather for a ceremony onboard Mausoleum 2069. But when a cloud of interstellar dust passes through the galaxy and eclipses Earth, the tenants within the walls of Mausoleum 2069 are reborn and the undead begin to rise. As the struggle between life and death onboard the mausoleum develops, Eriq Wyman, a one-time member of a Special ops team called the Force Elite, is given the task to lead the President to the safety of Earth. But is Earth like Mausoleum 2069? A landscape of the living dead? Has the war of the Apocalypse finally begun? With so many questions there is only one certainty: in space there is nowhere to run and nowhere to hide.

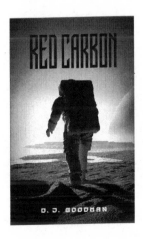

RED CARBON
by D.J. Goodman

Diamonds have been discovered on Mars.

After years of neglect to space programs around the world, a ruthless corporation has made it to the Red Planet first, establishing their own mining operation with its own rules and laws, its own class system, and little oversight from Earth. Conditions are harsh, but its people have learned how to make the Martian colony home.

But something has gone catastrophically wrong on Earth. As the colony leaders try to cover it up, hacker Leah Hartnup is getting suspicious. Her boundless curiosity will lead her to a horrifying truth: they are cut off, possibly forever. There are no more supplies coming. There will be no more support. There is no more mission to accomplish. All that's left is one goal: survival.

**SEVERED**PRESS

 facebook.com/severedpress
 twitter.com/severedpress

CHECK OUT OTHER GREAT SCIENCE FICTION BOOKS

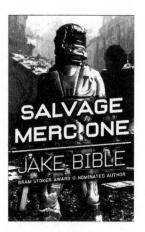

SALVAGE MERC ONE
by Jake Bible

Joseph Laribeau was born to be a Marine in the Galactic Fleet. He was born to fight the alien enemies known as the Skrang Alliance and travel the galaxy doing his duty as a Marine Sergeant. But when the War ended and Joe found himself medically discharged, the best job ever was over and he never thought he'd find his way again.

Then a beautiful alien walked into his life and offered him a chance at something even greater than the Fleet, a chance to serve with the Salvage Merc Corp.

Now known as Salvage Merc One Eighty-Four, Joe Laribeau is given the ultimate assignment by the SMC bosses. To his surprise it is neither a military nor a corporate salvage. Rather, Joe has to risk his life for one of his own. He has to find and bring back the legend that started the Corp.

SERENGETI
by J.B. Rockwell

It was supposed to be an easy job: find the Dark Star Revolution Starships, destroy them, and go home. But a booby-trapped vessel decimates the Meridian Alliance fleet, leaving Serengeti—a Valkyrie class warship with a sentient AI brain—on her own; wrecked and abandoned in an empty expanse of space. On the edge of total failure, Serengeti thinks only of her crew. She herds the survivors into a lifeboat, intending to sling them into space. But the escape pod sticks in her belly, locking the cryogenically frozen crew inside.

Then a scavenger ship arrives to pick Serengeti's bones clean. Her engines dead, her guns long silenced, Serengeti and her last two robots must find a way to fight the scavengers off and save the crew trapped inside her.

47621859R00146

Made in the USA
Middletown, DE
29 August 2017